Hitler's Twin

Jim Scott Books, Volume 32

Mike Jackson

Published by Mike Jackson, 2024.

HITLER'S TWIN

First edition. November 1, 2024.

ISBN: 979-8227490926

Written by Mike Jackson.

Also by Mike Jackson

Jim Scott Books
Baghdad Butcher
Back to Iraq
Dog Pound
Toboggan
The Tickleton Affair
The Saltwater Connection
Dead Silent Calm
Devil's Brew
Sedona Chip
Birth Of The Asps
The Zimo Hunt
Fido
Tears And Terrorists
Bear's War
Bullets And Baseball
Billy's Rescue
Father Mulligan
Adios, Amigos
Whodunit Did It
Horace Goes Home
How 'bout Both
Bob Becker P.I.

Bigfoot Bait
Pool of Blood
Back to China
Monster's Palace
Escape From Mexico
Assassin I Am
Dirty Bomb Crisis
Devil Two
Nohow Robotics
Hitler's Twin

Dedicated to: Don Fox

HITLER'S TWIN
A Novel
By
Mike Jackson

1.

On April 20, 1889, inside a very small clinic in the town of Braunau am Inn, Austria (then Austria-Hungary) a male child was born. The delivery was intensely painful, to the point that the mother of the child hardly knew the child had been born, nor as she had passed out, that a second male child, one she would never meet, was also delivered.

***

Well over a hundred years later, Kathleen (Kathy) Hogan of the Wentzville, Missouri Police Department was driving on her way to meet her boss, Detective Lieutenant Allen (Al) Felps, when the call that would change several lives came in. The department dispatcher requested a patrol officer report to a woman who needed assistance at her mother's home. After he gave the address, Kathy got on the radio. She informed the dispatcher that she would take the call, since she was less than two blocks away.

When she arrived, she left her car to meet the lady who was standing outside the home. Kathy could tell she was a bit agitated, so hurried toward the lady. After introducing herself as a police officer she asked, "What seems to the problem, ma'am?"

"I've tried several times to get my mother on the phone, so I came over. I looked in the garage and saw her car inside. She doesn't drive it much anymore anyhow. The spare key isn't where it's supposed to be, so I can't get inside. I'm worried about her. Can you help?"

Kathy told her she would assist her the best she could. Kathy first tried the door to make certain is was locked. After looking where the key was supposed to be located, then a few more likely places, Kathy asked, "Do I have your permission to pick the lock?"

"Yes, yes, of course."

Now inside, Kathy asked the woman to stay behind her while she started searching the home. The lady agreed, but shouted out for her mother as they started walking toward the living room to the left. Even when they entered the living room, Kathy could see through a breezeway-type opening leading to the kitchen. Looking through it into the kitchen, she saw the mother laying on the kitchen floor. Kathy turned to put her hand on the shoulder of the woman. "Please stay here...I see your mother on the floor, but need you to hold back for a bit."

The woman started to burst past her, but Kathy grabbed her. "Please."

The woman nodded, as she hung her head just a bit. She swallowed, so Kathy patted her on the shoulder, before turning back to go investigate the fate of her mother. Nearly all the way through the breezeway Kathy suddenly stopped. While she paused to take in what she was seeing it dawned on her what had caused her to stop. After the slight pause, Kathy continued on until she reached a crumpled throw rug. There she stopped again to take in the scene. After just a few moments, she turned back to the woman.

"I need you to go sit down. I can see from here that your mother is not breathing. I hate to tell you this but I suspect foul play, so this is now a crime scene. I know you want to go to your mother, but you will have to wait...please."

"Crime scene! What do you mean crime scene?"

"You see the throw rug between me and your mother?"

"Yes, I see that damned thing. I told mother it was a hazard for someone her age. It was always slipping and sliding on the floor. But so what about it?"

"A recent death in town had a throw rug arranged exactly like this one. Is that where the rug normally is located?"

"No, it's back here more, just at the edge of the living room. Can't I please go to my mother?"

"No, I'm sorry. Please go sit down while I check your mother's pulse, to make certain I'm right about her being deceased. Then I need to get some pictures. After that, I need to call my boss. He's nearby. I'll leave it up to him when you can go to your mother."

Not very happy about it, the woman turned away. When convinced she was going to do as asked, Kathy went to check for a pulse. There was none as she suspected. Then she quickly took a few pictures. When finished with that, she sent the one of the throw rug to Lieutenant Felps. Immediately after doing that she called him. "Al, this is Kathy. You need to get over to where I'm located ASAP. Check the photo I just sent you. Your hunch about something being wrong with the case you're working on was correct. We now have a murder to solve...actually two, because I'm just feet away from another one."

"Hold on while I look at the pic you sent."

Just a few seconds later, Al told Kathy he'd be on his way as soon as she told him where she was calling from. She did, then Al made another call to the medical examiner who had handled his case. He inquired if the body of the man on his case had been picked up, or if he still had it in the morgue. After being told the body was still with the medical examiner, Al explained, "Okay, we've got a new situation. We are now convinced this was a murder. We just picked up a second case indicating that to be the case. Do you have the time to come to the new crime scene, so the two connected murders can be examined at the same time?"

The medical examiner asked for more information, so Al told him what he knew to that point, but stressed the fact of the obviously intentionally arranged throw rugs. He also gave the address of the scene where Kathy was located, and stated that he was headed there. He must have told the examiner enough to convince him they were correct in their thoughts, because he agreed to leave immediately to the new crime scene.

Al knew the medical examiner was less than happy with this new development, because he had already declared the first case to be a matter of accidental death. Certain Kathy had now proven that to not be the case, Al drove to her location. When he arrived, Kathy introduced him to the woman, who by then had calmed down a bit. But she was still not pleased that Kathy had not let her visit her mother's body. Al did his best to explain that she could only do so after the medical examiner had arrived at the scene.

Al then left the woman sitting in the living room, as he went with Kathy to look the situation over firsthand. In almost no time he fully agreed with Kathy's assessment of the scene. "Good catch, Kathy. I had the feeling that something wasn't right about things at the first scene. It just seemed a bit off to me, but I couldn't put my finger on what it was. What made you think you had a murder on your hands?"

"First off, the rug of course. Even though it is different material, those three humps didn't seem right. Then it dawned on me it was exactly the same as the one on your case."

"Yeah, I always wondered about that darn rug. Anything else?"

"Yes, the lack of blood. She had to be already dead when the killer smacked her head on that counter. Just a bit of blood along with the skin on the edge of the countertop."

"You hit it. That is what I missed on the first case. Damn and damn. The M.E. missed that, too. We both should have our butts kicked."

"You said that, I didn't."

"Cute, shrimp, real cute."

While Kathy was only a tad over 5'5" tall, she didn't consider herself a "shrimp," but compared to Al who was a couple inches over six feet, she did realize that to him she was rather small. Like the other less than flattering nicknames he had come up with for her in a joking manner, she just ignored his comment, though she as a matter of course often called him "monster," or some other unflattering name for a rather large person.

Seeing he wasn't going to get a response to his comment about her size, Al jerked his head toward the living room. "Go hold the daughter's hand until the M.E. arrives. You might ask her if she knows of any connection between our two victims. Also ask for her mother's phone, and any address book she might have of friends. I've got a couple of calls to make."

First he called the Wentzville Chief of Police to let him know the situation, then he called a friend of the force by the name of Bob Becker. Bob was a retired Marine Sergeant Major and Navy SEAL. He lived in one of four nearly identical two-story homes on his estate with his lawyer wife Michelle. The estate also had a swimming pool with dressing area abutting it, that was open to all Police Officers of the Wentzville Department. In addition, it had a landing strip for two planes that shared a hangar. Two of the other homes were occupied by Bob's two partners in his detective/protection agency. The other home was now empty because a former partner and his wife had moved to Alaska.

Bob answered Al's call, "Hi, Al, what's up?"

"We've got two murders to solve. Need some help."

"Sure, shoot."

Al explained the situation, including the names and addresses of both victims, before he asked, "Will you run their names through that super computer you have available, to see if there is any connection between them? We'll work on it also, but I'd bet dollars to donuts you get to home plate before we do. We come up with anything, I'll let you know."

"Be happy to help out, Al. If I find anything, I'll give you a fast call. Um...how about tonight? Is that still on considering this mess?"

"Oh, yeah. See you about sixish."

***

By the time the medical examiner had come and gone with the body, the daughter had been given a ride to her home, which was only two blocks away (she had walked to her mother's home). Leaving the scene, Al returned to the police station with Kathy following behind. At the station Al made some plans.

First he asked Kathy to start the process of seeing if she could find any connection between the two unfortunate souls who had been murdered. As she started on that task, Al went in to see the Chief to report what they knew, or really didn't know, at that point. When he finished the only thing the Chief asked was, "Are we still on for tonight?"

"I see no reason to cancel...especially with all the people we've got coming."

"Okay, go to work. Good thought to ask Bob for help. Certainly glad you're comfortable enough in your own skin to get outside help...never hurts to have extra eyes and brainpower on a deal like this. Nice of you to check your ego at the front door...so to speak."

"The hell with my ego, I just want to solve this thing, before we have another one if this guy is some sort of serial killer."

With that, Al returned to what he jokingly called the "Detective Bureau," which was actually only two desks in the main station. While there were other detectives in the department, Al and Kathy handled serious crimes, such as murder, thus the "Detective Bureau" joke about their two desks. He walked to Kathy's desk. "Have you come up with anything yet?"

"No. The daughter was no help, as far as them knowing each other. Nothing of use on her phone, or her address book. I guess the next step is to check their credit card records to see if they may have met someplace along the line."

"About what I had in mind. I'll get right on those, while you see if there's anything on their phone records indicating they had ever contacted each other by phone. I'll also ask the county boys (St. Charles County Police) to send their forensics folks in to go over both locations. Though I'd bet against them coming up with anything. Since it seems like this guy is taunting us with the rugs, it's doubtful if he'd do anything like leaving fingerprints behind to help us."

Kathy just nodded grimly as she started back to work.

As Al had predicted, Bob Becker was the first one to come up with anything of value. He called Al. "Okay, I think we've got him…or at least a likely suspect. I know without asking the name 'Jimmy Bennet' will ring a bell with you. I remember that case, because Michelle told me you had it all wrapped up with a bow on it for the prosecutor…she also told me the jury set a record for bringing back a guilty verdict, the fastest ever in St. Charles County."

"Why do you think that punk has anything to do with this?"

"Both of your victims served on the jury that sent him up. In addition to that, one of the security systems I installed near your first victim has a guy about his height and weight entering then leaving the house at about the right time for the murder to have taken place. Couldn't see his face because he was wearing a ski mask, but it could be him. Didn't pick up much on his car except a dark sedan…no license plate. In checking the only car registered to him, he has a dark sedan. That enough to at least put him at the top of your suspects list?"

"You bet it is. Thanks."

"You're welcome. Before you ask, I've tracked down eight of the other ten members of the jury. Only one lives here in Wentzville. One is dead…died before Bennet got out of the joint two years ago. Three still live in Missouri, but well away from here. One in

Columbia, two near K.C. Two have moved to the Tucson area, one to Florida. The other two I haven't been able to find."

"Who are they?"

Bob told him, then Al replied, "That lady is now married and living in Colorado...got married out of the country, which is probably why you couldn't track her down. I have no idea about the guy. I only vaguely remember him from the trial. But, if you can't find him, I'd bet Bennet can't either."

"Okay, we can forget them for now. The other six—who no longer live here—should be warned, as well as informing their local police. Our local guy is a retired widower. Clyde is right now packing up some of our gear, we'll be heading over to install it at his place. Might be a good idea for you to meet us there. My thinking is someone needs to monitor him full-time until we nab this bastard. We can talk it over when you get there."

Al agreed to meet him after getting the address. Before he left, he told Kathy what Bob had found. He also told her the full details would be coming in on his laptop, which she could access because he had given her his password.

When he arrived, the three men knocked on the door of the man they would be protecting until Jimmy Bennet was captured or killed...assuming he was the killer they sought. Al explained the situation to the man, then Bob started installing an alarm system with several well hidden cameras. Before that job was completed, the three men who had arrived at his home, discussed a plan for keeping him under around the clock protection.

Bob agreed someone should be with him all the time, until Bennet was apprehended. The man questioned the need, at one point getting out his old Army WWII .45. There were a few pointed comments about that, such as would it fire, and could the man handle it. He assured them it would and he could, so they let it drop, but finally managed to get him to agree with the idea of someone being with him at all times. The thought of the three protectors was that one of them, or possibly Bob's other partner would handle the guard duty. When that planning was concluded, Al left to return to the police station while, Bob and Clyde continued with the installation of the new security system.

Back at the station, Kathy greeted him with, "I don't know how Bob came up with this so fast, but he certainly seems to have hit the nail on the head. Bennet has to be the killer. Where do we go from here?"

"First we get on the horn to all the other potential targets, and their local police departments, to give them a heads up. I want for us to be out of here by five-thirty, because I want to lay all this out over drinks and something to eat."

"Where do you have in mind to eat and drink while working?"

Al told her, causing Kathy to ask, "Is this some sort of a date or something? Sort of a working date?"

"Nah. Bob's gonna meet us there. Knowing him he'll pay for the food and booze."

"Pity."

Al gave her a funny look, even as Kathy wondered where that comment came from. While she wouldn't mind dating Al, had even thought of it often, but to blurt that out was just a bit embarrassing.

Al was thinking along the lines of maybe dating Kathy might not be a bad idea. He knew they got along well, and he had run the idea of asking her out through his mind a few times. But rather than pursue the matter now, both got to work with the task at hand. Al then suggested that he follow Kathy home, so she could ride with him to meet Bob. Kathy found that strange, but agreed...still feeling a bit embarrassed about her brief comment on finding out this wasn't to be considered a date.

2.

The fine eating establishment where they went, had a back room where large groups could have privacy. Al led Kathy to that room. When they reached it, he opened the door, and a throng of people started clapping, as Al patted her on the back. "Congratulations, *Sergeant.*"

She looked at all the people there and gulped. She also hit Al on the arm. "You're sneaky, Lieutenant."

Attending the congratulation party were the Chief of Police, with his wife, and all the off-duty Wentzville police officers (with mates or dates if they had them). Also attending were Bob, Clyde, their other partner Bill Hedden and his wife Amanda. In due time, Bob explained his wife and Clyde's were not there because they got hung up in Chicago, where they had flown the day before on a shopping trip. He also explained to Kathy that the man with him and Clyde was the next expected target.

When the party to congratulate Kathy on making sergeant was breaking up, Bob, Clyde and their "ward" spent a few minutes going over immediate plans for keeping the former juror alive. When she found out someone would be going home with him to spend the night, Kathy volunteered, "Since I'm now a sergeant, I guess I better start earning the big bucks that come with it. Plus which, in case no one has noticed, I'm smaller and can hide better in the back of his car."

Clyde joked, "I didn't have any trouble hiding in it on the way here, but you are a peanut."

Kathy sighed. "Okay, guys, I get it...I'm smaller than any of you."

The former juror piped up, "For my money, ma'am I'd a lot rather have you spending the night with me, than any of these guys."

Kathy smiled. "I hope that wasn't an invitation to share your bed, sir."

"Well, now that you mention it, I wouldn't mind that either, but I meant at my house. By the way, since these guys didn't mention it, I'm Emil Poepplemeier. Prior to becoming a target for this fella, I spent more years than a man probably should, in the United States Navy before retiring."

Kathy joked, "That may explain the strong come on, Emil. Nice to meet you. For your info, I'm well versed Navy men, because I did one enlistment there also. Both being Navy, we should get along well. Okay, since the plan is for me to hide out in the backseat of your car on the ride to your place, I'm ready. Who is gonna relieve me in the A.M., fellas?"

Al answered, "We can figure that out in the morning at our favorite eating establishment, if Emil is willing to drive you there, again hidden in his back seat."

"I am most willing to do so, if someone will tell me where it is."

Kathy answered, "I'll fill you in during our drive, or at your place. We'll see at least Al in the morning."

Both Bob and Clyde, knowing the café where several of the police force members often ate, told the others they would be there. After a short conversation, seven was agreed as the meeting time. That organized, Emil and Kathy left the restaurant. From the back seat where she was laying down, Kathy asked, "Hey, Emil, do you have a spare toothbrush for a watchdog?"

"Yep. You have your weapon with you?"

"I do. Almost always have it."

When they reached Emil's home, he pulled into the garage after opening the door with the remote in his car. Inside, they entered his home through the door connecting the garage and the house. It was early December, with a light snow falling as they entered his home. He took Kathy's overcoat to hang up with his in a nearby closet just out of the kitchen.

Kathy was wearing a fashionable pantsuit, the jacket of which covered her shoulder holster and gun. It was warm in the house, so she took off her jacket. When she did, Emil asked, "Would you like a nightcap?"

"No thanks. I've had more than enough to drink already. If the bad guy comes nosing around, I want to be able to shoot straight."

"How about a tour of the place?"

"That I'd go for. Be a good idea to get the lay of the land as it were."

They had entered the house through the kitchen and were now standing just out of it in the living room. From there Emil led Kathy through the house, showing her a den, a downstairs full bathroom, and a dining room that could be reached by another opening off the kitchen. Upstairs, were three bedrooms and two bathrooms. There was also a large linen/storage closet in one corner, next to the master bedroom.

While up there, Emil asked, "You want to use one of the bedrooms? Any of the three would be fine."

"Naughty, naughty. We already covered the ground of not sharing your bedroom."

"Never hurts to give a gal a second chance."

"No it doesn't, but in spite of missing out on what might be a wonderful experience, I think I'll sleep on the couch downstairs anyhow. It has a clear view into the kitchen in case this bozo actually shows up. Was me with evil in mind, I'd try coming in the back door rather than the front. I think I'll grab a comforter and pillow off one of the beds. You feel like rounding up a toothbrush for me? A tube of toothpaste would be nice, too, if you have an extra one."

"Coming right up."

By the time Emil got those two items, Kathy was already downstairs with what she had pulled off one of the beds in a spare bedroom. She took the offered teeth cleaning gear with thanks. Next she made certain all the blinds and drapes were tightly closed. She was happy to see they all were, and also nodded approval that both the front and rear door had dead blots that were locked.

Before Emil headed up the stairs intent on going to bed, Kathy instructed, "Anybody comes banging on the door or ringing your bell, you let me take care of it. You can bet I'll do so with my gun in hand. Actually, I don't expect he'll show up tonight if he's gonna at some point. There were two days between the first and second murder we think he committed. So my guess is if he keeps to the same schedule, it'll more-than-likely be tomorrow night. Which, now that I think of it, is probably why Al didn't try to discourage me from being your houseguest for the night. I bet he insists on being here tomorrow night."

"Okay, you answer the door, but I'll have your back."

Kathy smiled. "Thanks."

Kathy waited until Emil disappeared from view after he reached the top of the steps, before she started organizing herself for bed. She ruffled the comforter into the positon she wanted, tossed the pillow down, took off her jacket, pants, shoes, and socks. Her next move was to visit the downstairs bathroom where she used the toilet, washed up, brushed her teeth, and returned to the living room. There she took off her shoulder holster, removed her gun, which went under her pillow, took off her blouse, then paused. She really didn't like to sleep with anything on, but decided against stripping all the way down, leaving her bra and panties on. Satisfied, she turned off the only light still on downstairs, which was on an end table near the sofa.

After she snuggled down in the comforter, with about half of it under her and the other half covering her, she laid awake for a while before she sighed, sat, removed her bra, tossed it aside, and then tried again to sleep.

At a bit after two in the morning, Kathy was woken by the sound of a door latch being opened. Since his release from prison, one of the things Jimmy Bennet worked hard to learn was the art of picking locks. In his mind it had taken nearly forever to master dead bolts, but he finally reached the point where he was confident of picking any lock he might run into. He had just picked both locks on the rear door of Emil's home, and when he turned the door handle, the latch made the slight noise that awoke Kathy.

She wasn't certain what she had heard, but reached under her pillow for her gun nonetheless. The alarm system installed by Bob and Clyde had a one minute delay before making any sound. Kathy was sitting up on the couch, gun in hand, with the safety off when the soft chime of the alarm system announced an intruder...or at least someone entering the home without turning off the system within the allotted minute.

During that 60 second delay since he pushed the door open, Bennet had made it as far as the opening between the kitchen and the living room. There was only a small nightlight turned on in the kitchen but it was bright enough to silhouette Bennet as he paused. When he did that, Kathy rose up from the couch with her weapon pointed at him. "Freeze, police!"

Jimmy Bennet had no intention of giving up so easily. Kathy barely saw his weapon start to come up in time to dive to her right as she fired a shot at Bennet. He was hit in his right leg, but still managed to fire back at the flying target. His shot grazed Kathy in her left side just below the bottom of her ribcage.

In addition to being hit, Kathy landed hard enough on her right shoulder to jar the gun loose out of her hand. Bennet might have taken advantage of that, but for the painful realization that there was a bullet lodged in his leg. This being the case, he spun around and limped out of the house headed toward the street behind Emil's home. Survival instinct defeated pain, as Bennett made rather good time crossing Emil's backyard, then the backyard of the neighbor who lived directly behind him.

Emil, meantime, had been awakened from his sound sleep when the chime went off. He grabbed his trusty Army .45 and headed down the stairs, wearing nothing but pajama bottoms. On his way out of his bedroom, he heard the two distinctly different sounding shots.

When Bennet went out the backdoor he threw it open with enough force for it to clamor against a small porch railing there. Emil knew what that sound was so he ran through the living room to see Kathy recovering her weapon. Not knowing she had been hit, he kept right on going to the kitchen. When he reached the backdoor, Bennet was a step away from being out of view. That step caused him still more pain because Emil took careful aim with his .45. Bennet was stepping toward the neighbor's driveway when Emil shot. The .45 slug took a nice chunk out of his buttocks.

Before Emil could fire again, he lost sight of Bennet. He was standing there deciding if he should give chase in the snow with bare feet when he heard a car door slam, followed seconds later by the sound of the car starting. When it sped past the space between the back neighbor's home and the home next to it, Emil sighed as he turned around to see Kathy running in his direction with her gun ready, and her phone in the other hand.

He held up his hand. "He's gone...I'm pretty sure he drove off in a sedan...dark, maybe Chevy. I think I hit him with my shot, though. How bad I couldn't tell you."

Kathy nodded as she stopped hurrying. There was just enough light for Emil to see blood flowing down her side, so he flicked on the kitchen overhead light. Kathy asked, "Do you think that's a good idea?"

Emil was tearing off several paper towels from the holder near the sink when he answered, "Yeah, gives me a better look at you...*wow!*"

Kathy suddenly remembered she was naked except for her panties. She also saw Emil, who had turned back to her with the wad of paper towels extended toward her, was getting a good look. Seeing the blood running down her side onto her leg onto the floor, she decided that was a bit more important than modesty. She was also calling the police station after having put her gun on the table next to her. "This is Detective..."

Emil over spoke her with, "Detective *Sergeant.*"

"...Hogan. I've been shot...not too bad but need some help. Also call Al Felps to let him know."

Before ending her call, Kathy made certain the on-duty officer had the address correct. When she put her phone down, Emil suggested, "You do what you can to stop the flow of blood while I get my first aid kit."

With that Emil was gone as fast as a man of his age could travel. By the time he returned Kathy had more-or-less stopped the bleeding and was holding a couple of the folded paper towels hard against the wound.

Emil suggested, "Hop up on the table and lay on your other side."

Since it was obvious Emil was intent on taking charge of the scene, Kathy did as told. She tried to watch as he worked on her, but being on her side made it difficult so she finally just relaxed until he finished. At that point he helped her off the table. "That should hold you until the EMTs get here. I used three butterfly bandages to close the wound. It's not too deep, or very long. You got lucky. By the way you must have hit the guy because on my way to the back door I walked through blood, and you weren't here yet. You sure are a bloody mess. Do you want me to get a wash rag and a couple towels to clean you up?"

Kathy who had been watching Emil's eyes on her as he spoke, answered, "Not until you put away that weapon."

Emil noticed where Kathy was looking, so he looked down to the fly of his pajamas. He noticed something was protruding through the fly...something that was attached to him. He jerked his pajamas to one side, enough for the offending "weapon" to be hidden from view. "Maybe I better go get something else on. Be right back."

Kathy was laughing inside when he hurried off. She went to the sink, wet the dishcloth there and started cleaning the blood off her the best she could. She was using more paper towels to dry off when Emil returned. He now wore a robe and slippers in addition to the pajama bottoms.

Kathy smirked. "Better. Come give me a hand."

"I'll give you anything you want. As to what you saw, what did you expect? You're one of the hottest women I've ever seen, and you were standing there in nothing but blood soaked panties."

"Thank you for the compliment. Now, if you think you can behave, I'd like you to help me on with my bra. I guess any other clothing would be fruitless, because the EMTs would just take off whatever I put on when they arrive."

In the living room, Kathy slipped the bra on and turned her back to Emil. "I bet you've *un*hooked thousands of these in your lifetime, let's see if you can hook one."

Emil did as asked without comment, but after Kathy thanked him, he asked, "You want me to wash your panties? If I get them in the washer before the blood dries, they probably won't stain."

"Haven't you already seen enough of me, sir?"

"Nope, but seeing more of you at this point wasn't my intention."

"Yeah, I bet."

Just as she said that, they both could tell the ambulance had arrived because, in spite of the drapes being pulled tight, a bit of the flashing lights shown through at the edges. Without a word, Emil hurried off to open the front door for the EMTs.

When they came in, Kathy had returned to the kitchen table. This time she was sitting on one edge of it with her wound facing away from the middle of the table. One of the EMTs started working on Kathy. After a few minutes he told her the wound had been well taken care of, so there was little for him to do. Emil shook his head at that. "I didn't do much in the way of sterilizing it. I figured all the blood pouring out of her would do a good enough job."

The EMT shrugged as he took out a can of disinfectant spray. As he was using that on her side, Al hurried in. He looked at her with a worried expression. "You okay?"

"Oh, yeah. Emil took good care of me."

"What exactly happened?"

Kathy told him how she came to be shot, and stated she knew she had hit the intruder in return. At that point, Emil interrupted. "She definitely hit him. When I came charging in here, I stepped in a bunch of his blood. Kathy hadn't been in the kitchen by then. He was already gone out the back door when I spotted him. I think I got him too."

Before Al could respond to that, Bob showed up with Clyde right behind him. They knew there had been an intruder, because the alarm system was tied into a master electronic board in the homes of all three partners. After those two were filled in, Al decided to go take a look at where Emil had been pointing when he was talking. Bob tagged along. When they reached the front edge of the house behind Emil's, they saw blood spatter indicating to them that Emil had indeed hit what he shot at.

When they returned, the EMT was finished with Kathy, who insisted she wasn't going to "Any damned hospital" so they were getting ready to leave.

Al looked at the EMT. "Doesn't she need any shots or anything?"

"No, sir. She told me her tetanus is up to date, and I doubt if there is much chance of infection. The butterflies this gentlemen used should be good enough...will be good enough. *Sergeant* Hogan has made it very clear she that has no intention of going to the hospital for further care or attention.

3.

Though Kathy didn't need further care, Jimmy Bennet certainly did. While in prison he had made friends with another con who had given him the name of a doctor to feel safe in using, if he ever needed the very type of attention he now needed. In his careful planning he had contacted the doctor (actually a defrocked one who no longer had a license to practice medicine). He had pre-paid for any work needed to be done in the case of ever getting shot, or needing other medical assistance. On his way to see the doctor, he called ahead. The former doctor was none too pleased to be awakened, but agreed to see Bennet.

When he arrived, he was let in. Emil's shot had taken a rather large chunk out of his left buttocks, while Kathy's had hit him a few inches above his right knee. The medico grunted. "You must have gotten into some shootout."

Kathy's bullet was still in his leg, so it was dealt with first. In spite of the pain shot given him, Bennet nearly passed out in pain when the bullet was extracted. When he finished his work the former doctor suggested, "I've got a spare cane. You better use it for a few days. Come back in about five days, so I can make certain you aren't getting infected. Take it easy until then, obviously."

Bennet thanked him and started hobbling out using the cane. He was about halfway to his car when another car pulled up behind his. Both men did a double take as they met—with one leaving, the other one arriving, for the same type of medical attention needed. The other man asked, "Do I know you?"

Bennet thought about that a few seconds, before he replied, "Yeah, maybe. You do any time in Jeff City (Jefferson City Correctional Center)?"

"Yes, that's it. I'm Fateen Bassam...you?"

"Jimmy Bennet. You get shot too?"

"Yes, and the Feds are after me."

"You don't look shot."

"The back of my right shoulder."

"Oh. Well, good luck. I may have the local...Wentzville, cops after me. Probably do already, since they were waiting for me in ambush at my last stop. If not yet, I no doubt left enough blood behind for them to run DNA, which as you probably know, they have on everyone who has been in the joint."

"Look, I really have to get rid of my car since, there is probably an alert out to look for it. Maybe we could team up for a while...sorta help each other out. What I mean is work together trying to keep from getting arrested."

Bennet though about that for a few seconds, before he responded, "Yeah, maybe that's a good idea. I'll wait...out here, until you get patched up. Then we can dump your car. After that I need to change cars, too. I've got one they don't know I have. Set it up in another name, the one I'll have to use now that they're on to me."

"Good. I'll be out as soon as the doc takes care of me."

Both men were thinking the same thing: *"Work with this guy until he is no longer of use to me."*

When Bassam headed toward the door, Bennet hobbled to his car to wait. After Bassam was attended to, he came out. The two agreed that Bassam would follow Bennet to a likely place to dump the car, then go on from there for Bennet to exchange vehicles. The nearest place to get rid of Bassam's car without the likelihood of anyone noticing, was a shopping center's parking lot.

Bassam just left the keys in his car, hoping someone would steal it before the authorities found it. At the site where Bennet's second car waited, they got into it, leaving his car behind as well. Bennet drove to a small house, really not much more than a cabin, he had north of the Interstate. It was near a small stream in a heavily wooded area. He had purchased it from the proceeds of a robbery he had pulled off, with two men he had been working with to raise additional capital.

Those three had agreed that they would have one last, major, robbery before splitting up to go their separate ways. By the time he pulled up in front of the cabin, Bennet had already come up with an idea of how to best use Bassam. During the drive, Bassam had told him he had been planning a major terrorist attack when the FBI raided his apartment. During that raid, he had shot two agents, been wounded himself, and lost two of his co-conspirators with all his explosives.

Bennet could care less about the fact he was working with a terrorist, but that was what gave him the idea he had come up with. When they went inside, Bennet asked, "Do you drink, if so would you like one?"

"Yes. I am Muslim, but don't always behave as one. When I went to prison I wasn't inclined to terrorism, but I guess the authorities would say I was radicalized when there. That aside, I still drink. I also love bacon."

"Other than your name, I would not have guessed you are Muslim. What I mean is you speak English much as I do, with some of the same slang."

"I was born here, my parents are immigrants. I must admit I wasn't ever a very good Muslim, though I did attend services with my father. I now go to a different mosque. The imam there is connected with the imam from prison, who led me to terrorism. My father's imam is for more peaceful means to eventually take over America. You know, like was done in Lebanon and is presently well underway in Europe...most notably in France and England. The idea being to just out produce, children wise, other religions. The liberals in those nations make it easy. Abortion is a big asset. You may not be aware of it, but abortion is considered a major sin in my religion. But, for some, now like me I suppose, the wait for that to take effect is too long-term. Actually, I think that is the likely way to proceed, but in the meantime, terrorism helps reduce the numbers of non-believers while causing angst amongst them. I hope that doesn't concern you too much."

"Nah, as long as I'm not included in your plans as far as eliminating us non-believers. With luck, I'll be long gone before any such change comes about. My long-term plans call for evening some scores, then settling in some nice place like South or Central America. I've been working with a couple of other guys to get a nice nest egg built up, then splitting. As it is, I may not be able to settle all the scores I wanted to take care of...namely killing all the damned jury members who sent me up...and taking out the stinking cop who busted me. Now I may have to settle for just the cop. Well, also the lady cop who shot me."

While the two had been talking, Bennet had poured them both a liberal amount of vodka (his favorite drink). He handed one glass to Bassam, clinked his glass to the other man's then offered a toast. "To a successful partnership."

After they both drank some of their drink, Bassam asked, "Any way you can help me get some more explosives? My imam will help, of course, but contacting him might be dangerous. At least until the heat settles down. My hope is the Feds will consider the possibility that I have fled the country, after not being able to find me for several days."

"Yeah, I can help you out. In fact, I've got an idea how we can work together. My two partners and I have a big deal in the works. It would be nice to have a major distraction...like a terrorist event, to keep the cops busy while we do our thing."

"That sounds like a very good plan. I'll make a list of the things I need. At some point I'll also have to contact some associates, to help me carry out an event you will find satisfactory. With this deal I was just involved in, I'll have to find another target because too much of what I was planning was left behind when I got away."

"Good. We'll work together trying to find a good spot for your attack. Question...does your planning include some sort of suicide deal?"

"Hell no. At least not *my* suicide. But I am in touch with a couple of not-very-good-Muslim idiots I met in the joint, who will carry satchel bombs into any place in exchange for a nice payday...though, in addition to the money, they do like the idea of messing with the law. Of course, the bombs will be detonated by remote...a remote I have control of."

"I like it. Let's move on for a bit. We both need to change our appearances. You need to lose the beard, I need to add one. I've got a large kit that we can use, to do what we need to avoid easy identification. I have papers to go with the look I'll use. We'll have to be careful with you though, since I doubt you have a set of papers that will match the look I think you should use."

"You're right on that score. I have no other IDs, but can get them fixed up through my imam. However, as I said, I best not try to contact him for several days. When do you plan on this big score of yours?"

"My partners are still working out the details. We can ask them when they show up here. After the cops put out the word they're after me, they'll know to come here. They are the only ones who know about this place. I bought it in my alias. I wonder if the news is carrying anything about one or both of us yet. Let's see if we can find out."

The news about Bassam's event was all over the media by that time. It, of course, showed various pictures of him, but none were clean shaven. Nothing was being broadcast on Bennet, but that was soon to change.

In Emil's home, Bob was playing back various camera shots on Bennet as he entered the house. When he had come through the rear door, he had removed the ski mask he wore. He wanted Emil to see who was about to kill him, as he had done with the first two victims of his revenge campaign. Depending on the camera, various angles of the shootout were being shown. More than one very good picture of Bennet was shown. Bob dryly commented on one of those. "Little doubt who shot you, Kathy."

Kathy joked, "I like the one of him limping out of the house, better than the one of me getting shot with next to nothing on."

Emil disagreed. "Other than the fact that you got shot, I rather like that one. As I told you before...*wow*!"

"Thank you, sir...even if I get the feeling you're still trying to bed me. But, if you keep on, and I don't get any action before long, I might just take you up on your repeated offer."

Having found out during conversations with Bob and Clyde the previous day, Emil knew both were very happily married. So he had the feeling Al might be the intended target of that comment. That being the case he looked at him to see his response. The look on Al's face confirmed his thoughts on the subject, but he said nothing.

Before he stammered out something stupid, Bob came to Al's rescue when he suggested, "It might be a good idea to do a bit of planning on where we go from here, Al."

"I agree. Sure as hell Kathy isn't going to be spending the day with Emil. I'm planning on taking her home before too long. That leaves one of you two fellows to take the next watch."

Bob shook his head. "No worry about Bennet coming back here anytime soon. On top of that, Emil, I'd like to invite you to move in with me until this is over. If I have you safely tucked away at my place, the rest of us can spend more time trying to track him down."

Clyde spoke up, "Yeah, Emil, you'll love it there. Especially so when Bob's wife gets home. She's easy on the eyes...but you best not make a move on her, like you have on Kathy. Bob might blow your nuts off."

"If she's as hot as Kathy, I might take the risk."

Kathy grunted, "'Easy on the eyes' my foot. Emil, Michelle Becker is out of this world. Jo Feegle, Clyde's wife is beyond the pale also when it comes to looks."

Al changed the subject, "I like that idea, Bob. Emil are you game? It really would free up the rest of us to concentrate on the task of tracking down Bennet."

"Put that way, I guess I have no choice but to agree. But I'm not going anywhere until I clean up the mess in my house."

Al had an evil grin as he replied, "After I get a sample of Bennet's blood to take with me as evidence, Bob and Clyde will be glad to help you clean up. Once I have said sample, I'm taking Sergeant Hogan home, then putting out the word we're after Bennet for two murders, and an attempted murder of a police officer. Let's put a little pressure on this jackass."

While Al got his blood sample, Bob forwarded a video to Al's computer of Bennet firing, and getting shot in return. The video was to be used for airing with his release of information about Bennet being wanted for murder. Kathy, meanwhile, went to the downstairs bathroom to clean up and dress except for the blood covered panties. Those she handed to Emil along with the washcloth and towels she had used to clean up, when she came out.

He took those items and said, "I'll see you get these panties back all nice and clean, Kathy."

"No need. I've got another pair or two. Keep those as a souvenir. You can think about what might have been...or still might be."

Al shook his head slightly, but soon left with Kathy in tow. In the car he grumbled, "You certainly are something flirting with an eighty year old man that way."

"Ha, who was flirting?"

"To abruptly change the subject, but maybe not, after your 'pity' comment that our get-together last night wasn't a date, am I free to ask you out on a date, when you've healed up some?"

"I'm healed up. When are we going out?"

"If you're game, how about tonight?"

"You're on. Also, I don't need to go home. Let's go into the shop so we can get right to work on catching this guy before he kills someone else."

"You sure?"

"Of course I'm sure. I hurt a little bit, but not enough to take a sick day."

"Kathy, it's only five in the morning for Pete's sake."

"So let's stop to grab a bite to eat...but it doesn't count as our date."

Al just laughed at that. They were eating their 'non-date' breakfast when the Chief of Police called Al. "Where are you, Al?"

"Having breakfast with our wounded worrier. She insists on coming in to work. We'll be there in a bit. I want to put out a news release on Bennet being wanted for murder, and attempted murder of a police officer."

"You certain it's him?"

"Oh yeah. I have a nice video of him to broadcast. It clearly shows him shooting at Kathy...and receiving a shot to his leg in response."

"That may not be a good idea, Al. I don't want any crap from some ambulance chaser of an attorney wanting to get a change of venue for a tainted jury pool, because of broadcasting something like that."

"I get a shot at him, there isn't gonna be any damned trial."

"I didn't hear that, but share your sentiments."

Al drove to the station after they finished eating. It didn't take the Chief long to approve Al's idea on the press release. In fact, they did a fast video of the Chief making a statement about the situation that was made available to all the news outlets in the St. Louis area.

Bennet watched the entire presentation, including both videos, with Bassam. The terrorist commented, "Well, I guess we're both in the same boat, my friend. At least neither one of us looks anything like the pictures being broadcast."

"The police statements didn't mention Lieutenant Felps, but I'd bet anything he's the one who put it together. What I don't get is how he got on to me so fast, or how he got that video of me shooting at that dame cop. I notice they didn't show her getting hit with my shot. I only got a brief look at her, but she was nearly naked at the time."

"She good looking?"

"No...but has a nice bod. I got a few looks at her when keeping an eye on Felps, getting as much info on him as I could for when his time comes. But, as I told you, I'm putting my personal stuff on hold until we finish with our business. One good thing about this stuff coming out, I'll bet we get my two partners out here in the next day or so. That'll give us a chance for you to meet them, and them to meet you."

"Do you think there will be any problem with them having me in the know on your deal?"

"No. Not when I tell them what I have in mind, and that you've agreed. They'll love the idea of having a diversion...or diversions."

"I guess you're right about that. I don't suppose you guys would like to leave a little bomb behind when you do your thing?"

"Now there's a thought I like. What a nice icing on the cake...for both of us."

"Glad you like it. For now, though, I hurt and am about to pass out from lack of sleep."

"Yeah, you're right. We both better get some rest."

4.

Al worked with Kathy, and with Bob checking in a few times, until nearly five. During that time quite a bit had happened. First Bassam's car had been discovered. The FBI was called in to take charge of the car. Their team also had the presence of mind to check for any security cameras that might shed some light on where he might have gone from there. It took nearly two hours, but they discovered footage showing him getting into Bennet's car. It took only a few minutes to discover there was a want out on that car, and who it belonged to.

The upshot of all that digging resulted in Ken Langston, the lead FBI special agent in charge of the hunt for Bassam, to wind up in Wentzville Police Headquarters. He was led to Al with his partner. After introductions between those three and Kathy, the four of them settled into a long discussion about who would take care of what. During that conversation, Bob came in to meet to the FBI men. Al introduced Bob as an auxiliary Wentzville police officer (which he, and his two partners, were by special arrangement with the Chief).

It took the FBI agents only a few minutes of conversation with Bob to realize why the special recognition of auxiliary police officer had been conferred on him. By the end of the meeting, everyone was in agreement to share all information gathered, with the FBI being in charge of hunting down Bassam, while the Wentzville department would continue pursuing Bennet. This was nothing new, but it did open lines of communication allowing the two factions to avoid duplicating work.

Bob had left first, then the FBI team. So with five o'clock approaching, Al suggested that he drive Kathy home, so she could change clothes, while he would go to his home to do the same thing. They agreed he would return to pick her up at around six. When they left her home to go on their date, Kathy joked, "It certainly is nice to have undies on again. I'm not used to going all day sans them."

"More info than I really needed."

Their evening at a fine restaurant went well they both thought. However, Kathy was a bit disappointed that on arriving at her home, Al walked her to the door and said goodnight...*without* a kiss.

Al wasn't too happy with that either, but he had decided to go slow. He had been thinking about a relationship with Kathy for some time, but didn't want to 'blow it' by rushing things. Therefore, in the morning when Kathy arrived at work only a few minutes after he had, he was happy when she asked, "Are you game to come over to my place tonight for a home cooked meal?"

"You bet. That is if you know how to cook."

"Oh that was funny. Six at my place. Steak and potatoes okay?"

"Yup. I like my steaks..."

"I know, I paid attention when you ordered last night. Glad you don't mind steaks two nights in a row, because I gambled and got them out of my freezer to thaw during the day."

While Bennet wondered why his partners hadn't come out to his place yet, the hunt for him was going on without much success. His apartment had been visited on the sly by Bob because it was not located in Wentzville. Al had agreed to that idea, because he didn't want to involve other jurisdictions in the case. Bob reported there was nothing of use in the apartment, after he checked it out *very* carefully.

Bennet, fearing such a situation as he now faced, had been very careful never to leave anything the authorities could use to track him down. By the time Bob came in to make his report, Bennet's car had been found, obviously abandoned. There was nothing of use found in it either. That caused Bob, Kathy, and Al all to agree that Bennet was a careful man, one who might be a good deal smarter than any of them had thought likely.

A few minutes after five, Kathy left, asking Al to come to her home around six. He arrived promptly at six to be shown in. She had just put the steaks on, so his timing was nearly perfect. They had an enjoyable meal together, with Al liking both the meat, as well as the well prepared baked potatoes. Kathy was pleased to have Al help her with the clean-up, then he agreed to an after dinner drink in the living room.

On the way to the living room, Kathy stopped Al. "Hold on there, mister. This is our third date, if you count the party you arranged for me, which I do. I didn't get so much as even a kiss the first two nights, but I darn well expect one now after slaving over a hot stove for you."

Al smiled before he took her into his arms. He blew gently in her ear, then gently kissed his way to her lips. There the kiss became less gentle, until it turned into an all-out show of great feeling. When he got the response he hoped to get, Al suddenly swept Kathy up in his arms as he muttered, "Which way to the bedroom," though he had already started heading that way.

Kathy knew Al was well aware where her bedroom was, because he had helped her with a plumbing problem in her master bathroom about six weeks previously. That being the case, she just pointed as she replied, "That way," with the direction of her pointing nowhere near correct.

After they made love and were snuggled together, Kathy giggled. "What?"

"I just thought of the look on your face when I told Emil if I didn't get some action soon, I'd give him a try."

"You noticed, huh?"

"Yup," Kathy answered before she nearly purred, "I certainly hope you aren't planning on going home tonight."

"The thought never crossed my mind."

They made love again in the morning, then showered together. After they dried off, Al helped Kathy replace the dressing on her wound, which had gotten sopping wet. She let him do so, even though she had managed on her own the previous night. While they dressed, they both realized they didn't have time for much in the way of breakfast, so Al suggested, "You go on in. After I go home to change, I'll buy enough donuts to feed an Army, so we can pig out with still plenty left over for everyone else."

Even while eating more than their share of the donuts, they got busy trying to figure out what their next move would be. When both had eaten all they wanted, Al stood up. "Come on, we need to have a chat with the Chief."

Normally when information on something in progress had to be passed on to the Chief, Al did so without Kathy along. Thus she wondered why she should go to the meeting. Inside the Chief's office, Al pointed to the sofa as he sat down in the chair immediately in front of the Chief.

He got right to the point. "Chief, we've got a situation we need to bring to your attention. Kathy and I made love last night."

Kathy butted in, "And again this morning," then realizing how stupid her comment seemed to be, she shrank down in the corner of the couch.

Al smiled. The Chief all but bit his cheek. Al continued, "I for one, hope to make this a long-term deal. What is your policy on this type of thing?"

"We have no policy against fraternization between the sexes on the force, as long as they are consensual. You are well aware that we have one married couple on the force right now. By long-term, are you thinking marriage, or just fun-and-games for as long as it lasts?"

"Well, actually I was thinking along the lines of marriage."

"Me too," chimed in Kathy before she shrank further down in the couch.

The Chief laughed outright. "Okay, then we have a proposal made and accepted. Please invite me and my darling wife to the wedding. Anything else?"

"No. We'll get back to you on our case when we know something."

With that Al stood up, as Kathy bolted through the door while the Chief replied, "Please do."

Back in their area, Kathy sat down, but Al walked over to her desk. He spun her chair around, to face him. He went to one knee. "Kathleen Hogan, will you do me the great honor of becoming my wife?"

"You bet I will. Glad you still want me after I made a fool of myself while we were in with the Chief."

"I'm really pleased that you want me as a husband. I wanted my proposal to be more proper than what it was in there with him. I guess the next thing on our agenda, besides work, is to figure out when and where. About work, I'm really at a loss for now on how to proceed. Any ideas?"

"No."

More ideas were to take shape later in the day, when Al decided on a trip to Bob's home to talk about the case. The three of them sat around discussing the case with Clyde and Emil listening in when Kathy suggested, "It might be a good idea to check with someone at the Jeff City prison to see if Bennet and Bassam were close while there. I keep thinking about them both being shot. Maybe they went to the same doctor."

Al smiled, "I knew I was gonna marry well, dear. Good idea."

Emil asked, "What's this 'marry well' business? Don't tell me my dreams of bedding you, Kathy, are now shot all to hell."

"Okay, I won't tell you...Al can."

Clyde joked, "For God's sake, don't let Michelle hear about this. She'll get the 'great wedding planner' in here to take charge of getting you two hitched."

Michelle walked into the room just then. "You just told 'Michelle,' big mouth. But I like your idea of giving Holly a call to help me plan a nice wedding. When do you two want to get hitched? Oh, congratulations."

Kathy replied, "Thanks. But just who is 'Holly'?"

Bob butted in as he answered, "She's the wife of the guy who owns the computer I use to do wondrous things...Jim Scott. Al, you may as well give in without an argument on the wedding planning deal. Now that Clyde has let this cat out of the bag, it's all over for you two to even consider planning your own wedding."

Al looked at Kathy, who shrugged. He sighed, "Okay, Michelle, have at it. We've got a case to solve...or more to the point, a murderer to find."

"That's fine, Lieutenant, but I still don't know when you plan on doing this."

"How about after we have Bennet in jail...or dead."

Michelle grinned. "In that case I better get Holly to bring her other half with her. He's probably smarter than all of you sitting here combined."

Bob grunted, "Thanks for the nice compliment, dear. Though you're probably right. Now while you go get us some help, maybe we can get back to Kathy's great idea. Al, I'm thinking you should be the one to visit the Jefferson City joint to see what you can find out on these two. Expanding on the idea just a bit, since they were together so soon after the two shootouts, they may have visited the same doctor to get patched up. Also, if Jim comes to town, we best plan on working together on this deal here at my place. The Chief knows Jim, so will understand when you tell him this will be your headquarters while tracking Bennet down."

Al nodded agreement. "Thanks for the offer, Bob. I've heard of Scott, but hadn't met him. You're right, the Chief thinks highly of him. Honey, you stay here to continue working with Bob and whoever else, while I run to the shop to bring the Chief up-to-date, then I'll head to Jeff City."

Kathy was beaming inside at the use of 'dear' and 'honey' being used so freely by Al. She replied, "Yes sir, boss and soon-to-be husband."

By the time Al left, Michelle had already spoken to Holly Scott. She was more than pleased to find out the Scotts and another old friend, Hector Garcia, were actually flying in their direction for a planned visit to a medical complex a few miles from the Becker estate. Jim Scott funded the operation there that primarily dealt with supplying injured military personnel with bionic limbs, or normal replacement ones, to replace those lost in battle.

While those left behind at Bob's continued to go over the case, Al was on his way to Jefferson City. The Chief had readily agreed to have Al and Kathy transfer their operation to Bob's home...especially after being told Jim Scott was going to assist them. After his meeting with the Chief, Al had called FBI Special Agent Ken Langston to ask if he would like to ride along to Jefferson City. He explained why he was going, and the agent readily agreed. As Al drove, the two men talked, with Al explaining about the help he was getting, with more help on the way.

Ordinarily, Ken would not have been pleased about "outsiders" working on the case, but he happened to know of Jim Scott, and his many friends in Washington D.C. Those friends included the current Secretary of Homeland Security, the Director of the FBI, and at least three former heads of either the FBI or the CIA. Thus he asked, "Any chance I can meet Mr. Scott?"

"I don't see why not. By the time we get back he should be at Bob Becker's place, where Kathy is presently working with Bob on my case. I've never met Scott myself, but the Chief thinks highly of him. So does Bob, who is a first class fella himself."

"He seems to be. I was impressed with him in the one meeting we had together in your shop. What's the deal with Becker and his two partners as some sort of auxiliary cops in your department. Whatever 'auxiliary' means."

"Sorta what it sounds like. They're all on call for any emergencies, or other help we need. They even have Wentzville police uniforms, not very clearly defined as 'auxiliary.'"

"I do remember a while back, when Air Force One was shot out of the sky, they were first on the scene and offered quite a bit of assistance. Though I didn't remember that until after our meeting with Becker in your office."

"Yeah, that was quite a deal. But they help out with mundane stuff, too. They even help with traffic control, for things like our Fourth of July parade and celebration. They have also assisted with things like stadium security at our football games. Good guys, all three of them. Oh, and by the way, they receive the princely sum of one dollar a year payment for their services."

"Sounds like Wentzville is blessed to have them around."

"Amen to that."

***

While those two talked on their trip, Bob came over to sit down next to Kathy. "I tracked down what I believe is what you're looking for on Bennet's employment. Those periodic deposits into Bennet's account come from a used car lot in St. Charles."

"Maybe I should go ask a few questions. How long before your friends arrive?"

"From what Michelle said, it should be a couple more hours. I think it would be a very good idea for *us* to visit this place."

Michelle walked in as Bob was speaking. "Hold on there, husband. We've got a wedding to plan. Jo, Amanda and I are ready to get started. Holly can assist when she gets here...or more correctly, she can take charge."

Kathy grinned. "Maybe you could start without me, Michelle."

"Bob said that to me once, Kathy. I punched him."

"I can understand why, but this is different. I really should keep working on finding Bennet. I worry that every second we waste, he might be planning his next murder. Also, now that we know he's hooked up with a terrorist, it's even more important we track him down."

"I can't argue with that. Go. We'll work up some ideas, but will need your input at some point, since *you* are the one getting married."

That settled, Kathy left with Bob, who opted to drive. When they reached the car lot, it took only a few minutes to find out who the owner was. Kathy showed her badge, and identified herself as Detective Sergeant, but failed to mention that is was with the Wentzville department.

She introduced Bob, as also being a policeman, before she asked, "Do you employ Jimmy Bennet?"

"Not anymore, after I heard on the news he's wanted for murder. Actually, he hasn't been around for going on a week. But that isn't always unusual, because he worked on an open schedule. That is, he came in when he felt like it. I have two or three guys who do the same thing. Even though Bennet is wanted for murder, I have to admit he was about the best salesman I had."

"What can you tell me about him?"

"Not much. I knew he was an ex-con, but thought he had gone straight after getting out of prison. I had another guy who was an ex-con, who also sold for me from time to time. But he moved out of state after his parole was up."

"How come the special arrangement on when he worked?"

"I have a couple of other guys who work the same way. In most cases this is a sort of part-time deal with them. They call in and if I need them I tell them to come in."

"Do you have a phone number for Bennet?"

"Yeah, sure...hold on."

The number he gave Kathy was the same cell phone number they already had discovered for him. Feeling nothing else could be learned there, Kathy left with Bob.

5.

On the way back to his home, Bob asked, "Well, what do you think?"

"I think he was too smooth. I also thought he was a bit edgy. I'd say we should figure out a way to keep tabs on him."

"Very astute...I fully agree. Manpower is your issue, but I can help out there. There is no way the FBI could ever get a court-order for a wiretap, with no more than our gut feelings to go on. But if you had a friend capable of doing so without legal standing, it could be done."

"Is this where I say I didn't hear that?"

"It is...because I never said it. I noticed you didn't ask him about any car, or cars, he may have sold to Bennet."

"Good catch. Feeling as I did about him, I didn't want to give him any idea we thought he might be involved with Bennet, beyond being a former employer. Speaking of noticing, I saw you looking around getting a lay of the land. Might that have to do with what I failed to hear a moment ago?"

"You are sharp...yes. Al's a lucky fella to land you. Hot and smart."

"This is where I say, 'thanks,' but forget you said that, right?"

"Not really. Michelle is comfortable in her own skin, and knows I might flirt a bit, but am a one-woman guy."

Before Kathy could respond to that, her phone rang. "Hello, dear...by the way I really like saying that. What's up?"

"I want to apologize for being such an ass."

"What are you talking about?"

"When I made a big production of getting on bended knee to properly propose, I forgot all about a ring. We'll take care of that as soon as I get back."

"Al don't be silly. In the first place, things did get a bit rushed because of our chat with the Chief. In the second place, I don't want some klunky old diamond on my finger. All I want is a nice little gold band...and for you to say 'I do' at the appropriate time."

"Thanks for letting me off the hook. Um...is 'klunky' a word?"

"It is now. Other than all this, let me bring you up-to-speed on what I've been up to."

When she finished telling Al about her trip to the car lot with Bob (without mentioning the by-play between them), Al asked, "Good move, honey. Nice to know one of us can still think straight. I'll give you a call when we're on the way home."

"Okay, I'll see you at Bob's place. Bye."

Al glanced over at Ken, who had been smiling at Al's end of the conversation. "She only wants a gold band. I dodged a bullet there."

"Yes, you did. If you don't mind me saying so, this came about sort of suddenly...the proposal I mean. Seems to me when I met you two, there was no hint of love in the air."

"There wasn't. Just, bam, in a matter of forty-eight hours. But I had been thinking about asking her out before that. She told me she had been thinking along the same lines for quite a spell. If she sent any signals, I guess I'm just getting too old to read them."

"You said that, I didn't."

"Yeah, yeah."

They continued to talk until arriving at the prison. Al had called ahead so they were expected, thus after showing their identification, and turning in their weapons, they were led directly to the warden's office. During his call to the warden, Al had explained the reason for their visit, so the warden got right to the point. "I checked the record on the two men you mentioned in our call, Lieutenant. They both were released before I became warden, but I've got a few men who were here when those two were. Let me call them in."

The upshot of the conversation of the four men and one woman who came to the warden's office, was that none felt Bennet and Bassam knew each other. They did, of course, allow that it was possible they did have some contact, but all felt there was no close relationship between them. That being the case, Al asked, "Is there anyone here who might have known at least one of them that might have knowledge of a doctor who would treat wounds without reporting them?"

Between the prison officials, they came up with three names of men who might be most likely to be in the know for such information. When one of those names was mentioned, one of the prison guards offered, "That guy was pretty close to Bennet."

Al asked, "Any chance we can talk to him?"

The warden, who ran the man's name when it was mentioned, answered, "Yes, of course. You are in luck on him with having an edge in getting info from him. He's due for a parole hearing three months out."

Both Al and Ken smiled on hearing that piece of news. When they were led to a room to meet the prisoner, Al suggested to Ken, "It might be a good idea for you to keep quiet until I spring a little surprise on this fella."

"Oh, what's that?"

Al told him. Ken replied, "I love it. Good idea."

When the prisoner was led into the room, Al introduced himself, showed his identification, and then asked, "Do you know a former inmate by the name of Fateen Hassam?"

"No. Never even heard of him, why?"

"How about another former inmate by the name of Jimmy Bennet?"

"Yeah, him I knew. Didn't know him well, but did meet him a couple of times."

The two investigators exchanged glances at that lie, before Al replied, "Oh, is that so? We were led to believe you knew him quite well."

"Well maybe I did, so what?"

"Did you happen to tell him of a doctor who will take care of wounds received, without reporting it to the authorities?"

Suddenly wondering just how much these two cops might know, and remembering he had a parole hearing scheduled, the prisoner answered, "I don't think so. I'm not sure I know any doctor like that in the first place."

Al thought, "*Gotcha*" before he shot back, "It dawns on me that I failed to introduce the gentleman with me. He's a parole board investigator, who happens to be assigned to your case. On top of that, you have now lied twice to a Police Lieutenant investigating a double murder case, ones that your friend Bennet is definitely responsible for committing. Lying to me is in itself another felony, not to mention the effect it will have on your parole hearing. You sorta cleaned up the first lie, you want to try to do the same with this latest one?"

Before the inmate could answer, Ken jumped in. "For my money, even if you now tell the truth, I'm still inclined to nix your parole. You better be pretty convincing when you give us a straight answer, pal."

Knowing he was trapped, the prisoner told a partial truth. "I do maybe know a doctor who might do something like that. But I don't remember ever mentioning his name to Bennet. I do guess he might have overheard me mention the guy to someone else."

Al snapped, "Bullshit! Give me the name of the doctor right now, and tell me what you told Bennet."

Ken stood up. "I've had enough of his crap. Forget your parole, jerk."

"No, no, wait! I'll give you what I have."

Completely broken, in fear of missing out on the chance of parole, the prisoner gave them the name of the doctor, and admitted he told Bennet who he was. But insisted he had never even heard of Bassam. On being pressed, he gave the address and phone number he had for the doctor.

On their way back to Al's car, Ken patted Al on the back. "Nicely played."

When back on the highway, Al called Kathy. "I've got the name of the doctor who probably patched up Bennet, but we found no evidence that Bennet knew Bassam while in prison, so it's possible he met him at the doctor's place. Makes sense since they were both shot within a couple hours of each other. How about having Bob see what he can find out about the doctor. He should be spoken to. Oh, also...I love you."

Ken raised an eyebrow at Al asking for a civilian to do the checking, but said nothing as he placed his own call for his office to get the same information.

Bob called back ten minutes later. "Hi, Al, we've got the info on that doctor. He no longer has a license to practice medicine. I'm calling because Kathy has been kidnapped by the three wives out here and Holly Scott. Guess what they're talking about. Anyhow, obviously, Jim Scott is here, with, in addition to Holly, Hector Garcia. He's another friend, one who the Chief..."

"Also thinks highly of. No need to mention that, old friend. If he's someone close to you, that's good enough for me."

"Yeah well anyhow, Jim is gonna go talk to the doctor with a bit of help from Hector. Pity the poor doctor. I'd bet by the time you get back, they will be here with everything the doctor could possibly tell them that's of use. I'd go with them, but someone has to run errands for the gals. Clyde is with Bill taking care of some of our business...installing a new security system for a rich guy."

"I didn't hear any of that about those two having the conversation they are going to have. Thanks. Appreciate the help."

Al glanced over at Ken, before he told him what had been found out about the doctor, then added, "You probably will want to ignore what I'm gonna say next, that is I never said it. A couple of Bob's friends are going to have words with the doctor. Bob predicts by the time we get back to his place, we will know everything the doctor knows."

"You're right, I didn't hear that, but have an idea I'd just be wasting my time to even speak to the doctor myself. How did they get that info so fast?"

"My guess would be they used a friend's computer...which I've been told is better than anything the government has."

"I find that hard to believe."

"Believe it, trust me. If I need something quick, I always call Bob. As you can tell, it doesn't take him long to get answers. By the way, did I mention that the Chief told me Bob and some of his friends have White House passes?"

"No you did not. But thanks for doing so. I got the message to tread lightly where Bob and his friends are concerned."

Good to his word, there was an email from Bob for Al waiting when he arrived back at his police station. It had a summary of what the doctor had to say, which included an admission that he had treated both Bennet and Bassam. Al printed it out to give a copy to Ken. It was worded in a manner that the agent could say the information came from Al. Ken left the station still not having heard back from his office. He was shaking his head in dismay and amazement when he got in his car. He was never to speak to the doctor.

Al reported what had transpired during the day to the Chief, then headed to Bob's estate. Arriving at Bob's home, Bob opened the door with a grin. "The ladies are in the playroom. They want to see you."

The house had a large room that housed workout equipment, a pool table, a Ping-Pong table, dart board, wet bar, and several easy chairs. The ladies were seated in five of the chairs pulled together in a circle. When Al walked in, Kathy ran to him to give a hug and kiss, before she introduced him to Holly Scott. He tried hard not to ogle her beauty and fantastic body, but was only partially successful. Happily for him, Kathy pretended not to notice.

Holly asked, "Do you have time for a few fast questions?"

"Yes."

"Okay, we're working on guest lists. Anyone, like parents or siblings that you'd like to invite?"

"My parents, but they live in Arizona. No siblings. Other than that, no one except possibly some or most of our police force, if that isn't too many."

"We've already got them on the list. I'll take care of getting your folks here. Just give me their names and phone number."

Al did. Then Holly joked, "Okay, dismissed."

Al waved limply at Kathy before he went back to the living room, where Bob had set up shop. "I got booted out."

Bob laughed before he introduced Al to Jim and Hector. That out of the way, the men got down to the matter of finding Bennet.

***

While they cussed and discussed, the car lot owner, known as "Blowhard" Cardin was talking to one of his two partners in the thief ring, "Jitters" Donnelly. "Two cops came by the lot today about Bennet. I guess we should take the risk of going to his place in the woods."

"Or we could just cut him out of the deal. He's damned hot right now. I'm a bit jumpy about him getting us caught for no good reason."

"I would consider that except where are we gonna find anyone like him? He's got balls of steel. To bring someone else in now, it all might blow up in our faces. He may have a loose screw when it comes to wanting to kill everyone involved in the deal that put him behind bars, but other than that he has been a big help to getting us to where we are right now. A lot of the extra cash we've got from those jobs, is gonna be needed to put this thing together right. No way we can pull this off with just the two of us either. We need the third guy, and if we bring someone new in, how do we know for sure how he'd act under pressure."

"Yeah, okay, Hard. When do you wanna go see him?"

Donnelly called him "Hard" because Cardin preferred being called that, since he didn't care for the "Blowhard" nickname, but went along with "friends" using the shortened version.

"Tonight, around eight. I'll pick you up."

"Okay see you then."

Not knowing his partners were ready to come see him, Bennet was getting a bit worried about why they hadn't already showed up at his hideout. He didn't let on that he was worried to Bassam, but did mention if his partners didn't show up in another day or so, he would have to make a store run to get in supplies, something he wanted the partners to take care of, so he didn't have to show himself. His new look probably would be okay, but why take the risk if he didn't have to.

Bassam for his part, wasn't too concerned because he was still thinking about the things he'd need to do any kind of terrorist act. He knew at some point he'd have to visit his imam, but he felt he could put that off until he had things ready to move with any plan he came up with. The two "dopes" he was planning to use as unsuspecting suicide bombers were of no concern, because he had told them to just keep on with their normal lives until he was ready to move, at which point he would contact them. Though, the more he thought of it, he was considering contacting them, just to let them know he was still planning on carrying on after the problem he had with the FBI. The news reports concerning him had mentioned that he had been wounded in the shootout at his apartment, so he didn't want them to get any ideas along the lines of him being out of the picture.

After the two men ate, they took an evening walk, but near enough to the house that they could still see it. The obvious reason for this was to make certain no unwanted guest approached the house. The other reason was Bennet didn't want to miss a visit from his two partners. As they walked, Bassam brought up his concern about the two far less than brilliant men he planned to use as unsuspecting suicide bombers. "These two men, while loyal to me, are not the most intelligent men around. The growing fear I have is they might think I'm either dead, or on the run out of the area. If they get that idea, they might decide to take matters into their own hands, which would be a disaster because neither is bright enough to come up with a workable plan. They would only wind up being captured by the authorities or killed without doing any damage to anyone else, or trying to make a bomb and blowing themselves up. So I probably should contact them. I really don't want to use a phone, even a throwaway, because their phones aren't such. If the authorities are on to them, as they were me because of whoever gave me up, calling them might not be a very good idea."

"We can figure out how to get word to them without risking you, but only after my two partners come out here to speak with me. As I've mentioned, I expected they would be here sooner than this, but probably have very good reasons for not doing so."

"Would fear be one of the reasons?"

"Maybe, probably a real possibility. They knew I wanted to get some payback for the years I spent in prison. They had no objections, but they more than likely felt I could do so without being found out. On that subject, I still can't figure out how the cops were waiting for me at the home of my most recent target."

Even as he said that, Bennet had the feeling his clever idea with the two throw rugs might be responsible, but he still didn't see how Al Felps could have figured it out so fast, or how he was able to make the connection in the short time he had to ponder it.

6.

While those two were thinking and talking, the meeting in Bob's house continued. At one point Jim asked, "Al, on the car Bennet obviously dumped, he must have had another car nearby. I suppose you've checked out every angle on that."

"Oh, yeah. He picked a great place to make such a switch without being seen. If the car was seen by anyone, they probably wouldn't have noticed unless it was a car that would stand out. No cameras in the area, or homes where anyone would have noticed any strange car. It was a parking area where several cars are parked by commuters, taking a bus from there to wherever they were going. It would have been a good place to have security cameras, but none were there. Before you ask, Bob spent a good deal of time trying to find another car in his name, likely using your computer. We did the same thing...nada. The guy had a couple years to set up his revenge campaign, so if he was careful, he probably somehow developed a reasonably good false identity."

Bob agreed, "Yeah, Jim, we've covered that ground pretty well. No property in his name either. The guy has a second identity, I'd bet on it. How good it might be, there is no way of knowing. We aren't going to find this guy electronically. I don't know if it's cash or an account with his alias, but he kept almost no money in his known account. Money would go in, but wouldn't stay in the account long. Right now it has less than a grand."

Hector asked, "About the money going in, much other than what you said about the checks he got from the car lot?"

Bob answered, "No. Which raises another point. Where is he getting all the money he would have needed for things like the second identity, a second car, and a place to live where we aren't likely to find him."

Jim suggested, "Somebody, namely me, better run all the financials on this car dealer that Bob and Kathy think may be more involved than as a simple businessman who isn't opposed to hiring ex-cons."

Hector grunted, "We also better throw a big net over the fella. Might not be a bad idea for me to get some of my guys in here to help out."

Jim nodded, then looked at Al. "Now would be a good time for you to go help the ladies plan for your wedding."

Al tilted his head as he gave Jim a funny look, so Jim added, "Al, what I've got in mind to say next, you best not hear. At some point you may be called to testify in one trial or another on this deal. I have a feeling you know what I have in mind, but best have deniability that it actually went down."

"If you're gonna plant illegal bugs on the car dealer, I see your point. But couldn't I just go outside and play with Bob's dog?"

Al smiled when he said that. A few chuckles followed him as he went to join the ladies.

Jim got right to the point of what he didn't want Al to hear, "Okay, Hec and I'll do the bugging. I'm thinking about midnight or later. Hec, how say you?"

"Sounds good. I think six of my guys to blanket him should do it. But we gotta get them here. You want me to have them fly commercial, or should we ask Holly to do it? My other source of an available plane, as you know, Jim, is out of the country. They're in Hawaii visiting her parents."

"Yeah, I already thought about that. Holly can make the flight to pick them up. I'd bet Michelle or Jo, or both will be happy to give her a hand with the flying."

Bob agreed, "Yeah, I'd bet on both."

The three men then sat around discussing their plan in detail until Al returned. "They ran me off after putting up with me for a while. Hope you fellas are finished with what I don't have to un-hear if I'd stayed in here."

For their part, the other ladies and Emil laughed when Holly ordered, "Be gone with you, Al. We're finished with you."

Actually by the time Al came in, they were just about finished with their initial planning. About all he added was agreeing to the now planned date. It was Monday, and they had the wedding planned for Saturday, because as Holly put it, "I want to get this done before Al gets cold feet."

Kathy had stated that her mother and stepfather would not be attending because her stepfather was quite ill. Holly wasn't too thrilled with that, but let it go after asking if she could call Kathy's mother to at least give her the opportunity to attend. Kathy had agreed, just as Al came in to join them. He did stay long enough for Emil to volunteer to "Give away the bride, since I won't be able to bed her now that Al swooped in to pull the rug from under my feet on that idea."

That in mind, Al joked, "You two guys with wives here better keep an eye on that old devil Emil. He's gonna give Kathy away, because her stepdad isn't able to travel due to illness. So since he's given up on bedding her, he'll probably start casting his eyes around in other directions."

Jim bragged, "A turn in bed with Holly would probably do him in."

Hector joked, "Yeah, but what a way to go."

With the exception of Jim, who was working on digging out the financials on the car dealer, the men were still joking around when the women arrived with Emil. After they all found a place to sit, Hector asked, "Holly, do you feel like a fast flight to L.A. to pick up some of my men?"

"Yes, of course. I guess you mean right now?"

"I do. I already have them getting ready to travel."

Holly nodded, while also looking at Michelle and Jo. "You two wanna give me a hand with flying?"

"You bet, I can always use new pointers on how to become a better pilot," agreed Jo while Michelle just nodded.

Emil asked, "Hey, what about me? I could use a trip, and since you three are going to be on the plane, what a wonderful way to spend a day or so."

Al suggested, "If you don't mind, Holly, maybe you could pick up my folks on the return flight. That would save another flight later on."

Holly thought that was a good idea. "I like it, Al. I'll call them from the air. Hec, same place as always to pick them up?"

"Yes. Thanks, Holly."

Kathy looked directly at Al. "I'd like to go to, but I guess I have work to do here."

He grinned. "Nice try, dear, but yes you do have work to do. Maybe Holly'll give you a rain check."

"I will...anytime you want to go flying, Kathy, just let me know."

"Same here," chimed in Michelle.

Jo held up her hand. "Me, too. Anytime Kathy. That is anytime the slave driver will give you a bit of time off for good behavior."

After the foursome leaving said their "goodbyes," they left in Holly's plane.

While the plane was taking off, Amanda announced she was going to her home to get some work done. Before she left, she added, "Cook out tonight. Bob's cooking here. I'd like a steak."

Bob replied, "Yes, dear."

The rest of them sat around talking about various things until Jim came in half an hour later. "Al, go teach Kathy how to shoot pool."

Al joked, "More stuff I shouldn't hear I take it."

"Good guess. We'll join you when we're finished."

After those two left, Bob sighed. "Okay, wait before we hear what you have, Jim. I have to get some steaks out of the freezer. Be right back."

When Bob returned, Jim held court. "Okay, I found a couple of interesting things. First off, our neighborhood car dealer Cardin is using his place to launder money. Whose money, I don't know...maybe some ill-gotten money of his own. Bob, when you went to his car lot with Kathy, what did his inventory of cars look like?"

"Nice, Jim, real nice...not a pimple on 'em. Maybe a little pricey for the make and models, but if they run near as good as they look, still a real deal."

"About what I thought you'd say. He's buying derelicts for a couple of hundred bucks or so per. Then he's selling them for princely sums compared to what he paid. He has some expenses for paint and parts, but not anything like he'd need to turn them into something someone would buy for his prices. Also, he's only got one mechanic and one bodywork guy. They're being paid peanuts, well below what they should be getting. I'm betting he's paying cash for paint, parts and workmanship under the table. The question is back to whose money is it? Is he money laundering someone else's money or his own? Doesn't really matter."

Hector asked, "So okay, Jim, he's up to something, but does it have anything to do with Bennet?"

"Not certain. But the car Bennet dumped came from him...at a low price compared to what he's charging for the other cars. Bob, call that FBI fella Al went to Jeff City with. See if you can get a look at it, maybe test drive it."

"The FBI doesn't have that car, just the one the other guy, Bassam, dumped. Bennet's car is for now in the St. Charles County impound lot, or at least under control of the County cops."

"Well, wherever it is, get a look at it. Guess you'll need Al and his badge in on that. Hector, have Kathy drive you to the clinic to pick up a car. She can leave her car there until you get finished with what I've got for you. I want you two to whiz over to the area of the lot to check things out."

"Bob, you and Al take a look at that car. I want an estimate on what Bennet *should* have paid for it. If Clyde and Bill ever get back, I'll have one of them drive me over to the clinic to borrow another car. We'll also have to get three cars for your guys, Hec. We'll go with rentals for that."

"What I had planned on. I'll make the call while Kathy is driving me to the clinic. Bob, give me the phone number...and address, of the car rental outfit you'd like me to use. I guess I better get motel rooms for them too, so will need your recommendation there, also."

Jim held up his hand. "No need on the rooms, Hec. While in Bob's den..."

Bob interrupted, "Bob's former den, now Michelle's office."

Jim chuckled, "She certainly has you trained, Mr. Lap Dog. But, as I started to say, while in *Michelle's office*, I called the clinic to arrange for the cars we'll borrow. During that conversation, I asked about the possibility of a spare house. They had a three bedroom that won't be needed for at least a month. So four of your guys can use it, Hec...they can fight over who gets the couch. As you know, these places are fully furnished, with a good supply of non-perishable food."

Hector nodded. "Good move, Jim. The other two, with luck, will stay in a room or house I can rent on a short-term basis."

Shortly thereafter, Kathy was driving Hector toward the rehab clinic.

Less than a minute after those two drove down the long drive from Bob's home, Al drove Bob toward the St. Charles impound lot. Al had no trouble getting to look at the car Bennet had abandoned.

He also obtained permission to drive it around the block after explaining the reason for the test drive.

When they brought the car back to the lot, Al returned the keys Bennet had left in the car to the man in charge. He also chatted for a few minutes with him while Bob got on his laptop to check prices of comparable cars for sale.

While Al pulled off the lot, Bob told him what he'd found out, then added, "I'd bet not a single one of the same cars I found, is in as good a shape as that one. For God's sake, it even had new tires."

"Jim didn't mention what Bennet paid, but I've a hunch it was less than what you found on similar cars. If you don't mind, Bob, I'd like to swing by the station to bring the Chief up-to-speed. Guess I better keep the FBI in the loop, too."

"Goferit. Unless Jim comes up with something else for me to do, I'm free until I put the steaks on. Since Jim has attached us at the hips, at least for the day, you can give me a hand."

"I assume by that you do not mean applause."

"You assume correctly."

When Al finished talking to the chief, he made the call to Ken. On the trip back to Bob's home, Al thanked Bob again for all the help he was getting on the case, to which Bob replied, "Happy to help out, Al. You know that."

Back from their trip, those two started working on the planned evening meal, while Hector and Kathy "struck gold" as Hector put it. After driving to the rehab clinic to pick up the arranged car, they left in it rather than Kathy's car, because Hector felt her car looked too much like just what it was...a police vehicle. In spite of the change in cars, Kathy continued to drive because she knew the area much better than Hector. She drove by the car lot before starting to drive around the area so Hector could get a "lay of the land."

Satisfied with what he'd seen, in particular one house, Hector asked, "Did you see that two-story house about two blocks down from the car lot on the opposite side of the street?"

"Yup."

"Okay, good. Swing around and drive to it. When you get there, pull into the drive as far as you can. I'm gonna get out to look it over. You stay in the car while I do. I don't want to take any chance that you'll be spotted by our car dealer if he's around."

Kathy joked, "He'd have to be endowed with very good eyes to recognize me from that distance."

"Yeah, but not if he drove by when you got out of the car, or while you were walking around watching me check the place out."

"Point well taken, sir. Why the interest in that house?"

"If it isn't presently occupied, I'm gonna buy it for my guys...or at least the two who will babysit the lot."

"That's a lot of money to spend for what we hope will be a short period of time."

"I can afford it. Jim likes to say he has more money than sense. That applies to me, too. If I wind up taking a loss on the place when selling it after this is over, I can use the tax write-off."

After Kathy pulled to a stop at the end of the driveway, Hector walked up to the front door. There he rang the doorbell. Getting no response, he knocked. After still not raising anyone, he started slowly walking around the house, peering in the windows as he went. Satisfied with what he saw, he went back to the car. "Okay, Kathy, this place looks empty. There's some furniture, probably stuff the owners didn't want. So we may get lucky. This place, if I can buy it fast, will be perfect."

"From this distance? Hector, you can't see squat from here."

"Ah, my dear, with the gear my team is bringing, you can see the head of a pin from a mile or two. But, not to count my chickens, et cetera, I best call the realtor."

Kathy just sat there without a word in total disbelief as Hector not only managed to get a real estate agent to hurry out to the property, but had already settled on a price and immediate occupancy on the phone before ending the call.

Hector took a fast tour of the house, wrote a check for the full amount of the sales price and, as he handed it to the agent, he suggested, "Call your office to have them verify that I have funds to cover the check."

When he said that he flopped open his three-fold wallet to take out one of his business cards. It was a card to a business that was not his primary one, which was a major detective/protection agency. The main purpose he had in mind when getting the card out, was to make it easy for the agent to see his White House pass. She nearly fainted when she saw that.

He noticed and smiled inwardly. She was so impressed with his White House pass that she nearly dropped her phone, when calling her office with a request to verify funds for the check in her hand.

When all was said and done, Hector had the keys after explaining he had a team coming in to do some checking on a company he was thinking of purchasing. He told her the men would only be in the area for three months or less, but she would get the listing after they left, if he decided to re-sell the property. He did stress that he did not want any word of his making the purchase...or even his presence in the area...to slip out, because it might affect the pending deal he was working on.

When the agent got back to her office, she hurriedly told everyone that the purchaser had a White House pass in his wallet. Her boss told her that under normal circumstances such a fast deal including giving up the keys to the property for immediate occupancy wasn't a very good idea, especially since the closing on the deal would be done three days later. But he told her the bank he had called on the check had assured him any check Hector Garcia wrote in any amount up to a *billion* dollars would be covered. (Hector had called his bank earlier telling them to expect the call, and asked that wording be used when assuring whomever called that the check was good...it also happened to be true.)

7.

The house deal completed, Hector and Kathy returned to the clinic to pick up Kathy's car. When Hector returned to Bob's estate in the car borrowed from the clinic, with Kathy following in hers, she was gushing about how Hector operated the second she entered the home. Everyone else there, except Al, knew how those associated with Jim went about things, so there were just a few grins as they exchanged looks.

Al, on the other hand, was impressed that Hector had not only found a house that would do, but had somehow managed to get the keys before the closing, so his men could move in immediately on arrival.

After Kathy finished lauding Hector's accomplishment, Jim, who had already returned with Clyde driving another borrowed rehab clinic vehicle, spoke up. "Okay, I think I heard something about a cook-out. Clyde and I have salads ready, Amanda worked with Al on the potatoes, so, Mr. Becker, time for you to get with the steaks."

Bob nodded as he gathered up his cooking utensils before heading out the back door. The large outdoor barbeque pit was about fifteen feet out of the kitchen on a brick patio. He was gone for less than two minutes when he returned with his utensils. "It's too damned cold out there...cookout is gonna be a cook-in."

Kathy found that to be quite funny. While there had been a few other smiles or smirks, Al, Bob, and Jim all gave her a funny look. She asked, "What?"

Jim asked, "What's so funny?"

"Oh, nothing. Just something my grandma was quoted as having said years ago. Why back in the 1940s. It only sorta ties in to Bob's crying about how cold it is out."

Al asked, "Okay, give. You've got us curious now."

Kathy nodded as she replied, "Okay, but I'll try to make the story shorter than it really was. Seems their furnace, grandpa and grandma's, shot craps. It took a few days in the middle of one of the coldest winter snaps in years to fix. A day or three after they got it fixed, the family was sitting down to eat when the phone rang...you know one of the old fashioned things that filled your hand to use. Anyhow, grandma listened for a few minutes before she said, 'No, but it was four days ago.' Well grandpa asked her what that had been about, she replied, 'Somebody wanted to know if this was the icehouse.'"

Al was laughing at that even as he walked out of the kitchen to return wearing his overcoat. He gave Bob a dirty look. "And you, a Navy SEAL. It'll take all day to cook all those steaks on your stove."

With that he went out to the barbeque pit to start the fire. By the time he had it ready, a sheepish Bob was outside with the steaks. Kathy pitched in with Amanda to help out. Amanda offered, "Since this was my idea, I guess I really should lend hand."

Once the meal was finished with all the cleanup work done, Hector announced, "Full belly or not, I'm for some rest since Jim will keep me up half the night bugging."

Bob thought a second, before he offered, "Emil has one of the upstairs bedrooms, so you can have one Hector, while the other one will be for Jim and Holly."

Hector shook his head. "No, I'll take the downstairs maid's room. Let the young lovers have the other upstairs one. That is, Al, if you have already sampled the goods to make certain Kathy is worth keeping."

Kathy blushed, but Al responded, "Thanks, Hector, but we'll just go to one of our places."

Jim butted in. "Like hell, Al. You two are staying here on Bob's grand estate until we finish this deal. In case it hasn't dawned on you, if Bennet wanted to kill the jurors he probably isn't too keen on you either. Now that he left Emil's with a hunk of Kathy's lead in his leg, you can bet he'll want a piece of her hide, too. The maid's room has a big enough bed for Hector. Actually it has a nice queen-sized, so his feet'll be two feet from the end."

Hector all but ignored that while shaking his head on his way to the maid's room. That started an exodus from the kitchen, with Bill announcing he was heading home with Amanda. She agreed, but before leaving suggested, "Kathy, plan on spending Friday night with us at our place. You can bet Michelle will insist that you not see Al on Saturday until marching down the aisle. Holly will be just as bad on that subject, so considered it closed. The rest of you can bad guy hunt on your own Saturday until after the wedding."

Jim nodded agreement as he announced he was going to get some rest also for his nighttime plans with Hector. Everyone else went to the game room to shoot pool and talk about the case.

***

When Jim got up, he went downstairs to see Hector already had coffee on. Bob had laid out everything they would need for their bugging operation on the kitchen table, before he went to bed. Over coffee the two men checked to make certain they had what they wanted, so when finished with their coffee, they loaded up. Jim drove, while Hector navigated. It was nearing one in the morning when they reached the car lot.

Jim circled it twice before finding a good place to park. Getting out of the car he muttered, "I'm real happy that this guy has his place in a more-or-less residential location. With only a few other businesses in the area, at least we don't have to deal with a ton of extra lighting...or security cameras. When we get in, I'll try to find his other set of books. From what I could find out in checking Cardin's financials, I bet he's still making some profit above the money laundering operation."

Hector grabbed one of the two tote bags they had. When they started walking to the lot office he pointed at the side door to the building. "Probably easier to go in that way."

"Right. Hope he doesn't have too good of an alarm system."

Hector just grunted as Jim got out a piece of gear to work on figuring out the alarm system. He stood nearby watching Jim until his friend shrugged. "Here goes. I think there should be a control panel somewhere nearby. If he has it set with a minute delay, we should be okay."

Jim picked the lock to the door before the two men hurried in. Hector found the control panel first. "Here it is, Jimbo."

Jim rushed up to place another piece of gear on top of it. In a matter of a few seconds he entered what he was certain would be the correct code...it was. The elapsed time since opening the door was forty-seven seconds. Hector joked, "We'd be in the soup if he used a thirty-second delay."

Without further comment, they went to the office. There, Hector placed a bug under the desk, then bugged the phone on it. When he finished, he helped Jim hunt for the expected second set of books. Not finding them, they searched until they found a floor safe. Jim glanced at Hector. "I'm thinking this might take too long to fool with, Hec. How say you?"

"I agree. Let's hit it. Maybe if we get enough for a warrant, either Al or the FBI can deal with it. Well, not Al because this isn't in Wentzville."

"You're right there. You're also right about getting out of Dodge. Let's go put a homer on his car and call it a night."

They drove to Blowhard Cardin's home, planted a homing device on his car, and then headed back to Bob's estate. On the way, Hector asked, "I wonder where he was since his car was still warm when we got to it."

"Don't know, don't care, because nothing we can do about it now."

Jim might well have cared if he knew where the car had been, along with what the car dealer had been up to. He had driven his other partner to Bennet's hideaway. Jitters Donnelly ran the body shop at the car dealership...supposedly as no more than a hired hand. At the car lot he was always dealt with as though the two men were simply boss and employee. While Cardin was the so-called "brains" of the operation, the three partners were more-or-less equal.

When Cardin pulled up in front of Bennet's place, the lights had just been turned off. The two men in the car expected that because they knew Bennet had an elaborate security system. As soon as they had turned onto the road leading to his house, an alarm sounded inside. He pushed one button shutting down all lights inside and outside the house. With gun in hand, he peered out of a one way window at the top of the front door.

He waited until the two men got out of the car on their way to the door, before he put his lights back on. That done, he opened the door. "I've been wondering when you two would show up. I guess you have heard the news I nearly got caught. I got shot, too."

Cardin nodded. "Yeah, we heard. You okay?"

"Slowed down a bit, but good to go."

When Bassam walked up from a darker area, the two new arrivals glanced at each other. Bennet quickly introduced Bassam, then added, "We're gonna work together. We first met at the doctor's place...the one who patched me up...him too. He got shot during another deal, you probably heard about that."

Not too pleased to hear the terrorist would be working with at least Bennet, and probably him as well, Cardin replied, "Yeah, heard about the shootout he had with the FBIs. Now what's this about adding him to our team?"

Bennet quickly explained his idea to have Bassam create diversions, just before their major strike. While he spoke, he could tell the "brains" of the partnership was softening to the thought of having Bassam. He concluded, "So if we have three major explosions in crowded areas in different directions around our target, every cop and FBI agent in the area will be occupied. I propose that we give Fateen ten percent of the take of our deal. You two each give three percent, I'll give four. The cost of the explosives he'll use will come off the top, but we'll have to advance the money for what he needs. He already has made up a list of the items he'll need. You two will have to get them, because other than a fast trip for him to contact two of his men, and possibly a third, we better stay here even though our appearances have been changed. I'd also like for you two to round up some food and booze for us. What say you?"

Cardin nodded. "I like it. But two things. One, this is the last time I'll be coming out here until after we hit the armored car outfit. "The other thing is we can use some extra money as it is, so I have another small job to pull. One of those payday loan and check cashing places. The one I have in mind gets their money for their Friday business late the night before...around ten. Also, they get extra money in on the 15th and end of each month. This coming Friday is also the 15th so they'll have even more money than normal. The money delivery is normally a bit before ten, when they close. We'll hit them Thursday just after the armored truck departs.

"The reason I won't be coming out here again is because two cops came around the car lot checking on you. One was a gal, the other a big guy. But the gal did all the talking while the big guy was checking things out, including giving me the fish eye. I think I pulled the wool over their eyes, but don't want to take any chances. I only drove this time because the only two times Jitters has been out here I drove. I wanted to make sure he paid attention so he could find his way back."

Bennet thought a second before he asked, "What did the broad look like?"

"Short, maybe 5'5" or so. Not very pretty, but had a nice bod. Brunette."

"Sounds like that damned Kathy Hogan, the bitch that shot me. The big guy couldn't have been Felps, or he'd have been doing the talking. He must have been with her as protection. Probably another cop, or maybe even a Fed. Now that I think of it, how about a little diversion when we pull this payday loan deal?"

"That I like. Will we have to get more explosives and stuff for it?"

Bassam answered, "Yes, but we can just replace what I use for this smaller deal later."

The four men continued to discuss the overall situation, with it decided that Donnelly, who had remained silent for the most part, would round up the food. Cardin would take care of arranging the explosives and other things needed, but Donnelly would also have to pick up those items.

When Cardin left with Donnelly, they talked about the new arrangement on the way back to Donnelly's car. Cardin asked, "Are you okay with all this? I noticed you didn't have much to say all night."

"Yeah, I'm in...but that damned terrorist gives me the willies. When the big job is done can we just off the bastard?"

"Exactly what I had in mind."

Fateen Bassam had already decided that 100% sounded better to him than 10%, with the added bonus of having a nice hideaway once the three partners were dealt with.

**

Early Tuesday morning, Holly returned with Hector's six men and Al's parents. Hector drove one of his two men to the house he had purchased for their stay while in St. Charles County. The other man followed in one of the cars rented by Hector. They moved in with the equipment they had brought along. After Hector outlined what their job would be, he left his men behind.

He had told them to keep constant watch on the car lot when anyone was there. He had shown them where the nearest grocery store was on the way there, so they could take turns going for what they needed. He also told them to feel free to order whatever else they needed for comfort, and to have it delivered to the house. For any purchases they might make, they would use their own credit cards, with Hector paying their statements from the credit card providers.

The equipment they brought included two telescopes, and a long range listening device. Those three items were set up before Hector made it back to Bob's estate.

While Hector was getting those two settled in, Jim had led the other four men to the house he had arranged for them. They followed in two more cars rented by Hector. Their instructions were to keep constant watch on the car lot dealer when he was not at the car lot. Since his car had a homing device, they could just hang out at the house until the two men Hector had in place let them know he was leaving the lot, and which direction he was headed. Both cars now had gear that would allow them to trail far behind his car. When he drove home, the team on duty would have to stay in the area all night...there was to be no lack of coverage on him, day or night.

By the time Jim returned to Bob's estate, Al's parents had moved into Clyde and Jo's home. It had been agreed that they would stay until Monday, when Holly would fly them home. Holly had also spoken to Kathy's mother, who agreed to having a 24 hour a day nurse attend to her husband (paid for by Holly) so she could attend the wedding. Holly would fly down to pick her up on Friday, then Holly would fly her back home the day after.

With everything pretty well taken care of as to the wedding, Holly started helping the men with the hunt for Bennet and Bassam. At one point she volunteered, "Those four guys of Hector's are going to get worn to a nub if this lasts too long. What say someone join me to give them some time off every so often."

Jim smiled as he nodded, "Okay, wifee, you and me one team, Hector and Bob another. Hector figure out a schedule. That out of the way for now, if everyone will excuse me I'm off to work on the computer to see if I can stumble onto anything."

When Jim stood up, Al looked at Kathy. "We better go to the shop to see if there's anything else on our plates. While there, I'll give the Chief an update."

Jim, who had started to walk off before Al spoke, turned on a dime. "Hold on there. You two can go in, but someone is gonna tail you for safety's sake. Don't forget this Bennet bozo probably has you two in his gun sights. Anywhere you two go, some of us will follow along. Since Bob and Clyde are welcome at the Police station, they are hereby nominated."

Al grinned, "You and Hector are more than welcome at our shop, Jim."

"True, but I want to hit the computer, and Hector has to stay put to coordinate things with his men."

Emil asked, "What about me? Anything I can do to help out, Jim?"

"Yeah. You're in charge of flirting with the women around here. At least one of them is putting on some age so can use all the flattery she can get."

Holly shot back, "Cute, Stanley James, real cute. I'm certainly glad Bob has a nice big couch in his living room. The rest of you staying here, if you come downstairs during the night for some reason, that obnoxious sound you hear will be Jim's snoring. The older he gets, the worse it gets."

Soon after that, Al drove Kathy to the police station, with Bob and Clyde following along. When all four were inside, Al quickly looked things over before deciding on a course of action. "Okay, Kathy, we've got two not-too-important things that need our attention, and all of our other guys are busy. Clyde, how about you ride with her as she looks into both? I'll talk to the Chief, then clean up some of this paperwork stacking up."

Bob had other ideas. "How about those two do their thing while I tag along behind them? Nothing for me to do around here."

Al agreed, "Yeah, okay, good idea. Thanks."

8.

The next day Al and Kathy took care of any new items that came into the "detective bureau" that needed their attention, with nothing happening on the hunt for the two fugitives.

The constant surveillance of Cardin had accomplished nothing, except for lack of sleep for whoever was watching him at his home. The two men in the house Hector purchased also had little of any use to report.

Donnelly had made several trips away from the business, but to explain his frequent trips had told the mechanic that he was going out for paint, complaining more than once, "A person would think these damned paint companies would have what a person needs without all the special ordering. You've got it easy on the parts you need, because the auto supply companies always seem to be on the ball."

The two men listening in from the house just assumed the guy was actually just coming up with reasons to get out of helping the mechanic. They had found out that when not doing body shop work, he lent a hand with the project the mechanic was working on.

But later on, they listened in as Cardin took Donnelly out to a 1998 Chevy Impala. He pointed at the side of the car away from the view of the two watchers. "I don't like the way this door panel looks. How about repainting it."

Donnelly shrugged, but quickly got the keys to the vehicle to drive it into his area. Before he started on the car, he grumbled about the situation to the mechanic, but before long was masking off the *entire* car.

The two watchers paid little attention until he started painting the car black, covering the two-tone white and light blue paint job on the vehicle. One looked at the other one as he asked, "Now what in the hell is he up to? You don't paint a whole car for one panel that isn't up to snuff."

Neither man could figure it out until the mechanic entered the body shop. "What are you doing? Does the boss want this car changed to black?"

"Nah. He was pissing and moaning about one door panel. I just decided to paint the entire car...black. I never liked that stupid two-tone job."

"He's gonna be pissed."

"He'll get over it."

On their next report to Hector, the man who called in for a routine up-date mentioned the situation of the car being painted, along with the circumstance. Hector acknowledged the report but thought little of it.

On Thursday, with the now black car still in the paint shop, Donnelly told the mechanic, "I'm going after paint. If the boss comes back, let him know. I don't think he will, because he told me he wasn't feeling too good. I got thinking about what you said, so I better make sure I have paint to put that thing back the way it was, in case he explodes over what I did."

"Good idea. See you later."

Where Donnelly went was directly to Bennet's hideout...he had all the paint he needed. When he walked in, he asked, "You two all ready to go?"

Bassam growled in reply, "The bomb is ready, but it is very unstable. We drop it, or get in some sort of auto accident, it'll go off. I really need those other things you weren't able to find yet."

Three key components of Bassam's list of items he needed had not yet been found by Cardin. During the week, Donnelly had picked up and delivered everything Cardin had arranged, but the three remaining items on the list were turning out to be difficult to locate.

Donnelly didn't point out this fact to the terrorist, but did reply, "We're working on the other items you need. Do you have any ideas on where they can be found?"

"Perhaps, but I will have to make the contacts with the people who have them myself. It is a risk. For now, we can go with what I have. After this event tonight, we'll figure out how best to approach the situation."

"Good. Have you found the car I got you to be satisfactory?"

During the week, Cardin had purchased four cars in rough shape, three had to be towed to the car lot, but the fourth one, while a wreck to look at, ran rather well. That one Donnelly had driven to the hideout. Bennet had then driven Jitters Donnelly back to his own car. When Bennet returned to his hideout, Bassam drove the car around to check it out, with Bennet following him.

While far from being a "grand vehicle," it did run. On the way back to the hideout, both men had gassed up their cars. So they were ready for the night's planned "distraction" bombing, and Bennet's planned meeting with his two partners for the payday loan robbery.

Bassam nodded approval as he answered the question posed to him, "It will do. I notice the plates are about to expire."

Donnelly replied, "Not to worry. Just bring it back here. I have different plates for it. I also have some spray paint cans. I plan on giving it a fast color change, until I can get it back to my shop to do a better job of improving its looks. I'll take care of that when we meet you back here. Come, let's go."

Bennet rode with Donnelly, with Bassam following them until he made a different turn along the way to pick up the man he had decided to use for placing the bomb. During the week, he had used Bennet's car to contact the two men he wanted for the big events to take place, just prior to the major robbery Bennet and his partners had planned. He had explained to them what his current situation was before deciding which of the two to use for the smaller bombing.

On the way to the site of attack they would make, Bassam explained, "This bomb you'll be carrying in a backpack must be handled with care. It is unstable. You drop it, and you'll be blown to bits...got it?"

"Yeah, sure. I'll be careful, don't worry."

"What you'll do when we reach the target is put the backpack on, then walk to a bar and restaurant I'll point out to you. As cold as it's getting tonight, there won't be anyone sitting outside on their patio, so you just place it near a set of windows looking out on that patio. There is a drawstring you pull. I'll show it to you when you get ready to put the backpack on. When ready to place it, you pull the drawstring. It'll give you about two minutes to clear the area...do so as fast as you can without arousing suspicion. Walk as near the other business on that side as possible to cut down the angle, so even if you're too close when it goes off, you shouldn't be hurt too badly. When I see you headed my way, I'll start the car, then drive to pick you up at the bottom of the stairs you went up."

"Sounds easy. I really appreciate you selecting me to do this job."

"You've earned the right to become a full-fledged member of my unit. I could do this myself, except for not having a car standing by to pick me up. With luck, you'll be in the car before the bomb goes off. When we get there you'll see where I'll pick you up. That spot should be reached in less than the two minute time delay after you pull the drawstring. One thing, please remember you cannot drop the bomb. If you do, my unit will be minus a very good man."

Bassam continued to discuss the plan with his man until they reached the parking area of their target. He pointed at the steps leading up to the quaint shopping area. "Okay, you go up those steps. The bar and restaurant with the tables and chairs out front on the left is your target. Since it's so cold out tonight, as I predicted, there is no one sitting outside, which is a good thing. When you get there put the backpack on one of the outside chairs, pull the draw-string, then walk toward the door to the left as though you were going inside to purchase a drink. When you reach the door, keep going. Pick up your pace when you do that, so you can get back here before the bomb goes off. When I see you coming, I'll meet you right here."

Puffed up with importance, the man got out, putting on the backpack once out of the car. When he started up the steps, Bassam drove to the nearest parking spot he could find where he could see his man walking directly toward the eating establishment, which was several store fronts down on the left side of the enclave.

The bomb toter walked with a purpose until he suddenly noticed a security man headed toward him. Since that was not part of the plan, he panicked. Thinking fast, he pulled off the backpack, pulled the drawstring and tossed the backpack at the approaching man in uniform.

When he did that, Bassam screamed inside the car, "No!"

The security man saw what the man had done, and for some reason he'd never be able to fully explain, dove to get behind a nearby large decorative round flower pot some six feet in circumference.

The bomber turned after he tossed the bomb. He made only one long stride to start a run from danger. He never completed the stride as the bomb landed, exploding on impact. He was killed instantly, and the security guard was hit in the legs protruding from behind the flower pot. Several patrons in the restaurant were injured as a result of the flying glass, ball bearings, nails, and screws. Workers and patrons of other nearby establishments were also hit in the blast.

Bassam swore, but calmly started his car to drive off the parking lot.

Five minutes later, after having picked up Blowhard Cardin earlier, Donnelly pulled to a stop in front of the payday loan business just as the armored truck was leaving. Donnelly had picked up Cardin by parking on the next street behind Cardin's home, directly behind it. He called on a throw-away phone, to let him know he was there.

Now all three men got out to hurry inside, all wearing ski masks. As planned, Bennet was last in so he shut the door, turned the old-fashioned open/closed sign to closed, and pulled down the shade on the door. Donnelly closed the blinds covering the front window. Cardin, gun out, headed to the rear of the business just as the clerk came out.

In less than three minutes, they had the just-delivered money, and the money in the cash drawer out front gathered and were out the front door, leaving the bound and gagged employee behind. Donnelly drove Cardin back to where he had been picked up, then drove back to Bennet's hideout.

When they arrived, Bassam was waiting on them. On being asked, Bassam explained what had happened with the bomb. He concluded, "So, after I told him a hundred times if he dropped the bomb it would likely go off, he panics on seeing the rental cop and throws it."

Donnelly nodded in understanding. "I would say we better make every effort to get you the other items you asked for before we do our last job. For now, let's do a fast job of painting your car with the spray cans. You can change the plates after I finish that. I still have to get the car that I used back to the shop to re-paint yet tonight."

The fast job on the car Bassam was using competed, Jitters Donnelly drove the black Impala back to the car lot. He opened the large door to the paint shop before driving inside. After shutting the door, he pulled down a large tarp affixed to a metal bar above the door. He also pulled down a shade to the door into the mechanics work area. Only then did he start re-painting the black car back to its original color.

Hector's two men slept through his arrival and paint job, and didn't wake up when he pulled the car back to its original parking area on the lot the following morning.

While he had been busy, so had the authorities and emergency personnel on the scene of the bombing. FBI Special Agent Ken Langston had just finished making love to his wife when his phone rang. They had only been cuddling for less than a minute when the interruption came. His wife giggled, "Glad that call didn't come a minute or so ago."

"Yeah, me, too," agreed Ken before he answered the call, "Langston."

The Agent-in-Charge of the St. Louis office told him about the bombing, and instructed him to go there immediately to take charge of the scene. Ken explained to his wife what the call had been about as he quickly dressed.

By the time Ken arrived, all manner of police and emergency personnel were already on the scene. In addition to St. Louis County Police, several local police from surrounding communities, a few Missouri State troopers, seven FBI agents, and ambulances from several nearby hospitals were involved. With the approval of a just arriving St. Louis County Police Chief, Ken soon took charge.

In short order he had what had been chaos in some semblance of order. Before the night was out, the FBI Agent-in-Charge arrived to take charge of the scene while Ken was instructed to round up tapes from every security camera in the area. When that was done, with some grumbling from business owners about being awakened in the middle of the night, Ken took the tapes back to FBI Headquarters to start going over them. While he was working with the tapes, other agents and St. Louis County detectives started interviewing all witnesses, including those injured in the blast.

One of the more senior special agents interviewed the security guard, but got little from him, other than his dive to partial cover after the bomb had been tossed. Both men agreed the dive probably saved his life.

By five in the morning, most of the police and federal agents had left the still cordoned off area. Forensic teams were still working the scene, with a few St. Louis County police officers keeping the media, employees of the various other businesses, and nosey onlookers away.

At FBI St. Louis Headquarters, most of the agents had managed to catch a couple hours sleep during the early morning, but were hard at work trying to piece together what information they had.

At Bob's estate, everyone started getting up around six. Michelle was first down in her home. Before she started getting things ready for breakfast, she turned on the TV in the kitchen. She paused in her preparations at the news of the "terrorist" attack in St. Louis County. Bob walked into the kitchen with Jim. They saw her standing there with a spoon intended to be used to mix pancake batter. Both saw her attention to the TV, and also glanced at it.

Just as Jim was about to comment, Hector walked in. Jim pointed at the TV. After less than a minute, Hector glanced at Jim, who nodded as he took out his phone, while on his way out of the kitchen headed to Michelle's office. While gone, Jim made two phone calls to old friends: one to the Director of the FBI; the other to the Secretary of Homeland Security.

By the time he returned to the kitchen, everyone else was downstairs, watching the news. Even as he offered to help where needed with breakfast, two calls were made to the Agent-in-Charge of the St. Louis FBI office. The second came in before he could take action on the first. When that call ended, he summoned Ken Langston into his office.

"Have a seat, Ken. I just got off the phone with the Director and the Homeland Secretary. The message both gave me were nearly identical. Jim Scott, who you told me was staying with Bob Becker at his estate, is to get everything we have that he wants. We are to also give him any assistance *he* asks for. Other than that, we are to stay out of his way, while continuing to conduct our own investigation. You will be our liaison with Mr. Scott. As you told me, Wentzville P.D. Lieutenant Felps is also staying at Becker's place. Please give him a call since you know him. Ask him if you may speak to Mr. Scott. From there do what Mr. Scott wants. Got it?"

"Yeah. You don't seem too pleased about this."

"I'm not, but I *do* know of Scott's reputation. Before you make your call, what have you come up with at this point?"

"We know who the bomber was, but can't get an ID on the guy in the car. The plates on the car, while not bogus, don't fit the car. They came from a car that was totaled in an accident. Beyond that, not much. I was going to send a couple of guys out to the salvage joint that took in the car after the wreck, unless you wanted me to take care of it."

"No, send someone else. For now your job is to give Scott what he wants. After that, get back to me."

"On my way."

Back in his own office, Ken made the call to Al. On being requested to do so, Al handed the phone to Jim, telling him who was calling as he did. Jim asked, "Special Agent Langston, what may I do for you?"

"My boss here in St. Louis was asked, make that ordered, to be of whatever assistance we can be to you. He was instructed to give you anything we have that you might want. Also, to be of any assistance you ask for. Beyond that we are to stay out of your way while we continue our own investigation."

"You don't sound too pleased."

"When the big brass in Washington gives an order, we follow it...like it or not."

"What do you have so far?"

Ken told him much of what he had told his Agent-in-Charge, which prompted Jim to reply, "If you are unable to identify the man in car with the videos you have from the area cameras, any way I could give it a try?"

"It'll take me about three-quarters of an hour to get them boxed up, and drive out to Bob's place."

"See you then...thanks."

9.

While waiting on Ken to arrive, the group in Bob's home discussed the call for a while, before trying to figure out what to do in case Bassam had been behind the bombing as they thought might be the case. A few minutes before he arrived, Holly stood up. "Okay, time for me to head to Florida. You fellas can get along without Kathy until Sunday morning...she's going with me. One of my two co-pilots is going also...who?"

Jo and Michelle exchanged glances. Both shrugged, so Holly made the decision. "Jo, you come with me. Michelle gets to stay back to assist Amanda in making certain everything's ready for tomorrow."

Michelle joked, "Hey, that's not fair. I just decided I want to be co-pilot."

Holly shot back, "Snooze, you lose. Let's go ladies."

Those three walked out the back door, just as the chimes sounded indicating someone was approaching the sign near the end of long driveway. Ken had been warned by Al not to ignore the stop sign if he ever visited the estate. Without clearance from inside one of the four homes, anyone who didn't stop to announce who they were, and who they wanted to visit, would be in for a nasty surprise. By passing the stop sign without permission, two sets of steel, razor-sharp blades shot up. The result was the approaching car soon had four shredded tires.

Ken spoke into the voice box. "Ken Langston here to speak with Jim Scott."

Bob pushed a button that disengaged the trap blades, before he answered, "Come ahead, Ken."

Ken drove around to park in front of Bob's home, where he was greeted at the door by Michelle and Al. Al smiled. "Glad you paid attention to me when I told you to stop where indicated."

Walking toward those two, Ken replied, "Yeah, you scared me...but didn't tell me what would happen if I didn't stop."

Michelle introduced herself, before she told Ken about the system. Ken grinned as he shook both offered hands. Those three joked about the system while walking into the living room where everyone else was waiting.

Introductions out of the way, Ken picked up the large, double-wide briefcase he had set down before shaking many hands. The briefcase was handed to Jim. "This has everything we have to date, Jim. Well, nearly everything...what isn't in here, I can cover with you if necessary."

"Thanks, Ken," Jim replied as he sat down to go through what was inside. When he came to the discs containing all angles of security cameras that picked up the bomber, Bassam, or his car, he handed them to Bob.

Bob just nodded as he started inserting them one at a time into a player that soon was showing the images on a very large TV screen in the room. When they came to the best two shots of Bassam in his car, Ken spoke up. "We've tried to ID the driver but without luck to date. We ran the plates...they're bogus. Or at least they don't belong to that car. They came off a car that was totaled. We have a team of agents on the way to the junk yard where the car was sent. When I get a report on what they unearth, I'll let you know."

Jim quickly put both discs into his laptop. When both had been forwarded to his master computer, Jim started to work on enhancing the two best shots of Bassam. In less than ten minutes, one of the images of Bassam as he started to leave the scene in his car was covered over with "98% match." A second later his name appeared at the bottom of the scene.

Ken swore, "Son-of-a-bitch, how did you do that?"

Bob replied, "I told you, Ken, about Jim's computer. It really is better than anything the government has."

Jim added to the answer, "Ear match. With all the stuff he added to his face, no chance of getting a facial match, Ken."

"You think we haven't tried for an ear match? Hell."

Even while speaking, Ken took out his phone to call his Agent-in-Charge. "How are you doing with identifying the driver of the car?"

"Same as we were when you left...23% ear match. Homeland got it up to 41%."

"Yeah, well, Mr. Scott's famed computer we've heard about came up with 98%...it's Bassam. He did it in about five minutes or so."

"I was warned by the Director and Secretary to expect that. Good going, even if it's darned embarrassing."

"Yeah. Anyhow, do we put out a press release on this?"

Jim spoke up, "I wouldn't. No sense letting him know we know. You've already got half the world looking for him, so let's keep him in the dark about our capabilities."

Ken asked, "Did you hear that, boss?"

"Yes. I see the point. We'll sit on it for now, but I better check with the brass to see if they agree. I assume that was Mr. Scott's voice I heard?"

"It was. Let me know if Washington disagrees."

"Will do."

Ken told those in the room what had been decided by the Agent-in-Charge. After a few nods, he asked, "Do you mind if I hang around for a while?"

Jim answered, "Not at all. But, please don't be offended, if at some point we ask you to go play pool or something."

Ken agreed. Emil pointed down the hall. "Pool hall's that way. Al and I have been sent to the doghouse a couple times."

While all this was going on, Amanda and Michelle had been working at the kitchen table going over their plans for the day as it related to the pending marriage. While working they had the kitchen

TV on listening to the local news with only half an ear. They were listening closely enough that Michelle paused in what she had been saying to listen to a news alert about the robbery at the check cashing/payday loan business. As she heard what was being said about it, a light went off in her head, before she ran into the living room. "Hey, guys get the TV on the local news. I think this is interesting."

No longer needing the screen for what they had been working on, Bob quickly did as suggested. While everyone was watching the news of the robbery, Michelle muttered, "I wonder if this was somehow connected to the bombing?"

Jim asked, "What makes you think this might be connected?"

"Oh, you missed the first part of the story...it happened about ten minutes after the bombing."

When the news channel switched to their next story about the time she spoke, Jim nodded. "You may have something there, Michelle. We've been trying to figure out why Bennet was running with a terrorist. What better reason than to create diversions for other bad deeds. You can bet if there had been any type of alarm about the robbery, it would take a while for the police to respond. With every cop in the area at the bombing, there would be a discussion about who should check into it. Even a five minute delay would give the bad guys time to split."

Ken asked, "Should I pass those thoughts on to my boss, Jim?"

"Good idea. Please see if there are any security cameras that may have picked this up. If so, I'd like to take a look at them."

Al suggested, "Maybe we could nose around at the scene, Ken, even though neither of us has any real standing in St. Louis County. You do, but not on a simple robbery if that's what this is."

Ken stood up. "Let's go. You drive, I'll call my boss on the way."

By the time Al reached the payday loan business, he had another thought. With Ken still in the car, he called Bob. "Hey, Bob, you remember that big robbery about a year ago in St. Charles that has never been solved. Three guys did that job, too...all were wearing ski masks."

"Damn, you're right. Let me kick that around here...I'll get back to you."

Bob told the others about the call. Before he finished talking, Jim immediately set up a program on his computer to see if there were any other unsolved crimes with the same M.O. from anywhere in the near vicinity of St. Louis. Ten minutes later he was on the phone to Al. "Okay, we may be on to something. Including last night and the one in St. Charles you called about, there are a total of seven unsolved robberies in the area...all with the same M.O. I think we better ask Ken for some help running down tapes, if there are any, from all of them. He can get his people to round up what is available on each, then get it to us."

"Funny you should call. After I made my call to Bob, Ken remembered two others. He's already called his boss to round up what info is available on those. One was a bank in St. Louis, the other was a heist in Jefferson County."

"I think we've got those two on our list...which leaves three others. Let me talk to Ken. I'll give him what I have on those three."

"Okay, but hold on a few seconds. He's talking to someone here at the scene of last night's job. He heard me and is reaching for my phone. Here he is."

By the time Al and Ken returned to Bob's home with what was available from the most recent crime and the one from St. Charles, the St. Louis FBI office Agent-in-Charge had teams of agents rounding up the information on the other five robberies.

The first one Jim looked at was footage from two different security cameras from the scene of the most recent robbery. It took only seconds for Emil to say, "Hey, that one guy has a slight limp. I bet that's the guy Kathy and I shot."

Jim, who had noticed the same thing, smiled. "Good catch, Emil. The one with the limp matches Bennet in height and weight. Somebody go tell Michelle she may have got us on the right track by being alert on the news broadcast."

Bob joked, "Never mind, her head is plenty big enough as it is. Actually she split with Amanda on what they're working on. Just let her do her job, while we try to do ours."

Clyde asked, "What are they doing, exactly? It looked to me like they took a good deal of meat from your freezer, Bob. I noticed when I went for my last cup of coffee."

"Never mind. Let's concentrate on what we're doing."

Jim gave Bob a funny look, but continued on with the job at hand as he put the only security footage from the St. Charles robbery on the large TV screen. In short order everyone there agreed it had to be the same three men as those from the previous night. When the tape was complete, Jim summed up. "Okay, if the other five, or at least some of them, are the same, I bet we know where Bennet got the money he seems to have plenty of. If they are dividing up their ill-gotten cash on a more-or-less equal basis, I bet he has plenty of money to have a safe house someplace. The first of these seven hold-ups happened about three months after he was released from prison. So we have the fun task of trying to find any houses bought since then by anyone we can't readily identify."

Ken grunted. "That should be a snap. I bet there's no more than a quarter million homes have been sold in that time frame."

Jim shook his head. "Probably more than that...but we can cheat. We can...for now...eliminate any where a mortgage was involved. Also, any costing too much...perhaps anything over a hundred grand. He's not gonna want to draw attention to himself by buying a grand place. Remember he had a rather cheap apartment from what I discovered when running his financials. I'll just set up a program and put my computer to work. While we'll set it up for St. Louis and

the five nearest counties, we'll concentrate on places further away
from core locations. If we find him this way, I'd bet dollars to donuts
he didn't buy in St. Louis or St. Louis County...I certainly wouldn't
under the same circumstances. Of course, if he rented this will be a
waste of time."

Clyde joked, "Great, now we've got it down to 10 or 20
thousand places to check out. But, before anyone asks, 'no,' I don't
have a better idea."

By late afternoon, what the FBI had managed to find out about
the other robberies had been turned over to Jim and his team. All
but one of those cases had security camera material to check out. All
showed the same three men.

Jim summed up what they had found. "Okay, all three of these
guys must have a nice little stash of money. In my mind, we may also
know that Cardin, if he's involved, is probably using his part of the
loot in his car business...which explains who belongs to the money
I'm certain he's laundering there. Bob, you went with Kathy to the
car lot. I assume one of the two other thieves is about the right size."

"Yeah, Jim. On the last shot of the three standing there, the one
in the middle is about right for Cardin. The baggy clothing doesn't
help make me sure, but close enough to put him at the top of our
suspect list right alongside Bennet."

Hector got up and on his way out of the room muttered, "I'll be
right back. Jim send that shot to my laptop while I round it up."

Jim, certain what Hector had in mind, did as asked. Hector
used his laptop to send the photo Jim had forwarded to his laptop
to one belonging to one of his two men in the house near the car
lot. Finished with that, he called that man. "Anything going on out
there?"

"No, Hector. Not much activity all day here other than potential
customers nosing around. Actually, they did sell two cars today."

"Okay, I just sent you a picture. The shorter guy on the left is the fella I'm curious about. Open your computer and tell me if he is the same size as anyone else at the car lot."

There was a pause before the man replied, "Might be the body shop guy. The mechanic is taller and thinner. None of the salesmen fits either...or at least the ones we've seen since being here. Cardin has referred to a couple of other salesmen we haven't seen yet. In case you're interested, the body shop man hasn't been in today."

"The body shop guy have a name?"

He's been called 'Jitters' and 'Donnelly'...no first name ever used. Speaking of that, he's the only one there who calls Cardin 'Hard'...which is some sort of nickname I guess. Everyone else calls him by his first name or 'Mr. Cardin.'"

"Good report, thanks. Jim probably has Donnelly's first name from running Cardin's financials...his and the business."

When Hector returned, he filled everyone in on the conversation. When he finished, Jim nodded. "Yeah, I got his first name, and will run financials on him pronto."

After he did so, Jim smiled. "Got 'em, I think. I'm betting we can assume Cardin and Donnelly are Bennet's two cohorts. Ken, I'd like you to keep the lid on this for now. These two are still our best bet on finding Bennet and Hassam...unless we get lucky on the house search. I can make a call or two to get that request turned into an order if you need me to."

Ken laughed. "Don't think that will be necessary, Jim. We got the word to cooperate fully with you, which in this case would be to keep this info in-house...which I fully agree with. My boss will like the idea, too. Are you gonna need any help keeping tabs on those two?"

"Probably not, but if we do, I'll let you know. For now we're gonna pretty well shut this operation down until Sunday. If you haven't been told, Al and Kathy are getting married here tomorrow.

I'll work on the house hunting job the rest of the day and tomorrow, time allowing. We may need, will need, some help checking out the places I find that are possibilities. You can work on the same thing if you want, but I predict we'll come up with it quicker than you can."

"You'll get no argument from me on that score. I'm just pissed your computer is better than anything we or Homeland have. I also read into what you've just said that it might be a good time for me to head back to the office to bring my boss up to date."

Jim smiled as he nodded. "Talk to you Sunday...feel free to come out then if you want. Not too early would be appreciated."

As Ken stood up, Al asked, "You wanna attend the wedding...*and* reception?"

Ken answered, "No thanks. I hate to see a good man going down in flames. Actually, I see Saturday work in my immediate future."

Bob also stood up. "Ken, follow me to the garage. I'll give you one of our security by-pass gadgets."

In the garage, Bob gave Ken the remote by-pass 'gadget.' As he did, he opened the garage door, followed by instructions, "Just press the bar like a garage door opener. Be sure the red light on the pole with the voice box is off, and the green one is on, before driving past the stop sign. If it malfunctions and the red light stays on, you'll lose your tires."

"Got it, thanks. See you Sunday more-than-likely...but not early. How about around ten?"

"Sounds good. Thanks for all your help."

"Hell, I should be thanking *you*...and do."

10.

By the time Bob returned, Bill was getting ready to leave for his home. His parting words were, "Somebody has to keep the business running, see you guys later."

It turned out his going to check on the business phone in his home was a good thing for the detective/protection business of Bob and his partners. The phone was normally manned by Amanda, the office manager. One of the calls needed immediate attention. After returning that call, Bill called Bob.

They discussed the matter for a few minute before it was decided Bill and Clyde would have to take care of the problem. With Jim in Michelle's office working on his project, Al looked at Bob. "You have any ideas on how to proceed at this point?"

"No. How about you, Emil?"

"Haven't the foggiest."

Hector joked, "Before anyone asks, neither do I. Well, hold it...we could run by this Donnelly's place to put a homing device on his car, but will need to figure out who is gonna keep tabs on him. I hate to split my four guys who are following Cardin all over hell and gone. A job like that really needs more than a two man team."

Bob nodded. "Agreed. I guess we could get Ken so we could use the FBI to keep tabs on him, but at this point it would be hard to do without a homer on the car, put there illegally."

Jim walked into the living room at that point. "I heard most of what you said Bob. You guys thinking of tracking Donnelly's car?"

Hector answered, "Yeah. We really don't have the manpower to do much with it though."

"I agree. So, for now, other than my house hunting project, let's play pool or something until the wedding is over. Sunday, we'll revisit this idea. Back to the house hunting deal. I've got a program set up to make some sort of an attempt to cut the number of house sales to work on. The idea is to track the financials of everyone who bought a home in our desired area. Anyone who has financials going back three years or more will be sliced from the list. But I have the sick feeling that we'll still have too many to check out."

That said, the men went to Bob's game room. They were still there when Holly returned with Kathy's mother, who met everyone before Amanda suggested, "Okay, ladies, time for Kathy to kiss Al goodbye until the wedding."

It had been agreed that Kathy's mother would spend the next two nights in Bill and Amanda's home, as would Kathy for Friday night.

***

On Saturday, little was done other than getting ready for the wedding, which went off without a hitch. At the reception, after most wedding gifts were opened, Bob walked up to the happy couple. He handed Al a key fob. "This opens the door to the home in the middle of the line of three homes across the road from my place. You two are welcome to stay there as long as you like. My sneaky wife and Amanda spent most of the day getting the place livable, including stocking it with food. Al, the alarm system there is the same as the other two and my place. Before you leave tonight, I'll go over the system with both of you."

When the reception party broke up, Bob showed the newlyweds the alarm system and they left for their temporary home.

Early Sunday morning after breakfast, Holly flew Kathy's mother home with Jo again going on the trip as her co-pilot. Kathy didn't make that flight, after her mother told her to stay behind with her husband, since she knew they had work to do on the manhunt for Bennet and Bassam.

After those three left, everyone else, including Ken, who arrived a little after ten, gathered in Bob's living room to work on ideas on their manhunt. Jim started the meeting. "Okay, Ken we need you to put a tail on Donnelly. We'll take care of Cardin. Since you found what is assumed to be all the explosive material Bassam had, someone had to supply him for his little episode the other night. I'm betting on Donnelly, since we're pretty certain Cardin was covered...except for sneaking out for their robbery. Hector talked to his guys tailing Cardin and they informed him it would be no problem for him to have snuck out the back of his house without being detected. From where they were parked, they couldn't see if he went out the backdoor, through his back yard, and the behind neighbor's lot. No big problem for Donnelly to pick him up there. You can bet they're using throwaway phones, so no way for us to track them down that way."

Ken nodded. "Okay, no problem with my people putting a net over Donnelly. I'd like to think we're pretty good on that kind of operation."

Hector smiled. "No real problem if they mess up and get spotted. If so, Cardin will have to take care of supplying Bassam, unless he already has everything he needs for his next move. The way we have this figured out, Donnelly has been the one delivering to Bassam what he needs."

Ken sighed as Jim added to the thought. "What Hector meant when he said that about the possibility of your guys messing up, doesn't indicate a feeling that they will. Just that if they do, it isn't the end of the world. In fact, at some point I might even suggest they allow Donnelly to spot them. It could force Cardin's hand to the point that he leads us to Bennet and/or Bassam. For some reason, perhaps some sixth sense about the visit Kathy and Bob paid to him, he seems to be taking it very careful. I talked with Hector about this last night, and the guys we have tailing him seem to think he may have a hunch we're on to him...which we weren't at the time of that visit."

Ken smiled. "No problem with what Hector said, Jim...I didn't think he expected us to drop the ball. Let me go into the office you've been using, to make my call to get things set up for the tailing process on Donnelly."

While Ken was gone, the others chatted about a few things not really having anything to do with the problem at hand. That was capped off just as Ken returned when Bob asked Al, "Well, pal, how is married life treating you?"

"Good so far. The sex isn't as good as before we got married, and Kathy isn't much of a cook, but beyond that everything is okay."

Kathy had a fake pout spread across her face as she retorted, "Some people—and note that I haven't mentioned any names—should use a glue stick instead of chap stick."

Hector joked, "Oh boy, Al, you've got a feisty one here...good luck."

***

With those in Bob's home joking around, Bassam was on his way to visit the imam at his mosque, and the other man he planned to use for the big events that would distract the authorities, while Bennet and his partners conducted the large armored car robbery. By the end of his day's work, he had assured his man that the incident with the other man had simply been an error on the part of the dead man. He also had gotten the three items he needed to stabilize the future bombs from the imam. The mosque was loaded with various items needed for bomb making, because Bassam had systematically placed them there as a backup in case his apartment was ever raided...as it had been.

The imam also informed Bassam that two additional men needed for the coming terrorist attack would be made available to him. None of the three men who would carry the bombs would know they were to be "suicide bombers." They would be told of a location where they were to place the bomb they were carrying. In fact a throwaway cell phone given to each, at the same time as the bombs, would be rigged to detonate the bombs. The imam was aware of this because like Bassam, he wanted to cut all links back to himself. He was even considering doing away with Bassam when the next terrorist act was completed...but decided to hold off on that to give it some additional thought.

The imam and Bassam would use safe throwaway phones to finalize their arrangements when time for the event neared. Satisfied with that meeting, Bassam returned to Bennet's hideout.

**

On Monday with Holly and Jo sitting in on the group meeting in Bob's home, Ken informed everyone that Donnelly was now under surveillance by the FBI. When he finished speaking, Hector looked at him as he asked, "If I send one of my guys around to buy that car now repainted, and we turn it over to you to verify that it does in fact have a black finish under the current colors, would you be able to get a warrant to put a homing device on Donnelly's car?"

"Should be able to, Hector. Later in the day I'll touch base with my boss to see what he thinks. For now there isn't any rush that I can see, because we have him well covered."

Hector grinned. "You say so."

While that idea was put on the backburner for the day, it was totally forgotten on Tuesday because several things happened to keep it from being necessary. The first was Tuesday morning when Cardin walked into the mechanic's shop to ask, "You got time to change the oil in my car?"

"Yeah, I'm just about finished with this car. Was gonna ask Jitters to take it out for a test drive. While he's gone, I can take care of your car."

Listening in at the house Hector had purchased, one of his men looked at the other. "You better give Hector a call. That bird discovers the homer while he's got Cardin's car up on the rack, we've got a problem."

Twenty minutes later, after Hector had been informed of the possible problem, the mechanic did indeed spot the homing device. He had a pretty good idea of what it was so hurried to have Cardin take a look. Cardin swore before he told the mechanic to "get that damned thing off, then smash it."

Before it was "smashed," Hector received another call. Hector replied, "Call our guys and let them know they'll have to follow Cardin the old fashioned way. I'll try to arrange some help from the FBI."

Of that call, Hector looked at Ken. "You wanna go play some pool with someone or can you forget what I'm about to say?"

Ken chuckled, "I'll leave it up to you...since you know how naughty you've been."

Hector nodded before he told everyone about the problem...with Ken still in the room. Next he asked Ken, "You able to spare more men to help with the tail on Cardin?"

"Yes."

At that point Hector's phone rang again. He was informed that Donnelly's car would soon go up on the rack to see if it had a similar device attached.

Even if that wouldn't have been enough to end the thoughts of getting a warrant to place one on Donnelly's car, what happened later in the day completely ended the need. The FBI team following Donnelly followed him to a firearms store, where Donnelly pulled around the back of the building. Being watched by the agents with binoculars, several minutes later Donnelly came out the back of the building with another man. They were both carrying various explosive items. After they loaded them in the car, Donnelly took out a wad of cash and handed a good deal of it to the other man.

One of the agents urged, "Hey we got him red handed, get down there pronto."

"Don't you think we should call in for directions?"

"Hell no, get down there...now."

The other agent shrugged, started the car, and tore down the alleyway. When the car screeched to a stop, both agents jumped out, identified themselves, and ordered the two men to the ground. In short order they had both cuffed. Only then did they call into their office to report the arrest they had just made, and request help with the two men, and the load of explosives in Donnelly's car.

When the dust settled, Donnelly and the arms dealer were in the downtown FBI office. At that point the Agent-in-Charge called Ken. "I don't think you're gonna like what I'm about to tell you."

Ken listened until the Agent-in-Charge finished speaking, then asked him to hold on as he turned toward Jim to explain the situation. Hector swore, Jim sighed, but immediately stood up. "How about driving us down to your office, Ken. Let us talk to Donnelly...with no one else present...no recording devices in play."

Ken said into the phone, "You get that, boss?"

"Yeah, and with our orders about letting Scott have whatever he wants, get him down here. Meanwhile I'll call Washington to make damned certain that order includes this."

By the time those three reached the FBI office, and after introductions, a very disgruntled Agent-in-Charge led Jim and Hector to the interrogation room where Donnelly had been placed.

They walked in and sat down. Jim glared at Donnelly. "Okay, sport, this is how things are gonna work. I'll ask questions, you'll answer truthfully. Got it?"

"I want a lawyer."

Jim replied with ice in his voice, "No you don't. You don't cooperate here, you'll be turned loose. When you walk out the front door, my friend and I'll be waiting outside. You'll take a little ride with us. What happens after that I promise will be worse than spending the next twenty years to life in the joint. We aren't employed by the government...we don't play by any nice little rules. Now, are you ready to give me what I want?"

"You can't do this. Those agents out there won't go for it."

Hector spoke up, "Jim, you get the car. I'll have the guys out there cut him loose...I'll walk out with him."

Jim stood up. "Right. See you out front. I'm gonna make a fast call so slow walk it a bit."

Hector followed Jim out the door, then walked up to Ken. "We're running a bluff. Told him we're turning him loose...come on."

Ken grinned as he followed Hector back into the room. When they were both inside, Ken looked at Donnelly. "Up, you. Hector, do you want cuffs on him?"

"Yeah, good idea...tough to run fast with your hands behind your back, in case he gets any ideas about splitting."

Donnelly was in a panic. "Wait, wait, I'll tell you what you wanna know."

Hector pointed to the chair Donnelly had just gotten out of. "Sit. Ken, ask Jim to come back in."

What followed was the worst half hour of Donnelly's life to that point. Even before they started questioning him, they told him what they planned to do to him if he failed to cooperate, or raised any kind of a stink about his treatment. They also told him whatever charges were tossed his way, he would be expected to plead guilty to.

Jitters Donnelly wasn't a brave man...he gave them everything they needed. At one point, knowing they would get it all, Hector left the room and called his two men in the house near the car lot. "Go detain Cardin and the mechanic until the FBIs get there. Cardin will be arrested, the mechanic will be detained as a material witness."

Ken heard that call and sent four agents in two cars to take control of the two men when they arrived at the car lot. By the time those two were brought into St. Louis FBI headquarters, planning was already underway for the raid on Bennet's hideout.

It was decided the raid would take place after dark, to avoid Bassam setting off what explosives he had to avoid capture, if he wasn't surprised when the FBI burst into the building. Jim and Hector made several suggestions, including that they would stop by Bob's estate to pick up some gear, including sensor detectors they felt (correctly) were superior to anything the FBI had.

***

Earlier, when he returned from his activities during the day, Bassam had laughed at the sight of Bennet who was filthy dirty. Bennet explained what he had been up to. Now with darkness just around the corner Bennet was concerned. "Jitters should have been here hours ago with the explosives he was picking up. He normally is on time. We best be prepared for the worst."

***

When the raiding party that included six FBI vehicles arrived at Bob's place, everyone was invited in for a final briefing. While that was going on, Hector went to the plane to get the gear he wanted to take.

During the briefing, Al and Kathy requested that they be allowed to be part of the raiding party. Jim agreed, "Sure, you two can ride with Hec and me."

Ken, who would be in charge of the raid, nodded approval, but he joked, "You can have Bennet, Al, but we get the terrorist. Don't get greedy."

Al replied, "Yeah, okay, sounds fair. Hope you don't mind if I put my cuffs on Bennet a bit tightly, Ken."

"Not at all."

11.

Even before Donnelly had been arrested, far to the East in London, England, Margaret (Maggie) Littlefield, Chief of British Secret Intelligence Service (MI6), was cleaning out her desk. She hadn't told the Prime Minister yet, but she had decided to retire. Her intent was to gather up all personal items from the desk, and put everything else back in an orderly fashion. When she got to the bottom right-hand drawer, she emptied it, but accidentally dropped a pen in the open drawer. It made a strange, hollow, clunking sound when it hit.

Maggie took a few minutes to carefully look at the drawer, finally discovering that it was a good deal shallower on the inside than on the outside. Convinced the drawer must have a hidden compartment, she spent still more time trying to figure out how to open it. This took several minutes, but in the end she managed to lift the false bottom to reveal a large manila envelope. She picked up the envelope, and after a few seconds of contemplation, opened it.

Inside on top of several pages of written material was a picture of Adolph Hitler...with a neat bullet hole in his forehead! Her excitement growing, Maggie started to read the material...all fifty-two pages of it. When finished, she was stunned at what she had read. Not wanting to mistake what she had, she re-read the entire manuscript. In a faint voice, she uttered, "My God in Heaven."

Maggie sat back in her chair as she reached for a special cell phone given her by her longtime friend, Jim Scott. Only a very select people had one of the phones that were totally untraceable and absolutely secure from eavesdropping. She called her predecessor as Chief of SIS, Sir Anthony Henry. "Tony, I need you to come here to my office...immediately!"

Something in the sound of Maggie's voice alarmed Tony. She was one of the coolest, most unflappable people he had ever known. "What is it, Maggie? You sound frightened or something."

"'Or something' twice over, Tony. Please hurry in as soon as you can make it."

"Yes, dear, I'm leaving now."

"Thank you."

It was nearly half an hour before Sir Anthony walked into the office that had once been his. Maggie had already poured two generous amounts of the sour mash Jim Scott had gotten both addicted to. She had been sipping on hers before Tony arrived. Without a word, she pointed to the chair in front of her desk, and held out the material from the envelope. Tony just smiled as he took it from her, then after a sip of the liquid fire, started to read after glancing at the picture.

When he finished he took a larger swallow of the sour mash. "Where the hell did this come from, lass?"

"The bottom right hand drawer of the desk you turned over to me, Tony. It was in a hidden compartment. I assume, from your reaction, you know nothing of it."

"You assume correctly. I think it is safe to say Sir Alistair didn't either, or he would have surely told me prior to giving me the job."

Sir Alistair Baldwin had been Chief of SIS prior to Sir Anthony, and was now deceased. Maggie nodded, "Wouldn't think so either. But, if you remember, two Chiefs before him died in office. Due to the finding of this thing now, I would assume no one ever knew of it besides the person who put it there. That is the only reason I can think of, as to why this has never been followed up on...or maybe there was a reluctance to delve into it."

"That or just wanting to slow-walk it, to make certain the facts are correct, but they certainly seem to be from what's here. Remember at that time it was much more difficult to 'follow the money' as it were. He may well have been doing so quietly when he died. God only knows how to go about it now after all these years, but we certainly have to."

Just as he finished speaking, both said "Jim" at the same time.

Tony nodded. "Glad you agree. He is the one person who can do the job, if it can be done. Then there is the matter of lineage. Of the twelve men on this list, I know of two whose lineage died with them."

"Yes, I had the same thought. I must admit at least half of the men on that list are totally unknown to me. Actually seven, but I think I may have heard of one of those, but know little about him."

"I'm about in the same boat, Maggie. Who calls Jim?"

"I will. But, if it involves a trip to the colonies, will you go along?"

"Of course. If for no other reason than to see where this leads. Bringing Jim in works in our favor two ways...if it comes down to eliminating anyone, he has the stomach and ability to make it happen without getting caught. Not that we aren't capable, but I think we both admit, Jim is in a class of his own for such matters."

"Agreed. Let me call him. We may as well plan on going there, so he can use his computer at his home base in Montana. I, like you, have access to it, but don't have the capabilities to handle this like he does."

"Yes, either he or Sarah would be best. Call him."

Sarah Turner, who lived on Jim's Montana ranch with her husband, was an expert in using his computer, and ran the details of his vast financial holdings using it.

Maggie picked up her phone without comment, and pushed the "1" on the phone, which was Jim's number on the phone of those who had them.

Jim answered, "Hi, Maggie, a bit late in London isn't it?"

"Yes, Jim, just past eleven. I need some help. Tony is here with me, and we both agree you need to see what we have. It is of utmost urgency."

"I'm right in the middle of something, Maggie."

"Be that as it may, whatever you are working on is not nearly so important as this. It seems as though Hitler had a previously unknown twin. One of them died in the bunker, the other in Brazil years later."

"What!?"

"You'll have to see what I found in a hidden compartment of my desk, to think this is possible. We need your help, as I said. Tony and I can be in the air within the hour for Montana."

"Not there, I'm presently staying with Bob Becker at his place Missouri. You've been here, so should be able to find it."

"Right, no problem. See you in a few hours."

As he put down his phone, Jim looked at Holly, then glanced at Hector. "We've got company coming...Maggie and Tony. Seems she has something hot. If true, it certainly is."

Holly and Hector exchanged looks, as Jim stood up. "Let's go, Ken."

An FBI armored vehicle with a SWAT team inside led the way since it was the slowest. Ken, with three agents in his car with him was next, followed by Jim's car and the other four cars containing FBI agents trailing behind. About halfway to their destination it started to snow.

In their car Hector groaned, "We could do without this snow."

Al agreed, "Yes, we could. Damned weather forecasters get something right about once every blue moon, and it had to be now."

Off that subject, Hector glanced over at Jim. "I still think we should be in the front of the procession. Hope those SWAT guys follow orders."

Jim joked in reply, "If they don't, I bet Ken has their ass. He seems pretty solid, and not one to suffer fools."

When they turned onto the road leading to Bennet's hideaway, every driver in turn killed his lights. With the snow falling, all drivers were still able to easily see the vehicle in front of them, so the lack of light didn't pose too much of a problem, even if they met another car coming the opposite direction.

At the drive leading up to the target cabin, the driver of the armored vehicle should have stopped, but instead decided to just pull up onto the drive before stopping. Hector swore, as did Ken in the second car.

Almost immediately after the armored vehicle stopped, the lights inside and outside the cabin went out. As Jim stopped behind Ken's car, Hector swore again as he hopped out with his detecting gear. In seconds he called out to Ken, who was standing outside his car. "Start the dance, Ken...they've got sensors."

Ken ordered the SWAT team vehicle forward as he got in to follow.

But by then it was too late. Bennet had been quite dirty, because he had finished off a tunnel, leading from the cabin down to a boat he had well-hidden near the river behind his property. As he had explained when Bassam joked about the condition of his clothing, he had finished putting the last section of rails in the tunnel so the three carts he had placed there could move rapidly.

When he had gotten still more worried that Donnelly hadn't shown up as promised, he had told Bassam. "You better put all the things not easily replaced in a valise, and put it on the middle cart with the stuff I've put there. Jitters brings his ass along, we can always take the stuff out of the tunnel."

When the SWAT vehicle pulled up onto the driveway setting off the sensors, as a matter of routine, Bennet turned off all the lights and looked out. What he saw was the line of vehicles behind the

SWAT team truck in the drive. Without delay, he ordered, "Let's go. That's trouble. I knew something was wrong when Jitters didn't show up. I'll take the front cart, you take the last one."

The FBI had a drone fly over the cabin earlier in the day, but the boat was not spotted. Thus, when the two men reached the end of the tunnel, they were floating down the river in a matter of about two minutes, even as the SWAT team swarmed into the cabin, weapons at the ready. It took a few minutes to find the tunnel, which were minutes the raiding party didn't have. While the boat had actually been on land in foliage, it was a short push to get it into the water. With the delay in finding the tunnel, the snowfall had covered any tracks left by the men or the boat by the time two SWAT team members had found the end of the tunnel.

Those two reported back, "No sign of them. Maybe they had a boat or something. But they could just be running one way or the other."

Irate at the missed opportunity, Ken ordered, "Well send some of your men both directions. We'll also send agents in cars up a ways in both directions. If they are on foot, they can't have gotten far."

With SWAT team members running, spread out in both directions from the end of the tunnel, Ken sent two cars further down the road, and told them to fan out in search of the two fleeing men. Two other cars were sent the opposite direction.

By then Bennet had started a well muffled outboard motor, and was speeding further down the river. Bassam was impressed with Bennet's careful planning, and told him so before he asked, "Where are we headed?"

"Down this river is a nice place to pull in where we can sorta hide the boat. About a mile from there is a bar that has live music, and most often a pretty good crowd. I'll leave you with our stuff and go boost a car...then drive down a path to near where I'll pick you up.

This damned snow might pose a problem on that path, but we'll just hope for the best. From there I've got a dame who'll put us up.

"Funny about her, I went to her place to kill her. She testified against me at my trial. But in fairness to her, that damned cop Felps had enough on me to get me convicted without her testimony. Anyhow, I forced my way in when she opened her door. She, of course, recognized me right off, and started pleading with me not to hurt her. She said she'd do anything not to be hurt. Well the long and short of it is she did the 'anything' I wanted. Turns out she's a damn good lay. I guess she liked it too, because she told me she'd be more'n happy to have me back for another go, or several more goes if I was interested. I was, and been banging her ever since...even after it came out I was wanted for those murders. I think she gets off on doing it with someone outside the law. I've stopped by to get a little more of her a couple of times, since I hooked up with you."

"I have another question. How do you think the cops found your hideout?"

"I'd bet on Jitters. I bet they arrested him on something and he gave me up...probably made some sort of deal with them. I'm betting Cardin's in the soup, too. All of which leaves us with coming up with a new plan. I only know one guy who I can pull into this next deal. You got any ideas?"

"Yes, maybe...we'll see. But, if Jitters gave us up, what if he told about your next deal, too?"

"That's a thought. You could be right. Maybe I better just drop that one. But, I need more money than I've got to get out of the country, and be able to live nicely once gone. I'll worry about that after we're safely with my gal."

Bassam just nodded as he thought, *"You get more money, but you won't be going anywhere with it. I can put it to better use for what I want to accomplish."*

The two men talked hardly at all until Bennet found where he wanted to pull the boat in. Once that was done, the two men carried what they had brought with them, to where Bennet would return with the stolen vehicle.

The long walk to the bar through the snow tired Bennet, especially now that the adrenalin rush of "the great escape," as he thought of it, was depleted. Arriving at the parking lot of the bar, he started looking into vehicles to see if anyone had been stupid enough to leave their keys inside. He knew in this day and age it was unlikely, but he checked anyhow. He had checked six vehicles without success, when a racket at the front of the building caused him to look in that direction.

With the door open, the din of the music inside was now more pronounced, but the real noise came from the "bouncer" of the bar as he shoved a man down into the snow, "Get your drunken ass out of here, and don't come back until you can behave!"

Bennet quickly faded back into the tree line as the drunk picked himself up and staggered toward his vehicle, which was a small sized SUV. Somehow in his state, he managed to find his key fob and push the button to unlock the SUV. Seeing which vehicle it was, Bennet hurried to stand in the tree line less than fifteen feet from its rear.

When the man reached to open his door, Bennet raced up to him. The man hardly noticed as Bennet raised his gun to hit him behind his right ear. Down he went in a heap, out cold. After picking up the dropped key fob, Bennet grabbed the top of the man's coat at the neck line to lug him into the tree line. He pulled the man along until he reached a slight gully well into the trees. After rifling the man's pockets to find his wallet and a wad of cash, Bennet turned to leave.

Knowing it wouldn't buy him all that much time, he nonetheless turned and shot the man in the head, thus freeing the man's poor wife from further abuse. Before heading to the bar, the drunk had beaten his wife while in the midst of an argument. Without realizing it, Bennet had done a good turn for someone else, something he almost never did if there wasn't something in it for himself.

Back at the SUV, he got in and drove to where he had left Bassam. When they loaded up their things, he drove to the home of the lady he had been seeing. He pulled into the driveway and then went to the front door, with Bassam right behind him. When the lady opened the door, both men walked in. Bennet quickly introduced them, then asked for the keys to her car. She obliged, and both men went out so Bennet could put the SUV in her garage, while her car was parked in the drive.

That done, they went back inside where Bennet explained, "We had a bit of trouble and need to stay here for a few days."

She just nodded as Bennet, who knew she worked Monday through Friday and it was Wednesday, continued, "I'll also need you to call work in the morning and tell them you have the flu and probably won't be in until Monday, at the earliest."

"Okay."

That taken care of in his mind, Bennet went through the door leading from the kitchen into the garage and returned with the satchel containing his money. Without saying anything, he took hold of the young woman's hand and led her into her bedroom, carrying the satchel in the other hand. But just before he closed the bedroom door, he called out, "Fateen, there's another bedroom. Help yourself."

In the morning, Bennet saw Bassam sitting in the living room. "If you want a turn, have at it. As I told you, she's a damned good lay."

Later when those two appeared, Bennet looked at the young woman and could tell she was a good deal less than happy. "I thought you might like a change of pace."

She was disgusted with the episode because Bassam—unlike Bennet who at least made an effort to make certain she enjoyed herself in bed with him—had been very rough with her. He had come in, mounted her, did his thing and gotten off without saying a word. Worse, he hadn't even used protection. While that didn't pose a problem as far as pregnancy was concerned, because she had been on the pill since she was 14, she had to hope he didn't have a VD or worse.

That being the case, she replied, "You thought wrong."

Realizing he had created a problem, and quickly thinking he really didn't need Bassam any longer, Bennet pulled out his gun and shot the terrorist in the head. Even though she was happy to know she would never have to experience what she just had again, she nearly fainted at seeing someone murdered right in her kitchen.

12.

Back at Bob's estate, there was a bit of grousing about the missed chance, with Ken apologizing about his SWAT team not following directions.

Jim replied to that, "Not to worry, Ken. For some reason I have a feeling he was looking for trouble, so may have seen us anyhow, without the aid of the sensors. If Donnelly was supposed to take the explosives he was caught buying out to him, he was probably getting concerned why the delivery was taking so long. Whatever else Bennet may be, he seems to be a wily fellow. Especially since he had such a good escape plan ready in the first place. That tunnel was something right out of the '*Great Escape*.'"

When Ken gave Jim a funny look, Jim joked, "Guess you're too young for that reference. The "Great Escape" was a classic WWII movie, and they built a similar tunnel to execute their escape."

Ken sighed. "If you say so, but I'm still pissed at my guys screwing up like that. It wasn't like we didn't go over where to stop when on site at least ten times with them."

Hector nodded. "Yeah, Ken, but what is done is done. Now the question becomes how to find these guys. We better put our thinking caps on, because whatever advantage we had is now blown with the arrest of Cardin and Donnelly. That being the case, I think I'll send the guys I brought in back to L.A. It would be nice if a young lady, or two, would volunteer to fly them home."

Holly joked, "Since you said 'young' I nominate Michelle and Jo. I'm bushed from all the flying I've been doing."

Michelle and Jo readily agreed to take them back. After Hector thanked them, he added, "But in the morning. We all need to get some sleep. We can get back on the great hunt then."

Jim agreed, "Good idea."

Jim was first up in the morning, waking around five. He put on coffee and decided to get Hector up, also. Those two were having coffee when Holly came downstairs. She grunted, "I heard you get up, and couldn't get back to sleep. Coffee...now."

Jim was smiling as he poured a cupful for her. "You have every right to be bushed, dear. The amount of flying you've been doing would tire anyone...even a sweet young lady like yourself."

"Yeah, sex was good last night...thanks."

Hector joked, "I didn't hear anything about sex in what he had to say, Holly."

"You weren't listening...there's nothing 'young' about me these days...sweet maybe."

At that point Bob walked in. "I smell coffee. Smelled it all the way upstairs."

By seven everyone in the home was fed, and those from other homes on the estate started filtering in. Bill was the last to arrive, and reported, "Amanda is staying home to catch up everything she should have been doing for the last few days. I just came over to say 'hi' before heading back to dig in myself. Clyde, I'm betting it's you and me doing all the work for the next little bit."

"Yeah, I know. You guys don't need us here do you?"

Bob shook his head. "Nope. In fact I may give you guys a hand if needed. Not that any of us is gonna get much done with all this damned snow. Looks to be around six to eight inches."

Bill agreed, "This is the most we've had in early December in years...a lot of years. But we do have some sensors to put out on one job I can think of. Beyond that, not much I'm aware of. Amanda told me that nothing new has come in since all this started. All of which is to say we probably don't need your help, Bob."

"Good...you two can dig up the snow to put those sensors out without my help. If memory serves, you've only got about six to put in place."

Bill nodded. "Yeah, that's right."

Changing the subject, Michelle looked at Hector. "When are your guys gonna be ready to fly...and from where, here or the rehab clinic?"

"I told 'em to meet you at the clinic at ten. That'll give them plenty of time to pack up their personal stuff, and the gear the two were using in the house I bought. Someone remind me later to go by that car lot, and recover the bugs we had put there. Speaking of the car lot, Jim, did Ken tell you what they found in the safe we told 'em about?"

"Oh, yeah, I forgot to tell you. About a hundred grand and a couple of weapons...handguns. At Cardin's house they didn't find much except plans for their next job...the one Donnelly told us about. At Donnelly's place nothing of use...all of which raises the question of what happened to all the dough they got from those robberies. At some point I guess we should have Ken ask Donnelly about that. I'll mention it to him when he gets here."

Those words were just out of his mouth when his phone rang. He answered, "Good morning, Ken. What's up?"

"Hi, Jim. Early this morning we sent a drone up and down the river Bennet used for his getaway, and think we may have spotted his boat. I'm on my way there with a few more agents. I'm certainly glad the snow stopped. Weather guy on TV said it was six inches, heavier in places. I'll touch base with you when I know more."

"Okay, be waiting to hear from you. We're just sitting around Bob's kitchen twiddling our thumbs."

As he put his phone down, Jim told the others about the call. Before anyone could make a comment on that, Jim's phone rang again. "Hi, Maggie. Wondered when you might be checking in."

"It seems to me Bob's runway is warmed, so all this loverly snow I'm seeing won't be a problem on landing...which is going to be shortly."

"Is 'loverly' a word...never mind. Yeah, you're good to go. He's got the same system here as I do in Montana. No wind from the looks of things, by the way. Come on in. When I see you swoop in I'll come get you. Just the two of you?"

"Yes...just me and his lordship."

Jim could hear a wisecrack made by Tony before he replied, "Tell him we're all standing by to scrape and bow."

"Will do. See you in a few."

This time as Jim put his phone down, Hector asked, "Maggie and Tony?"

"Yup."

When Maggie landed, Jim was there to meet them in a dune buggy-like cart Bob had parked next to his home. Noting neither carried a bag, with Maggie carrying only the manila envelope, he started driving back to the house. One the way, he asked, "Do I get a hint?"

Maggie replied, "Hitler had an identical twin...one killed in the bunker, the other in Brazil years later. Evidently no way to tell the difference, so we don't know who died where. Also, the Third Reich is alive and well."

"Wow, Maggie, when you uncover something you really go overboard."

"So it would seem. Jim, we've got a lot of work to do. To start I want you, Hector, and Holly to see what I have in this envelope. Anyone else you wish to bring into the picture, I will go along with, since I trust your judgement more than I do my own...or Sir Anthony's judgement either for that matter."

"That's high praise coming from someone in your exalted position, my dear...thank you."

"High praise I agree with, Jim."

"Thank you, also, Tony...or is it my lord."

"Enough, Stanley James."

"You sound like Holly, Tony."

Jim then asked, "Does your Prime Minister know about this, Maggie?"

"No, no one but Tony. When I called the P.M. from the air, I only said I was going to the colonies to consult with a friend. The P.M., of course, asked if that would be you, and I admitted it was...end of conversation. Well, not quite, I was asked when the P.M. would be brought into the picture. Again I told the truth...I wasn't certain. End of the conversation with an unkind word on the other end of the connection."

Inside, Jim looked at Hector, then glanced at Holly. "Will you two please accompany the three of us into Michelle's office? The rest of you, I'm sorry but Maggie prefers only Holly and Hector be brought into the picture of what she has to unload on me...at least for now."

There were only three chairs in Bob's former den, so knowing that, Hector took two from the kitchen. When everyone was seated, with Jim behind Michelle's desk at Maggie's insistence, she handed the envelope to him.

He opened it, saw the picture, passed it to Hector, who passed it in turn to Holly. After reading each page, he would pass it along also. When he finished reading the last page he said nothing until Holly finished it also.

The document outlined how the British, not convinced Hitler was actually dead, had sent a team of SIS operatives to track down the various leads that "Nazi hunters" had uncovered. After several years, they captured a former German general in Brazil. After intensive questioning, the general broke and told all. His story began with a Jewish nurse who tried to bargain for her life in one of Hitler's concentration camps. She told the commander of the camp that she had been present when Hitler was born...Hitler and a twin brother.

Not being totally stupid, she refused to go into detail, until assured she would be spared death and removed from the camp.

Somehow the story was passed up the line to Hitler who was intrigued by it. He ordered the woman be brought to him personally. She had then told Hitler, in front of the general (who wasn't yet a general at that time) now telling the story, that an hour before Hitler was born, the Jewish doctor who delivered Hitler had delivered another baby for another woman. Just minutes before the birth of Hitler, that baby had died, but the doctor hadn't had time to notify the other woman of the death.

When Hitler was born, his mother passed out before the second baby was delivered. Swearing the nurse to secrecy, he decided since no but those two would know of the second Hitler boy, that child would be given to the first woman. The other mother was not Jewish, and still lived in the area. Her adult son had been wounded in WWI, but was more-or-less in good health at the time the story was being told to Hitler. He was, at the telling of the story, a low-level functionary in the government of a town not too far from where he and Hitler had been born. The former nurse told Hitler the name of his twin when telling where he lived. Her story complete...Hitler shot her in the forehead and had her body burned.

Then he sent the general—who became a general only after he succeeded in finding the man and bringing him to Hitler—to find his twin. The general telling the story to the SIS operatives was a little foggy on what transpired after that, other than either Hitler or the twin had died in the bunker, while the other had been smuggled into Brazil before the war ended. The general also knew where whoever had not died in the bunker now resided. His story complete, the general met with an accident...a fatal accident.

Knowing where the surviving twin was located, the three SIS operatives requested and received a ten-man SAS (Secret Air Service) team to assist them in rounding up the twin. It was a good thing they requested the assistance of the SAS men, because they wound up in a terrible gun battle, resulting in the death of all those in the twin's compound, and three SAS troops. But Hitler, or his twin, was captured alive. Unfortunately the man was "a raving lunatic" that the SIS operatives were unable to get any sense out of. In a fit of peevishness one of the operatives lost patience and shot the "lunatic" in the forehead..."picture attached."

However, they did find a wealth of documents. Vast sums of money, millions upon more millions had been stashed in Swiss banks. The fortune was divided into 12 separate accounts of almost equal amounts. Three men each from Germany, France, England, and the United States were to be in charge of one of the accounts to continue the Third Reich. The feeling was that if Germany lost the war, these men would be responsible for a re-birth of National Socialism. The accounts were set up so that if any of the men died, their nearest living *male* relative would be responsible for carrying on the dream. Due to intermarriage and untimely death, the list of the most recent men responsible was, at the time of the writing of the document being read in Michelle's office: three in the U.S.; four in England; four in Germany; but only one in France.

After Holly read the last page, she simply blew out a mouthful of air as she put it with the rest of the material from the envelope. Seeing her do that, Jim got right to the point. "Okay, Maggie, I've got two very pertinent questions: are you able to verify this document as being written by one of your predecessors; and where did you unearth this from?"

"I found it in a secret compartment of my desk, which as you probably know has been in the office of the Chief forever. Tony and I both verified the handwriting, and are convinced it is kosher, and the paper is from the correct period."

"Who wrote it?"

Tony answered Jim, then added, "As you may or may not know, he died while still Chief...rather unexpectedly. We were certain it had to be him, since no word was passed on to succeeding Chiefs. The three SIS officers who tracked down Hitler, or his twin, also died early in life...prior to his death. One of natural causes, the other two on an operation gone wrong. All that said, I am certain this document is authentic."

Jim looked at Maggie who nodded. "Me, too."

Jim asked, "Now what?"

Holly answered, "Now four of us fly to Montana leaving Hector behind to find these two guys we just missed. At home, Jim, you, I, Sarah, and Maggie get on the computer at four different monitors and get to work. We obviously have to trace lineage of the 12 men who were the gatekeepers, so to speak, of the ongoing efforts to resurrect the Third Reich. Tony can observe and help us by giving us lineage shortcuts from his knowledge of some of the families involved."

Hector agreed, "I'll take care of things here, Jim, as Holly suggested. I can also offer my guys in L.A. to do any legwork you might come up with. Now I have a question: What happens to the money that is left sitting in a bank if one of the bloodlines dies out? While asking questions, what do we tell our friends in the other room?"

Jim answered, "To the first one, there is no way of telling what happens to said money. There is nothing in here to suggest any special arrangements were made. Pity we don't have the original documents found. To the second question, I'll take care of it, but in a word we tell them nothing."

Holly joked, "That's more than one word, darling. Before we go out to join the others, one plane or two?"

Maggie answered, "One. I can't fly another mile. I'm working on no sleep, which I plan to correct on the trip to Montana. But we best take my plane, I don't want it sitting out here in plain sight, in case we stir up a hornet's nest."

"Or," suggested Hector, "you could park it in Bob's hangar."

Holly shook her head. "No, I'll leave my plane, we'll take Maggie's, and park it in our hangar. If we decide we need my plane at some point, we can use the other one at the ranch to fly down here to pick it up."

That said, Maggie put everything back in the envelope and stood up, soon following the other four back to Bob's living room where everyone still on his estate had moved to. By then Michelle and Jo had left to fly Hector's men back to Los Angeles, and Ken had arrived.

He had called Bob to let him know he was on his way after Jim didn't answer his phone, which he had turned off after reading the first two pages of the document. Jim quickly introduced him to Maggie and Tony, then added for everyone present, "Maggie, as a representative of the Brits, has asked for my help on a ticklish matter. Sir Anthony has also been asked for his assistance by Maggie. I'll be leaving immediately for my ranch in Montana, to use my computer in giving the help needed. I could do it with my laptop, but may need Sarah's help, so Holly and I'll be going home with Maggie and Tony. While we're gone, Ken, Hector will be the point man for me on anything coming up. When talking to him, you can treat it as if you were speaking to me. You have any problem with that?"

"No, Jim...I'll save you the call to Washington, with resulting call to my boss. I can assure you that he will go along also."

"Thank you, Ken. Everyone, I want not a word of this to leave this house. Ken, that includes you telling your boss. If my absence is noticed, I'm simply returning home for a few days on a personal matter. Uh, Ken, you can bet those in Washington will no doubt be asked for their help in this matter, because the outfall of it may well, in time, concern the U.S. as well as England. Michelle and Jo can be told the truth, but should also be warned to keep it to themselves. That said, we're out of here. Bob, Holly and I'll be leaving our things here so please keep our room reservations as they are."

Bob nodded. "Consider it done. Come on, I'll drive all four of you to your plane."

Jim corrected, "Maggie's plane, we're leaving ours. Good luck finding those two jerks. Bye."

13.

When Bob returned to his home, Ken joked, "I didn't even get to tell Jim the news I brought."

Emil replied, "All you told us was that you found Bennet's boat, Ken."

"I know, Jim came out at that point. To finish the story, Bennet and Bassam have been up to no good...again. When we got to where the boat was found we saw several tracks in the snow, or at least indentations that were only partially filled in by the continuing snow. I sent one of my guys off to follow one set that seemed to go a good deal further.

"While he was off doing that we found where they had placed whatever they took with them from the cabin. It appeared as though one of them stayed there to guard their belongings. Anyhow, we also found tracks where a vehicle had driven down to where their stuff was placed. A lot of tracks suggested they loaded up and left.

"Then it got interesting. By the time we were ready to leave where we were, I was starting to wonder what had happened to my guy. I decided if Bennet and Bassam drove out on the tire tracks we found, maybe we might discover something. So leaving one car back for my agent on foot, I drove over the tracks we'd found. About the time we reached a road, my guy called to tell me where he was, and I better get there 'pronto.' When we got on the paved road, and turned in the direction he had been heading we saw flashing lights at once. When we reached those lights we found several police cars and a Medical Examiner's vehicle.

"Well, anyhow, the big deal was a dead body that had been found. There is a bar and restaurant there. The body had been found several feet from their parking lot. The place opens early, serving breakfast, and two guys had eaten. When they came out, one of them decided he had to pee. Rather than go back inside, he walked into the tree line at the end of the parking lot. What does he find? The dead body, of course. The guy had been shot in the back of his head. After checking his ID, the local cops soon found out no vehicle on the lot was unaccounted for, so they sent two officers to the address they got off his driver's license. To make a long story short, they managed to find out he had driven off in a huff in his wife's SUV the night before. They had gotten in a fight, in fact the officers reported that she looked well beaten. We now have everyone looking for her SUV.

"It doesn't take a genius to figure out one of those two men we're after probably did the killing to get wheels. If they keep the SUV long enough, maybe we'll get lucky...if not, I have no idea where to go from here, other than the usual stuff of checking friends, et cetera...as we've already done. Any ideas?"

Hector sighed. "It's too early to have a drink, but beyond that, I've got nothing. I suppose it's too late to keep the discovery of the body from the media, Ken?"

"Oh yeah, they were already there by the time I arrived. When they saw my SUV with FBI plastered all over the side of it, I had to issue a 'no comment' on what I was doing there. I can almost bet I'll be on the evening news making said non-comment."

Kathy spoke up, "Well, we've already checked out anyone Bennet could have known in prison, or knew before he went. But I guess maybe we should retrace our steps there. By the way, Ken, did you ever track down if Bassam went to any particular mosque?"

"No. None of his known associates claim to know...which I found doubtful. The men he had with him in the raid on his apartment were all killed in the shootout. We've checked out their known associates...nada. But, as you suggested, Kathy, we'll all have to retrace the steps we've already taken. I'd bet we come up with squat."

***

While that conversation was going on, a very rich and influential man, Arron Jones, was having lunch in his Washington, D.C. penthouse with a high ranking assistant Attorney General, Barton Flake. After a sip of his wine, the host got to the matter of the meeting. "Barton, we have a problem. A fellow by the name of Jimmy Bennet, that's all I have, is now the only living male from the Ethan Murry tree that I know about. I have been unable to find out anything about him except he hailed from Missouri...on the eastern side of the state. I don't know his correct first name, or if he has a middle name. As you may recall, when Ethan Murry's brother died without having children since he was...um, gay, he named a nephew as his successor, and had briefed him. However, it turns out the nephew died in an auto accident two weeks before old Murry passed on. By then Murry was in a coma, so no way to ask him about this Bennet fellow. The only thing we had on him from Murry, was a notation that the only other living male from his family tree was Jimmy Bennet, and with a further notation of 'God help us if he would be the replacement.' We did a bit of digging and discovered information about a niece of Murry's having a boy in eastern Missouri. Her married name was Bennet. But we couldn't find out anything about her...even what her maiden name was. It seems she was some sort of a rebel, and was never spoken of by the family...and none still alive ever heard of her."

"That's strange, because I seem to remember hearing the name 'Jimmy Bennet' recently. Can't recall where, though. I assume you have a DNA sample from Murry, in case we can find this Bennet fellow?"

"Of course...so do our friends in Switzerland. Try to find out what you can about the 'Jimmy Bennet' you heard of. Obviously this is important. Those damned banks already have enough of our money tied up."

"Will do. Wait, I think I remember. It was mentioned by one of the FBI agents we have in the movement. I'll see what I can find out from him."

The two men continued to talk over lunch, then Flake returned to his Justice Department office.

***

When their plane landed at Jim's ranch, the four aboard went to the computer center where they found Sarah hard at work. Jim told her to stop what she was doing, then led her to the kitchen/conference room near to the computer set-up. "Here, Sarah, I want you to read what is in this envelope. After you have your heart attack, we need your help with what we're planning to do."

Sarah smiled as she took the envelope from Jim. As she read, Jim got five tumblers from the cabinet, a bottle of his favorite sour mash, and poured five healthy amounts of it into each tumbler. With all five sitting at the table, Sarah read about ten pages, before she took a sip of her drink. As she did, she looked at Jim. "Is this real?"

"Afraid so."

When she finished, and made a few obvious comments about what she had read, Jim explained what the plan was. When he finished, he added, "Holly and I'll work on the Americans. Sarah, you help Maggie with the rest. When Holly and I finish, we'll assist you two. Tony will, in addition to being our gofer, stand by to offer any insight he can on any names developed along the way."

As Tony made an unkind comment, the five headed to the computer center. Arriving there, Jim asked, "Honey, you want the lineage or the money?"

Holly answered, "You better take the money. You're better at that than I am."

Sarah and Maggie decided Sarah would take the money while Maggie would work on lineage. Then the job started.

They were still working away when Bear Turner, called that by everyone but Sarah who called him Al, the shortened version of his first name Albert, arrived. After greeting the four from the plane, he asked, "Hey, wife, what's for dinner?"

Sarah answered, "Whatever you cook, dear. We're busy....real busy."

Jim pointed to the kitchen area. "On one of the conference tables you'll find an envelope. Read the contents. No doubt you'll be getting involved in this, so you may as well know what's up."

Holly smiled. "Bear, darling, I took six steaks out of the freezer before we started."

Sarah joked, "Mrs. Scott, don't be coming with 'darling' when speaking to my husband if you please."

Bear just shook his head as he left the area for the dining room. When he finished reading the material, he came back. "Man-o-man, if that stuff is real, we've got a real mess on our hands."

Jim nodded. "Glad you worded that the way you did...because it seems to be in our hands thanks to Maggie and Tony, who have decided to get us involved. I hope your war bag and travel bags are packed."

Sarah butted in, "They are, as always, and you know it, Jim."

Their joking aside, with nothing other than a break to eat, they stayed at it until nearly midnight. By then Jim and Holly had worked together to arrive at Barton Flake as one of the current men in charge of vast amounts of Hitler's money. When they agreed, Holly groaned, "Geeze, a stinking assistant attorney general, no less. This is gonna be a pip, dear."

Then when they both agreed on Arron Jones, Jim made a similar comment to Holly's earlier one. Sarah and Maggie had started on the two men who Tony already knew that the most recent descendants were dead. They verified the remaining money seemed to be sitting idle in a Swiss bank. The next one they started on was an

Englishman. When they agreed they had their man, Tony's comment was very like that of Jim and Holly, "Blimey, that chap could have been P.M. if his party had not been defeated in the election a few years back. The current P.M. is gonna love it when informed of this mess."

After Jim had started on the last of the original 12 who were Americans, he called a halt. "I'm think we should all get some sleep...maybe about four hours...sound good?"

***

While those at Jim's ranch had been working, Bennet was on the move to rid himself of Bassam's body and the stolen vehicle. He drove the SUV, while his lady friend followed in her car. Driving behind him, she considered heading to the nearest police station and running in for help. But she didn't, because however evil he was—except for the awful episode with the now dead terrorist—he had treated her better than any man in her life...and he certainly was good in bed. There was also the promise of a grand life in a southern country. She had never traveled outside Missouri, so that really appealed to her.

Satisfied with the location he planned on dumping the SUV, Bennet simply got out with the keys left inside. As he approached the car, he announced he would drive them home. Thus ended his brief relationship with the terrorist.

As it turned out, an alert patrolman of St. Louis County, where the SUV had been left, happened to spot it. Luckily for him, as he drove right up to the rear of the vehicle, neither of the men being sought was alive inside, or he might well have died for not calling for backup as he should have.

By the time the FBI had been notified that the vehicle they were looking for had been found, and then Ken had been told to investigate, it was after eleven. Convinced he was looking at the dead body of Bassam, he called Al. "Okay, I got my man. I have an idea your man may have killed him. Head shot, body found in the SUV they boosted at that bar and restaurant. As soon as I get the slug out of Bassam's head, we'll try to match it with the other ones you have from Bennet's misdeeds. When you pass this on to Hector, let him know I'll continue to help as I can on the Bennet search. But Bennet is a local matter, so I guess my boss will check with Washington to see how much help I can offer."

"Thanks, Ken. Glad you got your damned terrorist off the street, no matter how it came about. At least we shouldn't have to worry about bombs going off now...unless Bennet picked up some pointers from Bassam."

"I really wish you hadn't said that, pal."

***

While Bassam's body was being disposed of and found, Barton Flake had visited Arron Jones again. He had called Jones after finding more out about Jimmy Bennet. "Have you eaten yet, Arron?"

"Yes."

"How about inviting me over for a drink?"

Jones was alert enough to know this was an out of the ordinary request, and realized what it might be about. "Come on."

Neither man bothered about a drink when Flake walked in and started speaking, "I have information about Bennet...at least a Jimmy Bennet I had heard mentioned the other day. He's being sought for a string of murders in Missouri. He seems to be running with a terrorist by the name of Bassam. The very bad news about this is Jim Scott is helping in the manhunt."

"What, Scott...are you certain?"

"Afraid so. The St. Louis FBI Agent-in-Charge has been told to let Scott run the show. You know the rumor about Scott being involved in taking down the group we spent years setting up."

"Rumor, hell. Two of those now dead or presumed dead men, called me with news that Scott might be hot on their trail. Within twenty-four hours one was killed, the other disappeared...has never been heard from again. They were working on trying to take control of Nohow Robotics. Blew up in their faces."

"Yes, I know. I had a couple of those gentlemen contact me, too. Though they didn't know for sure it was Scott behind their problem, only suspected it."

"Well it was, or at least the two I heard from thought it was. Enough of this. We have two things to do. One, obviously, is to find this Bennet first, to see if he is the same Jimmy Bennet we're looking for. You should be able to find out more about this Bennet, but if we get to him first, we'll, of course, have to prove it out with DNA. The other thing is maybe we should get Scott out of the way before he becomes too big a problem. Contact Harris to take him out of the picture. He's been a problem long enough."

"I'll take care of it first thing in the morning. On second thought, I better do it tonight. Maybe have Harris do both...find Bennet and take care of our Scott problem. I'll also do what I can to see where the St. Louis FBI office is with tracking him down. I guess I better make a trip to St. Louis. I can come up with some reason for it...maybe to consult with the U.S. Attorney for that district on something. I'll also have a couple of our guys over at FBI Headquarters dig out what there is on Bennet."

"Good. While you're doing all that, I've got a couple men who I'll send on the Bennet mission. We simply have to find him first. Better let Harris work independently of them. What do you think?"

"Yes, I think so. Harris doesn't play nicely with others, as you know. But I will tell him we have others looking for Bennet, but we better not let your men know. We want them doing their best without the thought that they don't have to work too hard finding him, if we have someone else doing the same thing. With Harris, there is no worry on that score."

"Nor is there with the men I'll send. But, as you wish, they won't be told."

Once back in his car, Flake called Cam Harris. "I have two jobs for you. They are connected. Meet me at the usual place."

Flake had used a throwaway phone, and the number he called was another one. The only use of those two phones was to each other. Harris agreed to meet Flake.

The "usual place" was a long abandoned manufacturing plant. Flake was there first, so when Harris arrived, he walked to the passenger side of Flake's car and got in. Knowing Harris wasn't one for wasted words, Flake got right to the point. "A man by the name of Jim Scott needs to be eliminated. Also..."

Harris cut him off, "Scott is a hard one. Others have tried...they have died. I will take the job, but do not expect an overnight success. I have no intention of going off half-cocked when after someone like Scott. I will not even consider trying to take him down at his home in Montana. I have had associates who went there to do the deed, only to never be heard from again. One was perhaps the best assassin I ever heard of. Now about your other task."

"There is a man by the name of Jimmy Bennet who is wanted in Missouri for several murders. He must be found before the authorities do. He is desperately needed...alive by me and my friends. He has what might be called the "keys to the vault" as it were. Scott is also looking for him. In the morning I will get a file of everything the FBI has on him. I'll get it to you as soon as I have it."

"Yeah, I've heard on the news that there is one big manhunt going on for him."

"Yes, that's the man. We are sending others to look for him, but not to take out Scott. That is your job alone. Those men do not know you will also be looking for Bennet."

"Very well. Call me when you have the file on Bennet. In the meantime I'll arrange a private flight to Missouri. The St. Louis area according to the news."

"That's correct. Remember, Scott is also looking for him...working with the local police and the FBI."

"That's interesting. Might make the job on Scott easier."

14.

In the morning, Flake had no trouble getting what was known on Bennet, but when he tried to gather information on Jim, he found everything on him, including his military career and time at the CIA was sealed. Knowing the connections Jim had in Washington, this didn't really surprise him. He did find out more on the situation in St. Louis, including the fact that Jim was staying with Bob Becker, at Becker's estate near Wentzville, Missouri.

He took what he had to the meeting place with Cam Harris. After Harris looked at it all, he shrugged. "This guy Bennet is something. With half the world looking for him, I'll be damned lucky if I find him first. As to Scott, what you have should help. I guess the question becomes should I try to tail Scott hoping he leads me to Bennet, or just take him at the first chance I get?"

"Take him out. But, finding Bennet first is beyond urgent. Again, I remind you that we need him alive. He is of no use to us dead."

As he spoke he handed him an envelope containing thirty thousand dollars in cash. "This should cover your expenses. You need more, let me know. Million for Scott, another million for Bennet alive, are yours on success...satisfactory?"

"Yes. I'll be on my way to St. Louis within the hour. I have a plane standing by."

From his car, Flake called Jones. "Harris is on his way."

The executive jet Harris hired for the trip landed at a small airport outside St. Louis. There, Harris rented a car, found a nice motel between St. Charles and Wentzville, and did a drive by of Bob's estate. He was impressed. He had researched Bob on the flight, so knew his business was detective/protection. With that knowledge he suspected, correctly, that the likelihood of the estate having an ample supply of sensors was almost a certainty. It wasn't like Cam Harris to go charging in blindly, but fearing Bob would have sensors protecting from surprise visitors, raised his cautionary approach to the problem even more than normal. Still, he needed to get a good look at the goings on at the estate, so started looking for a safe place to leave his car. South of the entrance road (leading nowhere with a turnaround less than a quarter of a mile in) that led to Bob's long driveway, he found nothing. He drove on down the two-lane highway until finding a good place to make a U-turn. That accomplished, he headed back north. There was a now snow-covered dirt road that led down to a large pond. With the snow as an added problem, he chose to bypass that for now. He was on a small incline and less than half a mile up the hill, when he saw a road to the left. He tried that to find it led to several homes, but went nowhere else. While there was a tree line with underbrush that might do, it was not what he was looking for due to the snow.

Disgruntled with that, he went back to the highway to continue the trip uphill. As he crested it, he soon came to a road to the right. He turned onto it and in time found it led to what had to be a farm or ranch. He turned around, with some difficulty, and drove back to the highway. On the drive into Wentzville, he carefully checked out the landscape before going back to his motel. In his room, he kicked back with a glassful of the brand of Scotch he preferred. Sipping the drink, he started to consider what he had found out on his scouting mission. While doing that, he fiddled with the picture Flake had managed to find of Jim. It was the only thing given him on his target, and it was dated fifteen years previously. Harris wondered how much Jim may have changed in appearance in those fifteen years, because he was considering making an attempt on Jim as he drove back and forth from the Becker estate. Nothing else he came up with made any sense, so he decided he simply must find a way to get a better look at Bob's property...but how was the question. In the end, he decided to get a good meal and sleep on the problem.

***

While Harris was considering his options, Jim and his group were making good progress on their project, but not liking what they were finding. Convinced they had Arron Jones and Barton Flake well covered, Jim and Holly had reached nearly the end of the line on Ethan Murry. They had discovered the now also deceased nephew, and information that the long-ago disgraced niece had married a man by the name of Bennet. When they found that, Holly joked, "Wouldn't it be a trip if the gal had a kid by the name of Jimmy?"

Jim, who was busy trying to track down more about the niece replied, "Yeah, that would be something. I'm not having much luck here tracking her down, including if she ever had any kids. I'm thinking I should just put this aside for now and give Sarah and Maggie a hand. You can start on the financials of one they haven't started on yet. I'll probably hang it up on the niece pretty soon if I don't find anything."

Sarah and Maggie were further along due to a couple of reasons. The two family trees that Tony had predicted were without living males proved to be just that. Sarah, working the financials, had determined that those two accounts had been dormant for several years. Thanks again to help from Tony, they had uncovered the two Englishmen found to be the standard bearers for the accounts they were in charge of. One was from an English family tree and presently served in the House of Commons.

The other came from what had originally been a Frenchman, who married an English lady, who bore him a son and daughter. He died when the children were very young, so the lady returned to England. One of the Englishmen originally assigned one of the accounts mentored the young boy until he was old enough to be approached with his heritage. Eventually, that was passed down to still more Englishmen on that family tree. The current man in charge of the account was now quite old, but a son had been briefed, and accepted his heritage. The son had run for office twice without success, but was doing quite well in financial circles, recently having moved up to a high position in one of England's largest banks.

Putting those two aside, after a few unkind comments from both Maggie and Tony, the two ladies next had looked into the lone remaining Frenchman in charge of still another of the accounts. When satisfied they had him nailed down, they had moved right along to the present day German who had wound up in charge of one account much as had the other French account now turned English.

They were part way into checking on another German account when Jim finally gave up on his project, to assist Holly who was looking into another of the German men in charge on one of the accounts. As Jim started working on the financials, Holly looked over at him. "Honey, got something strange on this General Maximilian Bachmeier. A few years after the war, he seems to have moved to Brazil, then three years later moved back to Germany with a son I can find nothing on...that is Bachmeier never married, and there are no birth records of the son in Brazil. I know their record keeping leaves a lot to be desired, but how in the heck did he get him back go Germany without at least a birth certificate?"

Tony spoke before Jim could respond. "Hold on there a second, Holly. There is no way Bachmeier could have fathered a child. I saw his name on the list, but didn't give this a thought at the time, as I should have. After the war he was in custody and considered for the Nuremberg Trials. But because of the injuries he had suffered, and not being considered to be too high up in the pecking order, he was never charged. I know this because back when I first started with MI6, I was assigned the task of organizing everything we had on the Third Reich. Anyhow, those injuries included, in addition to losing an arm at the elbow, having a leg so badly damaged that he never walked properly again, he had his um...delicate parts severed. Both his testicles and penis. What are the dates of his trip to Brazil and return to Germany?"

Holly told him, then added, "Even though he was originally from a part of Germany that became East Germany, when he returned he lived in West Germany. I have gotten as far as being certain the son became the next in line after Bachmeier died. Tony, who do you think might be the father of that boy if not Bachmeier?"

"The obvious answer is Hitler or his twin, whoever wound up in Brazil. We hadn't gotten to whichever one was there yet, by the time Bachmeier returned to Germany, if we have the dates figured out correctly, as I'm certain we do. The correct answer, however, is we'll likely never know. But it will certainly be very interesting to see where that family trees ends."

It was two in the morning when the team digging far into the past finished—with the exception of the Murry tree—tracking all twelve of the accounts and present men in charge...or the two dead-ended by death. At that point Jim suggested, "Let's get some sleep. We're too shot to come up with sensible ideas on what we've found. Also, I'm in no mood to get back to the Murry situation."

While they slept, Harris was up early since he decided to find out what he could about the security system at the Becker estate. He didn't even take time to eat, but did have a thermos filled with black coffee. It was still well dark when he drove down the highway leading to Bob's place. On reaching the turnaround street leading to Bob's driveway, he put down the passenger side window and aimed a sensor detector across the street from Bob's estate with his right hand, while steering with his left,. The detector showed nothing, so when he reached the end of Bob's property, he turned it off, and put the window back up.

After turning around where he had the previous day, he drove back up the highway, this time pointing the detector at Bob's property. Immediately, the device started pinging. Before he could turn it off, the ping changed in pitch. He swore, shut the detector down and sped up the road at less than safe speeds. He knew the change in pitch meant his detector had been detected. He also knew any thought of ever making a try for Scott on that property was likely out of the question, as he suspected it would be...but he might give it one try to at least get a good look at Bob's place.

His next order of business was to change cars. His foresight to have the license plates covered over with dirt and grime to the point whatever cameras Becker had out would not be able to read the number paid dividends. Changing cars had been in his game plan for the day anyhow, so he stopped to eat, went back to the motel, placed all his things in the room, and after putting the "do not disturb" door hanger out, went to the car rental agency.

There he traded the car he had been using for an SUV. From the rental agency he drove to a sporting goods store. His plan thought out, he purchased a bicycle, a rack for it, a tight-fitting black bike riders outfit, including goggles, and a dark-colored helmet. He asked for help from the store in placing the rack and bike on the rear of the SUV.

When all that was accomplished, Harris drove back to the highway passing next to Bob's property. On his last trip down the highway, he had spotted another side road that looked to be overgrown, and nothing more than a path. This time he drove directly to it, turned in and drove until it ended without much of a good place to turn around. He managed, and when pointed back the way he had come, he noticed the sloppy tracks he had left. It had warmed up to the point that some of the snow was starting to melt, so he realized he best not use the path for the time being. That decision made, he drove back to his motel to wait out the weather to see if there was a chance the snow would melt all the way, and the path would dry up. As it was, he wasn't going to park his SUV and leave it. He also thought he better spend time plotting exactly what he was going to do, though he already had an outline of a plan to at least monitor the comings and goings from the Becker estate.

***

While Harris drove through Wentzville on the way to his motel, he was being discussed in Bob's home. Present were Bob, Al, Kathy, Ken, Emil, and, of course, Hector. Michelle and Jo were still in Los Angles after taking Hector's men home, because they wanted to do some shopping. Amanda was home working, while Clyde and Bill were also on a job for the company. They were installing gear on a new customer's property.

When Harris had driven by with his sensor detector setting off alarms in all four homes on the property, no one was up quick enough to see him...but Bob's camera array was much more sophisticated than Harris would have ever imagined. While not the best picture in the world, one of the cameras had managed to record what Harris looked like. It took nearly an hour, but Hector, using Jim's master computer from his lap top, had run a facial recognition program.

When the name Cam Harris popped up, along with what was known of him, Hector muttered, "Well, well, a half blast from the past."

Bob asked, "What means 'half a blast from the past'?"

Hector answered, "This guy, Cam Harris, is the half-brother of none other than Bill Harris, the former casino operator from Las Vegas."

Then, looking at Emil, Hector continued, "Emil, this Bill Harris guy was real bad news. He was involved in some very dirty business and disappeared."

When Hector said that, Bob nearly burst into laughter, but managed to swallow the urge. Two of Hector's men had kidnapped Bill Harris, taken him far into the desert, and left him there with little or no way to leave. His body had been found months later, and it was determined that he probably committed suicide...which he had. Later in the day, when Ken arrived and Hector told the same story the same way, Bob had left the room to keep from laughing.

But now, before the arrival of Ken, Hector continued, "At any rate, this Cam Harris is a very bad man. A gun for hire as it were. According to what I found here, he murdered a young unwed woman and her infant child. It was believed he was paid to do so by a married man who was the father of the child. Neither man was ever charged because there simply was not enough evidence to have hope of a conviction. He has also been suspected in other murders, but never served a day in prison for any of them. I note that in one case, a federal one, there was enough to get a conviction, but somehow the prosecution erred to the point that the judge had to dismiss the charges."

When Ken arrived he was brought up-to-speed on the drive by, and what he had found out on Cam Harris. When he finished, Ken asked, "Who do you suppose he's after?"

Hector answered, "We've been discussing that very thing. We haven't come up with a sound answer. Bennet wouldn't hire someone else to do his dirty work. If not him, then who is the question? If someone is after Jim or me, it makes a bit of sense...we've rattled the cage of more than one dirty operator. But, if so, I haven't the foggiest idea of who it would be, or how they would even know we're here, or Jim was until recently. That leaves Bob as the most likely target, but he has no idea of who it could be either, right, Bob?"

"Nah. But, like you and Jim, I have a few people in the world who would like to see me pushing up daisies."

Ken nodded, then asked, "Okay, so what do you plan to do about this?"

Emil joked, "They're gonna sic me on him."

Ken replied, "Probably as good an idea as any. But, back to Harris for a moment, what was the deal on the case the government had on him that went crossways due to some sort of goof? What more do you have on that?"

Hector held up his hand, found what he had turned up on Harris, and turned his laptop in the direction of Ken. Ken looked it over. Then he rubbed his chin before he muttered, "I seem to remember something about his case, but can't remember what it is. I may do some checking around to see if anyone else in my office remembers the details."

Hector didn't reply as he picked up his phone to call Jim and fill him in.

Only a few minutes earlier Jim had found what he had been looking for on Jimmy Bennet. He grumbled, "This isn't possible...the world isn't that small."

The other three on the computer, quickly turned their monitors to the screen Jim was using. Holly was the first to respond, "Oh for God's sake, give me a break. That idiot is next in line to handle one of these accounts. Jim, are you absolutely certain that Jimmy Bennet is the Jimmy Bennet we've been looking for?"

"Afraid so, honey. I tracked down the birth certificate...it has to be him."

As he spoke his phone rang. "Hi, Hec. Wait until you hear what we've unearthed."

"Yeah, well, wait until I tell you what's been going on here."

Before Jim could reply, Hector started telling him about the situation with Cam Harris. When he finished, Jim laughed. "My best guess would be he's after you and me, pal. Or at least me. Now let me tell you what we've got. The individuals in charge of the three American accounts are, in order: Barton Flake; Arron Jones; and, drumroll please, the one and only Jimmy Bennet...our Jimmy Bennet, the killer we've been trying to track down. And, I'll bet you dollars to tacos that Bennet has no idea he's in control of millions...or, as the account now stands, billions. The last man who controlled that account was a fella by the name of Ethan Murry...who died, with the only living male on the family tree being Jimmy Bennet. Also..."

Hector interrupted, "Oh, bull poop. Give it a rest, Jim...no way."

"Way. And why 'bull poop' rather than the less refined version?"

"Kathy is here with us. Didn't want to say the other version in front of such a refined lady who just got married."

Kathy was laughing at that, even as Jim replied, "You didn't let me finish, Hec. These three accounts were heavily involved in the original funding for most of the guys we took out who were behind the Nohow Robotics deal."

Hector sighed, "This gets worse and worse, or better and better...take your pick. Now what?"

"Good question. We're getting ready to talk this thing out here, then we'll head back to you. In the meantime, keep your head down...I'd hate to lose you after all these years. However, it wouldn't hurt to take Harris and bleed him of whatever info he has."

"Who here can I tell what to?"

"All of it to whomever can keep their mouths shut. Use your own judgement."

"Yeah, okay...so long."

Hector looked around those in the room, settling his gaze on Ken. "Special Agent Langston, as much as I'd like to tell you what Jim just gave me, I think for your own protection I'm gonna ask you to leave...not the room, but the house. Go back to your office to see what you can dig up Harris...but *do not* follow up on the court case where the ball was dropped. I already know. You will, too...in time. For now, forget it. On second thought, forget all about Harris, too."

15.

While Hector was saying goodbye to Ken, Jim and his group had taken printouts of what they had unearthed, and moved to the conference room. Once there, with drinks in hand, Jim held court, "What we've got is one hell of a mess. Of the twelve accounts, we have three dormant due to the death of the last man controlling it, with no living male to take over...two in England, and one in Germany. We've also got the account controlled here in the U.S. that would be run by one Jimmy Bennet if he is ever found. If by us, no problem. If by Flake and Jones, God knows what.

"We'll get back to our two, and your two living ones a bit later, Maggie. For now let's move right along to the Frenchman and his slew of living males on his family tree. We can't, won't, go around killing the entire lot of them, especially the male children. The four Germans are a mixed bag of just one or two living males on their trees, but the other two have several, including still more children.

"So, my friends, at this point I have no idea what to do about this. First off, I suggest your P.M., Maggie, and my President be brought into the picture...at the same time with the four of us who flew in here with this hot potato present. Sarah, Hector, and those Hector saw fit to inform of this mess can, for the present time, remain in the background.

"One other thing: there is no doubt in my mind that one or more of these fellows in control of various accounts may know someone has been nosing around. You can bet when we go popping into the White House, they'll know the four of us are involved. Someone already has this Cam Harris guy hot on my trail, and maybe Hector's as well. Tony, Maggie, how say you to my outline?"

Tony grinned as he pointed at Maggie, so she replied, "I agree the P.M. and President should be brought up-to-speed...by the four of us at a simultaneous meeting in the White House. Or maybe we can protect Tony by letting him miss the meeting."

Tony shook his head. "No, in for a penny, in for a pound...I'll attend the meeting and stay with you until this is over, Maggie. But we damned well should have our loved ones protected with both SIS and SAS personnel."

Maggie replied, "Already thought of, Sir Anthony. It will be my first call, before I even contact the P.M."

Tony smiled as Holly spoke up, "This is all well and good, but we should have some plan on what to do with this mess before we contact those two heads of state. Also, we better make damned certain there is no possible way either the President or the P.M. could be tainted with association with any of the remaining nine men in control of these accounts. Which means we do some more hacking. To go into their personal finances, going back at least two generations. Because if this ever goes public, as it very well might, we don't need any nasty surprises."

Jim nodded. "Yeah good thought, honey...but while at it we may as well go all the way back to the start of this deal to check on that. Okay then, for now we get on with that task. All six of us will also jot down any ideas we have on how to present a suitable plan to the President and P.M."

Bear had entered the room about halfway through the conversation so Jim looked at him. "Notice I said all six of us, Bear...so that obviously includes you, too."

"How about I just go shovel more horseshit?"

"How about not."

***

Jim had been correct on one point...their digging had been discovered by more than one of the nine men. In addition to two Germans, and one Englishman, Arron Jones was made aware that his personal accounts had been hacked...by person or persons unknown. But he felt he knew who, because he was well versed on the ability of Jim Scott and his computer. Barton Flake had told him more than once that nearly every agency in Washington had complained often about Jim hacking into their systems...but never with any proof. Anyone who could bypass his various safeguards had to be both good, and have one very powerful computer. From what he had been told, it almost surely had to be Scott, or some foreign government. He dismissed out of hand that any government would even attempt to do so.

With this new information, he called Flake and invited him up to his condo once again. When Flake arrived, Jones asked, "What is the situation on taking out Scott?"

"I have Cam Harris on the job as we speak. I know he is already in the St. Louis area."

"Do we have anyone else to put on the job? My two men sent to the area are good, but probably not good enough. Scott is a bigger problem than I first thought. Someone seems to be onto our overall plan. My personal account, and the main Reich account I control have been hacked. It has to be either Scott or some foreign government. I'm betting on Scott. From what you've told me about him and his computer, he has the ability to do so. The question is just how did he get onto us, if in fact he is? After all these years without even a smell of our activities being discovered, what changed?"

"I have no idea. But, remember, that long ago matter in Brazil had to be done by someone, who...no one ever knew. If this is in any way connected, why sit on the information for so long? Is there any other reason you can think of why, or how, anyone, Scott or someone else, could possibly have thought to start checking?"

"No."

The two men talked for another half hour before Flake left wondering if Jones had Scott on the brain for some reason unknown to him. He had to admit that the possibility of Scott being behind the death or disappearance long ago of the 11 men set up by various Fourth Reich (as they called themselves in secret) members was likely. But there had never been any proof of that situation, nor was there any proof that Scott was behind this breach of what up until now had been considered to be an impregnable wall of secrecy. He knew that someone had to be responsible for the death of Hitler (or his twin) in Brazil, but since it had never come to the surface how could that have been the reason.

Rather than Scott, Flake seriously considered one of the other eight living men was responsible for the current problem. It certainly could not have been the now deceased Ethan Murry, because he had been the most avid supporter of the idea of a new Fourth Reich, had in fact been the best planner on the team of nine men. Flake was convinced the weak link in their organization was one of the two remaining live English members...and he had an idea which one it might be.

***

Meanwhile, in Wentzville, Hector had finished bringing those still in Bob's home at the time of Jim's call up-to-date. Before he did, he had posed a question to Emil, "Do I need to ask you to go play pool or something, or can you keep your mouth shut, probably forever, about what I'm about to explain about Jim's call?"

"You can trust me to keep quiet, Hector, after all," he added in a joking manner, "as far as I know I'm still cleared for Top Secret material. I got that clearance while in the Navy."

"Two things on that, pal: one, this is so far beyond Top Secret that I can't even begin to give it a name; and second, clearance has always been on a need to know basis. A person can be cleared for Top Secret without having access to material they have no need to be privy of. But I trust you...especially since you had the good sense to openly pursue Kathy before good ol' Al did."

That out of the way Hector then brought everyone up-to-date on what Jim had told him. When he finished, there was stunned silence for a few seconds before Emil joked, "How do I go about unhearing that?"

Kathy chimed in, "Me, too."

Just as she spoke, Clyde and Bill, finished with their work for the day came in. Clyde asked, "You, too, what Kathy?"

Bob butted in, "She wants to eat. You guys finished for the day?"

They both nodded as Clyde answered, "Yeah, and if the great man-hunt team has nothing I'm needed for, I'm going home to clean up and feed myself."

Bob replied, "Go, we're at a dead end for now...brains fried. Ken is gone back to the FBI, since his guy is accounted for, and we're nowhere on a solution."

After those two left, Hector looked at Bob and raised an eyebrow, causing Bob to answer the look. "Enough damned people know what you just told us, Hector. I trust those two guys with my life, but I'd just as soon keep them in the dark. That goes for the other ladies on the grounds...when the two missing ones return. We know all we can do about this is to find Bennet first, which everyone can help with without knowing the new problem. I, for one, wish I didn't know. All the crap we've heard over the years about did Hitler really kill himself in the bunker now comes down to this. Knowing, but not knowing, because of a twin. No way will anyone ever know."

Hector nodded, "I thought that might be the case. Since food was mentioned, let's get to it...I'm hungry."

Over supper, they talked about the hunt for Bennet. But as she finished swallowing a mouthful, Kathy asked, "Hey, has anyone given consideration to what Bennet might do next? What I mean is, if he's still around with his other plans ruined with the two arrests, he might get the bright idea to go on with his killing spree. I know we've got the other jurors covered, but what about anyone else involved in the trial? Al, what about witnesses, who were they?"

"Not many besides me. Two forensic folks who only testified that the reports entered into evidence were accurate. They weren't even cross-examined by the defense. Neither was some gal who gave a sorta identification of Bennet. By that I mean, she was only 'pretty sure,' as I think she put it, that he was the right guy. She wasn't questioned by the defense either. I sure got a long, grueling cross-examination though."

Emil said, "If it was me, and I was Bennet, the first person I'd have killed would have been his defense attorney. That guy was a moron. He fired question after question at you, Al, but each carefully worded answer you gave only further buried Bennet. But, with the evidence you provided, I don't think it mattered how good or bad the defense attorney was. You had him dead to rights."

"Thank you for the kind words, Emil. It almost makes me forget how you were hot after my gal."

Kathy joked, "Ha, he hadn't been, I might never have gotten you in bed."

Hector held up his hand, "Hold on there, everyone. Kathy is onto something. We better track down everyone else involved, to make certain they are protected. Might not be a bad idea to talk to them to see if they maybe have any inclination they might be in danger, what with the word out about the murders already committed. First thing in the morning, Al, we better get what we have on everyone involved. Good thinking, Kathy."

They were all enjoying after dinner drinks when Ken called Hector. "The slug that killed Bassam, was from the same gun as the slug he fired at Kathy. Of no particular interest that I can think of off the top of my head, the autopsy showed Bassam had sex not too long before he was killed. We ran DNA on the fluids found, but no match came up. Other than that, noting else of interest."

"Thanks for the info, Ken. We're sitting around trying to think...not going too well. The best we've come up with is to get back to basics and check out all his known contacts. But I'm not in the mood to think on it any more tonight. Maybe we'll talk to you tomorrow. See ya."

As Hector put his phone away, Kathy gave him a funny look. He noticed. "For now, let's keep Ken in the dark on what we're doing or thinking. For his own protection, I want to keep him at arm's length with this new development. From what Jim told us, we have a dirty senior Assistant Attorney General to consider. I'd bet dollars to donuts he shows up in St. Louis before too long. If Ken runs into him, as I suspect he will, I don't want to depend on Ken's acting ability to keep the lid on what we know."

***

At that very moment, Burton Flake *was* on his way to St. Louis. He was using the excuse of wanting to check with the U.S. Attorney for the district office located in St. Louis, on a major drug case, that he actually had little interest in. He mentioned to the Attorney General that while in St. Louis, he would drop by the local FBI office...his real reason for the trip. Obviously, while in St. Louis, he would check in with Cam Harris, and the two men Arron Jones had sent in to find Bennet. He would also feed those three any new information he picked up from the FBI on the matter.

By later that night, with Flake now in St. Louis, those at Jim's ranch had pretty well worked out their game plan, so Jim suggested, "Okay, as much as I hate to suggest this, I think we better move pretty fast. It's time to head to Washington to drop me, then you three going on to England can keep on with your flight. I'll call the President first thing in the morning. Getting him to agree will be easy. Maggie, your job will to be to get your P.M. on board...without disclosing what we have. I know that may not sit well, but such is life. Let's hit it. I'll have the President call the P.M. to encourage acceptance of the plan to meet in the White House...should make your job easier. I'll let you know when I've got that arranged."

Jim and Holly had long had a condo unit in Washington, D.C., which is where he would stay until morning. When Maggie landed in Washington, Jim left the plane to a waiting rental car Holly had arranged on the flight. The reason she was going the rest of the way was to share flying with Maggie, so each could get some rest on the long flight with the expected fast turnaround.

In the morning, with Maggie already on the ground at the SAS base outside London where she normally kept her plane, Jim called the President...on the special phone he had given the man. The President answered, "Good morning, Jim. What can I do for you? Please don't tell me you have somehow uncovered another sinister plot to bring America down."

"Sorry, but I do have a rather pressing matter I need to discuss with you and the British Prime Minister. It turns out that the fellas who were behind the situation with Nohow Robotics were not the tip of the iceberg."

"Oh for God's sake, Jim...not again. Tell me what you have."

"I'd like to wait until we have you and the P.M. in the situation room, sir. We have a document you both need to read at the same time. Also present in the meeting will be my wife Holly, Sir Anthony Henry, and present Chief of MI6, Maggie Littlefield. Those three, Sarah Turner who oversees my finances, and is a master at using my computer, and I have worked up a plan to deal with the situation, but will need the approval of you and the P.M."

"Fine, when do you want to meet?"

"How about tomorrow morning, whenever is best for you?"

"Let me check my schedule. Ten would work, I have a few things that can be pushed back. How long do you think this will take?"

"Probably a couple hours. One more thing, would you call the P.M. and suggest it would be a good idea to attend the meeting?"

"Are you absolutely certain I won't wind up with egg on my face over this? That is, as to suggesting the P.M. attend with little or no upfront information."

"I guarantee you will find this to be the most important meeting of your Presidency, depending on how far along the planning of the men in question has progressed. This is scary stuff."

"Do I even get a hint?"

"Adolph Hitler had a twin brother."

"What! What kind of nonsense are you talking about?"

"You wanted a hint, sir. Please trust me on this. When you see what we have, you'll be glad you agreed to this meeting...if unhappy this threat exists."

"Very well, I *do* trust you, but this seems to be something...never mind. I'll do as you ask. When should I contact the P.M.?"

"Now would be a good time, sir."

While the President was making his call, Jim called Maggie. "The President is on board, but I had to tell him about the twin...but no more, other than there is a grand conspiracy at foot. Give it about fifteen minutes, then call the P.M."

A badly shaken Prime Minister answered the call from Maggie with, "This better be good, young lady."

Maggie assured her it was, and after a few minutes, the Prime Minister agreed to a secret flight to Washington in Maggie's plane. They worked out timing, then Maggie went back to sleep at the SAS base where she had arranged accommodations for those on her flight.

16.

Maggie's plane was granted landing permission at Joint Base Andrews. When down, it was met by three armored SUVs of the Secret Service. Those aboard were driven to the White House, where they joined Jim and the President in the Situation Room. Only Jim had carried anything to the meeting, it was a large legal type briefcase. After greetings, Jim looked at Maggie. "You have the floor, Maggie."

Maggie explained in detail how she had discovered the envelope Jim withdrew from the briefcase. She then explained seeking the assistance of Tony, Jim, and Holly...and later Sarah. She concluded, "We have been working the last few days to gather what information we could on the contents of the envelope. Jim, your turn."

Jim took the contents from the envelope and handed the picture on top to the President. "Mr. President, I will hand you each page of this material in order. When you have finished reading each, please pass them on to the Prime Minister. When you both have read the entire package, I will give each of you a copy of the data we have uncovered. From there, we will have a discussion, with me outlining what our plan is for dealing with the situation."

When both had completed reading the material from the envelopes, the President looked at Maggie and asked, "Are you absolutely certain this material is real?"

"Yes, sir. Sir Anthony and I verified the handwriting of the SIS Chief who died while still in office. Also, we did a bit of digging in SIS records and are satisfied we know who led the team who killed whichever one was found in Brazil, well after the end of the war. I hadn't even mentioned that to Jim, because it really doesn't matter to the problem at hand. As you will see when you read the data we have assembled, the facts you have just read are pretty well proven out."

There was a brief discussion about the contents of the envelope before Jim handed a copy of the gathered information to both the President and the Prime Minister. There were a few less than polite comments by both of them about the current men in charge of the accounts as they read.

When finished, the Prime Minister asked, "How did you manage to gather all this...specifically the banking information?"

Jim answered, "With a lot of hard work hacking into various places. As to the banks, I happen to have a good deal of money in all three of them. Using codes to get into my account, I managed to figure out how to get into other accounts. I have no doubt all three banks are aware someone compromised their security systems, but not who. I would guess right about now they are in a sweat, because they realize someone knows they have been handling very dirty money. Thus, I would assume they will make no loud protests, because several of these transactions should never have happened. By the same token, not much we can do about their misconduct without admitting how naughty we were. I am also certain some of the individuals are aware we have penetrated their records. There is already a well-known assassin who seems to be interested in my whereabouts."

The President cut in, "That is an uncomfortable bit of information. But, that aside, you mentioned a plan. May we hear it?"

For the next hour Jim and Maggie took turns outlining the rudiments of the plan they had come up with. When they finished, the President leaned back in his chair as he looked at the Prime Minister. When he gave a gentle nod, the Prime Minister asked, "What of the living male children? You both seemed to gloss over that situation, other than to say you have no stomach for the killing of innocents, particularly children."

Maggie answered, "That will take a bit—more than a bit—of careful planning and execution. With one or two exceptions, we noticed that almost immediately on the death of one of the men in charge of a given account, someone stepped into the void and took over. Therefore it would seem as though there is someone designated to take charge of the account. Our thinking is if we can determine beforehand who the next in line will be, that individual shall meet with an accident within minutes of the first death. By continuing to monitor the account in question we will be able to determine if we were successful."

The President looked at Jim as he asked, "You do realize you are asking the Prime Minister and me to authorize the outright murder of any number of people, don't you?"

Jim answered without delay, "Yes, sir. If either or both of you order otherwise, we shall comply with whatever you order. In fact, given my druthers, I'd just as soon give a redacted copy of this material to the German Chancellor and let them deal with the four Germans. The redacted portion would be anything relating to the other accounts. Also, with the original document Maggie found typed up to omit how this information was obtained in the first place."

The Prime Minister nodded. "I like that idea. But what do we do if they do not handle the matter in a satisfactory manner? Also, what of the money lying dead in the accounts no longer active? Shall we just let the Swiss banks have it as a bonus for being naughty?"

Maggie answered, "If Germany fails to take care of business, we can always revert to our plan. As to the money sitting there unused in Swiss banks, that would seem to be a political matter for you and the President to work out. It would seem to me that at least a portion of the money can quietly be forwarded to the treasury of our two nations."

The Prime Minister looked at the President and shrugged. The President thought a second before speaking. "I like the idea of letting Germany handle the problem of the Germans. Since the Chancellor is not thrilled with either the Prime Minister or me, getting the information to Germany would be done how...and when, Jim?"

"Since our plan calls for nearly simultaneous actions as regards to our two, England's two, and the Frenchman, I would say about then. How is a matter to figure out. At this time I do *not* have a good answer."

The President asked, "Assuming we agree to your plan, and I do, by the way, when will you implement it?"

Jim answered, "As soon as we are satisfied we have found out as much as we can about how deep this runs. What I mean is, I want to finger as many people involved as we can. We best not rely on picking up the guilty parties and simply questioning them. We'd never know if we got the full story. That of course will be much easier to do, after we have more information. I would say at least two more weeks of constant digging."

For the next hour, *after* the Prime Minister joined the President in agreeing to the plan, those present discussed the matter further. When the meeting concluded it was decided that Maggie would fly the Prime Minster back to England, with Holly assisting with the flying. Jim would have Sarah fly another plane to Washington to pick him up, and he would help her with the flying to pick up Holly.

With Maggie's plane headed east, Jim called the ranch and spoke with Sarah. "Hi, hon, I need you to fly into D.C. to pick me up. I'll help you with the flying to London to pick up Holly. Bring Bear along, have him bring his war bag."

"Got it. We'll be in the air within the next half hour."

***

While Jim was sorting out flights, Flake arrived in St. Louis. His first stop was to have a discussion with the U.S. Attorney there about the drug case. It actually was a rather big deal, so no one thought he might have other things in mind behind his trip. After a conversation with the U.S. Attorney, Flake announced he wanted to stop by the St. Louis FBI office to see where things stood with the matter of the now-deceased terrorist, and the follow-up investigation surrounding his activities.

In what seemed to be just idle curiosity, Flake asked to see the file on the entire matter, including what the FBI had on Bennet, the murderer still on the loose. That request granted, Flake sat in an unoccupied office to go over the files. With no one else in the room, he quickly took pictures of the entire file on Bennet. On the flight from Washington, he had weighed the pros and cons of having the FBI get more active in the manhunt for Bennet. Since he had created time to stay in St. Louis, by stating his desire to attend the trial of the major drug dealer, he had decided to hold off on pushing the FBI to get more involved.

After completing his copying effort, he gave the two files back to the Agent-in-Charge and asked to speak to Ken, who had been the lead investigator on both men. Ken was surprised at the number of strangely worded questions on Bennet, but answered everything to the best of his ability. Satisfied he had all the information available, Flake left to return to the hotel he had checked into. There he used his throwaway phone to call the two men Jones had on the "Bennet hunt."

He told the man who answered the highlights of what he had copied, as well as asking if they had made any positive progress...which they hadn't. Finished with that call, he arranged for Cam Harris to come to his hotel room. When Harris arrived, Flake asked about his progress on his "Scott assignment."

Harris told him in detail about his plan to get a better look at the Becker estate, including the matter of the sensors Bob had protecting his property. Then he gave Harris his phone to review the material on Bennet. Harris made several notes as he went over it carefully.

Just prior to finishing, the phone rang so Harris handed it back to Flake who answered, "Yes, what may I do for you?"

The way Flake answered the phone warned Arron Jones that someone was with him. "I'll make this brief. Jim Scott, his wife, the British P.M., and two other people...one believed to be the MI6 Chief, Margaret Littlefield, just conducted an unannounced meeting with the President in the White House. The meeting took place in the Situation Room. None of the visitors were logged in."

"What do you make of it?"

"I have no idea, but with the recent interest in the finances of some of us, I don't like it."

"Very well, thank you for the information."

As he put his phone down, Flake thought a moment before he explained at least part of the call, "Scott is in Washington, doing what I do not know."

"Actually that might be a good thing. Becker has a landing strip at his place. There is a cart path leading from the house to the landing strip. At some point, if he's coming back by plane, it will be an easy shot from the spot I picked out to observe the goings on there. Though as cold as it's getting, I'm gonna freeze my ass off up that tree."

"If you get Scott, it will be worth it. I'm prepared to pay you double if you get Scott in the next few days."

"Okay, I better get on with it. I'm not gonna worry about Bennet for the time being."

"That's alright. Scott first, even though in the long run, Bennet is more important...if taken alive. If the authorities get to him first, we'll just have to figure out a way to free him. In the meantime, I'm going back to D.C., even though I had planned on staying here for a few days. The U.S. Attorney here is expecting me to attend a big trial starting tomorrow. I'll just give him a call and tell him something else came up...but that I'd get back as soon as possible."

"Bennet must be damned important for you to be talking about jail breaks. But, as you said, Scott first."

***

While that conversation was taking place, Ken was on the phone to Hector. He called and asked, "What have you come up with on finding Bennet?"

"Not much. Got a few ideas we'll be following up on, but more than anything just to occupy ourselves until we come up with something better. Doing something is better than talking this thing to death. How about you, are you still actively involved in the Bennet hunt?"

"Not really. Spent some time today with an Assistant Attorney General. He seemed more interested in Bennet that he tried to let on."

"*Which* assistant Attorney General?"

"Fella by the name of Barton Flake, why?"

Hector thought for a few moments before he answered, "You still have the bank robberies that you know Bennet was involved in. Tell your boss you want to pursue him on that basis...that it was suggested by Jim...in fact your presence out here was requested. Then get out here as fast as you can. It's time to give you the whole story as to what's going on...but keep that to yourself."

"Yes, sir. See you in an hour or less."

"Less would be better."

There was something in Hector's voice that seemed to Ken as having a bit of stressful urgency. That being the case, he was in his car less than ten minutes later. The Agent-in-Charge, mindful of the order he had been given concerning Jim Scott, readily agreed to Ken doing as requested.

By the time Ken arrived at Bob's place, a number of things had been talked out by those on the estate. Clyde and Bill had returned from their day's work, and the two ladies had returned from California. When everyone was assembled in Bob's living room, he held court. "Michelle, Clyde, Jo, Bill, and Amanda, something of great urgency has come up. This new matter, while not actually part of our hunt for Bennet, does add to the need to track him down...to be taken alive if at all possible. This new deal is on a need-to-know basis. You five do not need to know. However, Hector—who is responsible for the who needs-to-know—has granted me the option of including you five. Honestly, I would prefer not to inform any of you. But I will leave it up to each of you, or in the case of you two married couples, both of you...do you want in on something that is hot as hell?"

Bill looked at Amanda who shrugged, so he answered, "If you don't need us on whatever this is, no need for us to know. But, for one, I think I'll lock my doors tonight."

Clyde nodded. "You need me, or us, lay it on us. If not, no need to give us the whole story."

Before anyone else could speak, Michelle did. "Since I'm gonna be living here, I may as well know what's up. But, I gotta tell you, husband, the way you've approached this scares the dickens outta me. You make it sound as though the future of mankind is at stake, because I know you, and I've never seen you hesitant about anything before."

Clyde joined that thought. "That's about the same feeling I had, Bob...so I repeat...you need me or us, I'm in whatever it is."

"Thanks, Clyde. I know I can count on all four of you if it comes to that, but hopefully it won't. But Bill's idea of keeping his door locked is a good one."

Bill took Amanda's hand as he got ready to leave. "Talk to you in the morning, pal. Forget business, we can handle anything that comes up...if not I'll give you a holler."

Clyde nodded agreement as he followed those two toward the backdoor, with Jo right beside him.

When all four were gone, Michelle asked, "Okay, what gives?"

Bob told her. When he finished, she asked, "How do I go about unhearing that? For God's sake...Hitler! After all the speculation about Hitler, it seemed as though that had been put to rest a long while back with claims that he did in fact die in the bunker...now this. Do you believe all this stuff, dear?"

Before Bob could answer, Emil joked, "You just said the same thing about unhearing that I made when I heard this."

Bob then answered Michelle, "Yeah. The follow-up work Jim and those working with him came up with pretty well proves it. Last we heard from Jim, he will stop by here sometime tomorrow to give us a full briefing."

Hector added to Bob's comments, "Michelle, I've spoken with Jim few times since he left, and he is convinced the situation is not only real, but quite dangerous. Another thing, we had an assassin drive by your property using a sensor detector. He probably is after Jim."

Michelle asked, "What are you gonna do about this guy?"

Hector answered, "Try to capture him, so we can ask him a few questions before he has an accident."

Michelle chuckled, "I know the kind of 'accident' you're talking about, Hector. I guess if Holly isn't around, I'll get to dump the trash over the Rockies."

Bob nodded. "Probably, dear."

Emil shook his head. "You folks are something...and I love it. Wish I could play a more active role, rather than just hiding out here like a scared rabbit."

Almost at the same time, Bob and Hector made the same comment: "Careful what you wish for, Emil."

17.

While this conversation was going on, Cam Harris was making his final plans as he ate what might be his last good meal before he started his planned stakeout. After leaving Flake, he had made several additional purchases. Other than the dark thermal clothing he had, the most important item had been a very expensive thermos that would keep coffee hot for an extended period of time. As an afterthought, he had gone back and bought a second one he planned to put hot chocolate in. He had also bought several foodstuffs to eat on while up the tree he hoped to find that would do for his observation of the Becker estate.

Finished with his meal, he went back to his motel room. Once there he made several sandwiches to go with the ample supply of energy bars he had. Since the weather had turned quite cold, he felt safe in using the dirt road without leaving additional tracks. His plan was to spend long stretches of time up the tree, but come down for three hours' sleep each morning between two and five, leaving the tree at one-thirty, to return at five-thirty. He knew the four hour gap might cause him to miss Scott, but he reasoned that in time he would succeed.

At 5:00 PM, with it already starting to get dark, Harris left the motel with everything he planned to take up the tree, including the case holding his broken down sniper rifle. When he reached the turn off road, he didn't worry about leaving any tracks because it had gotten even colder. He did, however, drive slowly when passing through the foliage. Satisfied to that point, he loaded everything he was taking with him in a very large backpack. Then, after getting his bike off its rack and climbing on, he set out for his planned "observation post."

On reaching the road down to where he had discovered several homes, he turned onto it, then peddled about a quarter mile further.

There he turned left into the tree line. The going was too rough to ride his bike any further, so he got off and pushed it along until opposite Bob's estate. He kept on until he found a very large old oak tree. There he put his bike down before taking out another of his purchases...a foldup grappling hook. With a deep sigh, Harris tossed the hook up. It took two tries to snag the lowest tree limb. Then he unloaded a few things from the backpack before he put it back on for his climb. Roughly two-thirds of the way up the tree, he found an ideal spot to set up shop. There were three rather large branches pointing in different directions, but close to one another. Standing on one that pointed in the opposite direction from Bob's estate, he hung the backpack on one pointing in a direction more-or-less parallel to the highway running past the property.

The limb he planned to sit on was aimed in the general direction of the first of the three houses with rear exposures facing the highway. From it, he could tell he would be able to clearly see the landing strip and hangar where he knew a plane could land and park. The hangar doors were shut, but another plane (Holly's) sat well forward of the hangar nearer Bob's home, which was turned the other way so the exposure of it was limited to one end.

Harris took out a thick blanket which he placed on the limb he would sit on. His next move was to take out his sniper rifle, which he assembled. With it slung over his shoulder, he took the bag of sandwiches with snack bars, and one of the thermoses up to his perch. Every half hour or so, he would get down to stand on the lower limb to stretch his legs, but for the most part he sat and waited. Finally at nearly two, he decided to give it up for the night.

The food and thermos went back into the backpack along with his rifle, which had been put back in its carrying case. Back on the ground, he got his bike for the return trip to his car. By nearly six in the morning, he was back up his tree to continue his watch. He was very happy to see no additional plane on the property. He, of course, had no idea when Jim might be returning, but was prepared to wait however long it took.

***

While Harris waited on him, Jim was flying the plane Sarah was in. She had picked him up in Washington with her husband Bear sitting in the right seat, even though he was anything but a pilot. Those three had flown to the secret SAS base outside London. Once there, Jim had spent some time with Maggie and Tony before leaving for the return flight to the United States with Holly aboard. On this flight, it was agreed that Jim and Holly would do most of the flying to give Sarah a chance to rest up, because once they reached Bob's property, she would fly the plane solo back to the ranch in Montana.

Before leaving Washington for the flight to England, Jim had called Hector to let him know he would arrive at Bob's estate sometime between 10:00 AM and noon. He told Hector he would call back and firm up his time of arrival when back in U.S. airspace.

While waiting on Jim's arrival, Al and Kathy decided on a fast trip to their office. With Bob following behind them in another car, they left a little after seven, and returned by nine...making only one stop on the way.

When they returned they discussed their activities since leaving, so Hector held court on what their plans for the rest of the morning would be. Jim called just before ten to announce he would arrive sometime around noon. He and Hector had a rather long conversation, that ended with Jim suggesting, "Just don't miss," which Hector found amusing.

When Holly, who was sitting left seat, touched down on Bob's landing strip, it was ten minutes before noon. Michelle drove out to meet them in one of the dune buggy-type vehicles on the property.

As soon as the plane touched down, Harris sighted in on it with his sniper rifle. He stayed on the plane until it stopped. When the door opened causing the steps to extend down to the surface of the concrete, Harris was ready. He slid his hand down to the trigger but with his finger not yet on it. Flexing his fingers in the cold, he waited patiently for Jim to appear in the open doorway. Bear was first off, causing Harris to wonder who he was, but knowing it wasn't his target. Next to come down the steps was Holly. Before she reached the end of the stairs, Jim appeared at the top. Just as he started to move his finger to the trigger, Harris felt his hand explode. He felt pain almost at once as he looked at his hand with fingers dangling from what was left of his hand.

Hector had fired the shot. His sniper rifle was loaded with anti-personnel exploding rounds. A split-second after penetration the bullet would explode. The round had gone through the back of Harris' hand. When it exploded the bones of his hands were shattered, the palm blown away. Now his two smaller fingers were only attached with a few strands of skin, with the other two and thumb only slightly better off.

Stunned, it took Harris a few seconds to realize what had happened. By then Hector had fired again, further damaging the rifle that had suffered damage from the first shot to Harris' hand. Knowing his rifle was now useless, Harris dropped it, then using his left hand, got a knife out of his coat pocket. The knife had been used for various things as he set up his tree camp. Now it was used to cut a large strip of the heavy blanket he had been sitting on. The cloth was wrapped around what was left of his hand.

Then, realizing time was of the essence, he started to climb down the tree. While he knew he had to hurry, he also knew that with one hand that was going to be difficult if he wanted to avoid falling all the way to the ground.

Long before he started down the tree, Hector said into the communication set everyone on Bob's property was tuned into, "Bob, hop in one of your buggies and go get him. If he gets to the ground before you arrive, I'll convince him to not misbehave. Bill, check out the cameras to make absolutely certain they operated properly."

With those two doing as told, Harris was making slow progress in getting down the tree. As he went, he was wondering just how they were onto him in the first place. He knew whoever shot him had to have been watching him for some time to be prepared to make the shot he made just prior to the shot Harris himself planned on making.

That was all thanks to a very alert Kathy Felps earlier in the day. With Al driving, she had been sitting in the front passenger seat on the way to their office. As they passed the path Harris had used to park his rental SUV, she exclaimed, "Al, stop the car...right now! Pull to the shoulder."

Knowing Kathy wasn't the flighty type, Al had done as told. As soon as he stopped, with Bob pulling in right behind him, Kathy was out of the car, reaching for her weapon. Seeing that, Bob hurried out of his car, with Al soon following along. Kathy ran to what she had noticed...the ruts in the path, most noticeably the thin tire track of the bike as it had cracked the frozen snow.

With a close look it was easy to see the various tracks, slight as they were, that had been left by the vehicle. She pointed, "Someone has been riding a bike here recently. And look at the car tracks. I wonder if that Harris guy is responsible."

Bob just nodded when he started down the path with his weapon also out. Al only then decided that was a good idea since the other two had theirs out, so he pulled his, too. At the SUV, it took only a few moments for everyone to figure out what must have taken place here. Bob immediately called Hector to explain what they had found. Hector's only reply was, "Get back as soon as you can. I'm filling in the others, the ones who don't know yet, about Hitler's damned twin and what goes with that story."

By the time those three had returned to Bob's place, after a *very* brief stay at the police station, Hector had informed Bill, Clyde, Amanda, and Jo of the full details of the information as known to him. He also had sent Clyde on the way to the gun port in his home to start looking for Harris. All four homes on the property had gun ports at both ends. All around the second floors of all four homes were what seemed to be decorative matte black slabs. At the gun ports, those slabs could be raised up to a foot. Inside all gun ports everything was matte black also. Anyone inside the ports normally wore all black, including ski masks.

Clyde had driven back to his home with Jo as though there was no rush. Arriving there, he had quickly changed into black clothing, grabbed a ski mask and hurried to the port nearest the central home, now being used by Al and Kathy. He raised the port slab just six inches and started using the scope on the sniper rifle in an effort to spot Harris. It took nearly twenty minutes, but when he spotted his target, he called Hector. "Got him, Hector. He's in a big old oak tree that is about thirty or forty feet back from the highway. It's in the middle of the gap between the house Al is staying at and Bill's. I can't make out much of him from this angle but enough to know without a doubt someone is there...oh, more than halfway up the tree."

"Good, thanks. Do nothing unless you see him taking aim at someone...if so shoot what you can see."

"If he decides to take a shot, I'll be lucky to even see his weapon, which I cannot see at this time."

When Al, Kathy, and Bob returned, everyone was outfitted with the communication sets. Plans had been made and efficiently executed, resulting in Harris now trying to get down the tree without the use of his right hand. Those plans had called for Hector to be in his present location inside the gun port nearest Harris in the house Al and Kathy were living in. Hector had also called Jim to let him know what the plan was, which led to Jim's comment about not missing the shot.

In addition to shooting Harris' hand, two time and date stamped cameras had been set up, one pointing at Harris, and one where Jim's plane would park. This was done so there would be absolute proof that Harris was about to take a shot at Jim when he was shot by Hector. While everyone knew that the tapes from those two cameras would be thrown out of court, in fact never even presented, they would allow extra pressure to be brought on Harris when he was being questioned.

When Bob reached a spot on the highway directly in front of the oak tree, he pulled his cart in as far as he could without losing traction. With a first-aid kit in one hand and his weapon in the other, Bob approached the tree with care. He needn't have bothered, because Harris had made it down to his grappling hook, but when gripping the attached rope, he had lost his grip after only a few feet, falling the rest of the way to the ground. While not badly injured in the fall, he was in no mood to offer any resistance when Bob, roughly, helped him to his feet.

After finding the man's handgun and tossing it near the shattered rifle, Bob led Harris back to his cart. Once there he growled, "Sit here and behave while I retrieve your weapons. The guy who shot you has you lined up in his sights. Any silliness and you'll have another wound to repair when I return."

Hector, of course, heard Bob on his comm set and chuckled at that comment, while Bob turned to go. Bob returned with the two weapons, leaving everything else belonging to Harris behind. As he drove the cart back to his property he asked, "Hey, Hector, should I just take him to the hangar to question?"

"Yeah, I'm already about to walk out of Al's front door to get the cart I have here. See you there."

Ken, who had spent the night in the same house Hector was now leaving, and who had one of the comm sets, asked, "Can I come with you, Hector?"

"No. You don't want to be around when we question this bird. Just head back to Bob's home with everyone else. We'll be along in a while."

Al and Kathy walked up at that point, and Al asked Hector, "How about a ride to Bob's place?"

"Yeah, hop in, all three of you."

Harris, who couldn't hear any of that, saw Bob smiling and wanted to hit him. He also considered trying to overpower Bob, but decided he had lost, so he may as well take whatever kind of medicine he was due. He realized even if he did manage to take out the "smiling jackass" as he thought of Bob, he couldn't get far in the cart. Any thought of trying to take the cart and head toward where Jim Scott was didn't even cross his mind.

In a matter of a few minutes, he came face to face with the man he had sought to kill. With friends like Jim Scott seemed to have, it was no wonder the man was so hard to kill. Bob led Harris into the hangar, while Bear was busy refueling Sarah's plane, with her help. By the time they finished, Bob had done what he could about the injured hand, first cutting off the two dangling fingers. As he did that, he told Harris it was likely that the other two and his thumb would have to come off, also, but for now he would just wrap everything up. Harris wasn't impressed with that idea, but kept his mouth shut.

After Sarah announced she was leaving, both Jim and Holly asked her if she was certain she was alright to fly on back to the ranch without spending some time resting up before the trip. She assured them she was fine to fly, and soon had the plane in the air.

Only then did the questioning of Harris begin. In less than five minutes, Hector had the man broken and ready to tell all. His reward for cooperating was getting to live, and stay in one piece, save the fingers and thumb that likely would be amputated in the near future.

He readily admitted he had been hired by Flake to kill Jim. He was surprised when Jim asked at that point, "What about Jimmy Bennet?"

"What do you mean?"

Jim looked at Hector. "Do you think this guy is that stupid?"

"Could be, Jim. Hey, bozo, do you know why Flake wants Bennet?"

"Not exactly, but I know he wants him alive."

"Why didn't you tell my friend here, the guy you tried to kill, what he wanted to know in the first place, so we didn't have to do all this dancing around?"

"He caught me off guard. I didn't know you knew Flake wanted Bennet."

Hector nodded. "Makes sense. Jimbo, what do we do with the guy?"

"Good question, Hec. The answer is what to do about Flake at this point? A case could be made against him, but with a good lawyer he would claim Flake doesn't know what Harris is talking about. If we hide him out for now, it would put more pressure on Jones and Flake."

When Jim mentioned the name "Jones," Harris' eyes opened just a bit in surprise that they know about Jones, too. Jim noticed, but kept on without seeming to, "The next question is where do we stuff this guy and for how long?"

Hector answered, "Take him to the ranch and put him in that dungeon of yours. Of course, we do have three cops, well two cops and an FBI agent, sitting in Bob's house who know we have him. I think they're solid, but still..."

Jim interrupted, "They'll hold their water, Hec, when we tell them why. Let me go talk to them. Bear, keep an eye on this fella."

18.

When everyone was gathered in Bob's living room except for Bear and Harris, Jim brought them up-to-date on all aspects of the situation, except the plan he had proposed. When finished with that, he continued, "Then we come to the plan devised by me, with input from those who helped with the discovery of the facts as we know them. That plan has been approved by our President, and the British Prime Minister...but it is strictly *illegal*. Three of you here are sworn to uphold the law. If you would prefer to visit the game room for the next little bit, I will understand. If you choose to hear the plan, and it is implemented, you will be guilty of conspiracy to commit any number of crimes that could include murder. How say you? Ken, first."

Ken thought for a few moments before he answered, "I'm in. Knowing that Barton Flake is part of this atrocious plan of evil, and knowing he might very well get by with it if not stopped by any means, including those beyond the law, I'm willing to not only hear the plan, but to assist in any way I can. The law be damned."

Al looked at Kathy who nodded before he replied, "We feel the same, we're in."

Jim sighed. "Okay, here's the plan."

When he finished, there were several questions, some of which Jim had no answer to because they involved "what ifs." The questions over, Jim expanded on his no answers to those questions he was unable to answer. "In some cases, obviously, we'll have to play things by ear. The one thing we all agreed on is we're not in the business of killing children. We may make a few orphans from our actions, but none of us has any desire to kill children.

"That out of the way, let's move on to our friend Harris. First thing with him is to take him over to the clinic to get his hand fixed. After that, we stow him someplace...probably at my ranch. I know he should be arrested for his failed attempt to potshot me, but for now we'll overlook that. Which means, in effect, we're kidnapping him. But I have an idea he won't mind too much. I'll need a volunteer to go with Bear to take Harris to the clinic."

Hector cut Jim off at that point, "I'll go. Jim, did it seem to you that for a tough thug, Harris gave in with ease...too much ease?"

"Yeah, I noticed. For now, don't press him. What he gave us jives with what we already knew, some of which he had no way of knowing we already had. So I'm thinking there is something else there, or he had a reason for giving in so fast.

"Okay, after Holly and I get some rest, we'll get back to the Bennet hunt. We know why they want him alive. What they plan for him after they get him is beyond me at this point. A loose cannon like Bennet probably isn't going to behave for them, any more than he has for society as a whole. When checking lineage of the U.S. guys on the list, Holly discovered that the document left behind by the former SIS Chief indicated the next in line to take control of a given account was to be the nearest living male relative. However, she discovered that in a few cases, the man taking charge of the account wasn't the *nearest* male relative. That seems to indicate whoever is in charge can nominate, or direct, that another male in his family tree take over the account on his death. So either the document Maggie found is incorrect, or these guys have worked something out with the banks to make that change. By the way, Maggie and Sarah, helped out by Holly and me when we finished with the U.S. guys, found the same thing when working on the others.

"Anyhow, while my bride and I catch up on sleep after all our flying, you folks put on your thinking caps. We'll help out when we come up for air."

As Hector stood up at the same time Holly did, Jim held up his hand. "Hold on. One more thing. Kathy, Hector told me I may well owe my life to you...thanks for being so sharp."

"Aw heck, Jim, Hector wasn't gonna let that guy take a shot at you. You can bet he wasn't gonna let you land without making damned certain Harris was nowhere in the neighborhood."

"Be that as it may, thanks for being on the ball. Al, you married well."

"As I know, and have been told several times in the last few days."

With that, Hector headed toward the back door to grab a cart for the drive to the hangar. Jim followed Holly up the stairs. When they reached their room, Holly started taking off her clothes. As she did, Jim did as well, but took the time to admire his wife's beauty and body. "Hey, hot stuff, you're still the best lookin' gal around."

"Thanks, hubby. You ain't bad either. We have time for a little fun and games before sleep?"

"You bet."

While Jim and Holly were making love, Hector and Bear loaded Harris in the cart for the drive back to Bob's home. Once there, they put him in the car Hector had been using, for the drive to the rehabilitation clinic.

They were still not back by the time, three hours later, that Jim and Holly came downstairs. Everyone else had already eaten, but Michelle offered to fix them something. Both thought sandwiches would do, and after eating they joined the main group in the living room. Clyde and Bill were gone to take care of a few business items, while Amanda was home working as well. Jo was still there, with Bob, Michelle, Emil, Al, Kathy, and Ken.

As Holly and Jim sat down, Bob started bringing them up-to-speed on what had been discussed in their absence. About finished, he added, "One more thing. Clyde reminded us about the fact that Bassam had sex seemingly not too long before he was killed. Al came up with the fact that the only known lady in Bennet's past split the area after he went to prison. We did a fast check and found her to be living in Kentucky. As it happens I have a SEAL buddy who lives in the same city she does. I called him, and he took time to find out she was still there. He checked in to find her at her job, so she wasn't the one making Bassam's day before he bought it.

"Then Kathy remembered Al saying a while back that one witness against Bennet at his trial wasn't too hard to look at. That prompted Al to remember that at the trial she gave tepid testimony. At the time he thought it might have been out of fear, but could have been something else. I was just about to go interview her with Kathy when you came downstairs."

Jim shrugged. "By all means, have at it. If nothing else, it'll check off another box. Also, you might give her warning that he's on the loose and likely to do most anything. Al, how about you and I start double checking on the others involved. Bob and Kathy can give us a hand when done with the gal they're gonna check on first. Where's the list of everyone involved in the case, with present locations?"

Bob dug through a stack of papers on an end table and handed the list to Jim. He also had a copy in his hand. He joked, "We've got about five copies."

Emil spoke up, "The tree huggers are gonna be pissed, with you making a ton of copies of everything. That aside, I guess I get to stay here twiddling my thumbs."

Holly looked at Bob. "Give me a copy of the list. Come, Emil, time for you to get to work. You're with me. Michelle, Jo, you two can guard the home front."

Michelle shook her head. "Or catch up on my work, in my case. Jo can make certain she still has an art store."

Jo shot back, "I've been staying in touch. Everything's running well. My associates have even made a few sales. One big enough to keep the doors open for another few months."

Ken asked, "What about me?"

Holly grunted, "You're with me and Emil...we can use your credentials."

"Nice to know I'm needed for something."

***

While the group went to work on finding Bennet, one of his former co-thieves, Jitters Donnelly, was sitting in his holding cell at FBI headquarters wondering about several things, and worried about another. He wondered why he was still in a holding cell, even though he had been asked if he "minded" the inconvenience...to which he had agreed because Hector had told him to agree to anything posed to him. He also wondered about why he had heard no word about the arrest or killing of Bennet. The other main thing he wondered about, in addition to things like the decent food he had been receiving, was why he was being deprived of any contact with the outside world...no TV, radio, even newspapers, or any indication about what had happened to Bennet. He knew Cardin had been arrested, but that was all he knew.

But the main thing on his mind was the money well hidden in his home. Evidently the FBI had not found it if they searched his house...surely he would have been asked to about that. The worry about Bennet was if he hadn't been captured or killed. Bennet knew he had most of the money from their robberies hidden someplace, but not where. If he was still at large he would eventually get around to thinking to look for it...if he hadn't already. Donnelly's hope was that if he went to prison, as he almost certainly would, if the money was never found it would still be there when he got out.

Donnelly had reason to worry about that, because the thought of that money had crossed Bennet's mind more than once. With the time passed since the raid on his hideout, which he correctly assumed either Donnelly or Cardin had been responsible for, it might be safe to look around Donnelly's house to see if the money was there. He thought the amount of that money would be close to a million dollars (actually it was nearly three times that much), and with an extra million he wouldn't have to stage another robbery.

That in mind, he considered taking his "girlfriend" with him when he went to search the house. If he took her with him, she might be able to help search the house. But, with her along, if the police showed up, and he got into a gun fight, it might push her over the edge if he killed anyone else in front of her, especially if it was a cop. She had already been on edge since the experience with Bassam, and then watching as he killed the terrorist. The first night in bed after those two events had shown her feelings when she begged off sex for the night. The promise of taking her with him when he left the country had the desired effect of calming her down, but it had taken all of the next day to get their relationship back to near where it had been.

Based on all of those thoughts, Bennet sat next to her on the couch where she sat reading. "Ellen, I have to go out. I have the general location of where some money—enough for us to leave the country on—is hidden. I'm gonna try to find it. If I have any luck, we can head south yet today."

He could see her excitement at that thought as she replied, "Okay. Just in case you succeed, I'll start packing a few things. But, we'll have to buy some things for you so we both have luggage. Otherwise it would look suspicious for us to take a flight out of the country."

"Very wise thought, darling."

Ellen Jennings nearly melted when Bennet called her "darling."

Certain things would be okay leaving her behind, Bennet left for the small house belonging to Donnelly. It was located nearby in St. Peters, Missouri so the trip didn't take him long. He parked in the street in front of the house and saw the crime scene tape left behind by the FBI when they searched it. He got out of Ellen's car and walked around to the rear of the house. He ignored the crime tape left there and quickly busted in by forcing the lock with a heavy kick using the bottom of his foot.

Bennet knew from having visited the house once sometime back, that from the rear it was unlikely anyone could see him do that because of the high fence at the rear and the foliage on both sides, as well as a good deal of brush near the back fence, that actually belonged to the house behind Donnelly's property.

Inside he started his search. He knew Jitters was a careful man, so knew he would have hidden the loot from the robberies with great care. But he also realized that with repeated use of the stash as they added to it each time they pulled a job, it wouldn't be all that hard to get into.

While Bennet was searching for the money needed to get out of the country, and to live a carefree life somewhere south of the U.S., two men pulled their car to a stop just short of Ellen's home, on the opposite side of the street. As they both reached for the door release handle on their side of the car, Bob drove up. He pulled into Ellen's driveway. The men in the other car froze as they watched Bob and Kathy get out of Bob's car.

At the door, Bob knocked while Kathy pushed the doorbell button. Ellen came to the door. Kathy pulled her badge. "Hello, we're with the police. Are you Ellen Jennings?"

"Yes."

Kathy asked, "May we come in, please? We have a few things to discuss with you."

Frightened that something bad had happened to Bennet, Ellen nodded dumbly as she stood aside.

Inside, Bob asked, "Do you live here alone, or are you married?"

"No, just me. What's this about?"

Bob told her about Bennet and his killing spree, including that Kathy had been wounded in an attempt on another member of the jury. When he finished, Ellen looked at Kathy who was looking out the window at the car with the two men, "Are you alright now?"

"Yes, thank you for asking. The terrorist Bennet killed was responsible for that café bombing you probably heard about on the news."

"Yes, I heard about that bombing. Heard on the news about the two jury folks, too...but not about the terrorist. Glad you're okay now."

For the next few minutes, they both asked Ellen a few more questions, then left after warning her to be careful about who she opened her door for. As they left the house—and *after* Kathy made a point of shutting the door behind them—she whispered, "Bob, that car to the right with the two guys."

"Yeah, I spotted them, let's just head for the car."

That said, Bob unzipped his overcoat as he got in the car. Kathy reached into her purse as she got in. They needn't have been getting ready for a shootout, because one of the men in the car blurted out, "I think they made us. Let's get the hell outta here."

The other man was already reaching for the key to start the car. "I had the same thing in mind. That must be the two cops we were told about. Big guy with a short dame."

As the car drove off, the other man replied, "Yeah, probably doing the same thing we were about to do. We can check the gal who lives there in a day or two. Let's try the court reporter next, but make it hard for that guy to follow us."

"Way ahead of you. He's just backed out of the drive, I'm turning left at this next street."

In his car Bob glanced over at Kathy. "Wonder who in the hell those two are. No way to follow them without being seen doing so. What say you?"

"Follow the bastards. I couldn't get a plate number...yet. Who the hell cares if they know we're following them."

"Okay, potty mouth, I'm after 'em."

Kathy chuckled, but found it less funny when they reached the street the car had turned onto. It was nowhere to be seen. Not only had the driver made a hard right at the first cross street, he had the presence of mind to turn left at the next street, then followed up with another right. On that street, he pulled to the curb in front of a parked car, backed up next to it, and shut his car off.

His partner nodded. "Nicely done. If they were gonna follow us, I bet you lost 'em. Let's sit here for ten or fifteen minutes."

"What I planned to do."

Bob decided to give up the chase when neither he nor Kathy spotted the car they were after once they had passed three more streets without making a turn. "Okay, we lost them. I'm heading on back. What did you think of Miss Jennings?"

"I thought she was a bit uneasy...even before you told her why we were there, and what Bennet had been up to. She seemed too...something. I'm not certain just what the right way to describe it is though."

"Yeah, about what I thought. The last time you and I agreed on a feeling of something not quite right, we hit it on the head with Cardin. But, like you, I can't put my finger on it with her. She didn't seemed frightened, but apprehensive sorta."

"That's pretty close to what I was thinking. You think we should stake the house out? I've got a funny feeling, but again, not sure what it is."

"I think it should be staked out, but maybe not by us. She's seen us and our car. I wonder if she noticed those other two guys."

"That's a good question, one that there is no way of knowing the answer to. Should we give Jim a call?"

"Good idea. Here, use my phone. It's one of Jim's special phones."

"I got one, remember? He's number one on it, right?"

"Yeah. I did forget you got one, Al, too. Call him...yes, he's number one."

Jim answered, "Hi Kathy. If you don't have anything hot, let me get back to you in a few."

"Not certain how hot it is, but Bob and I both have a funny feeling about Miss Jennings. Also, there were two guys that seemed to be watching her place. They took off when we came out from talking to her."

"Okay, I'll get back to you soon. For now just head back to Bob's place."

19.

The reason Jim didn't want to talk longer was because he and Al had just knocked on the court reporter's door. Her husband opened it just as Jim was ending the call. Jim noticed the man was of an age with him, and liked the cut of the man immediately. He quickly introduced himself and Al, to which the man introduced himself before tilting his head toward his wife and introducing her.

Jim got right to the point of their visit. "As you've no doubt heard, this Jimmy Bennet fella has been on a murder rampage. He killed two jurors, and made a try on another. Then he killed the terrorist he was running with. We're trying to track him down, but thought we better alert everyone involved in the case that he might be coming around."

The husband grumbled, "He comes around here, he's gonna get his ass blown off."

Jim smiled. "I take it you have a gun, and know how to use it."

"I do...I'm a Marine."

"Semper Fi, fellow jarhead. You look to be about my age, so guess you got in on the desert fun."

"Yup, both times. A bit more action in Desert Storm. Shoulda retired before the second one, but stayed in longer than my bride wanted me to. From the way you said that, guess you did, too."

"Just the Storm. Right after it, I got kidnapped by the CIA, stayed there until just before the second one. Have managed to find a little action here and there since."

"How about a drink, fellas?"

Jim nodded. "I'm game, but make it light. We've got a lot to do yet tonight. How about you, Al?"

"May as well, I can't dance worth a darn."

After the husband offered bourbon, which was accepted by both men, he poured more than a "light" amount into four tumblers.

When all four touched glasses, he looked at Al. "I know your Chief a little, saw you around a few times. If memory serves, you were the copper who got the goods on Bennet to see him sent up the river."

"One in the same. Thought I recognized you, too. My recently wed wife is working the case with me. She got wounded by Bennet, so I have a personal grudge."

"Well, good luck with that. Like I said, he comes around here, you won't have to look any further for him," the husband stated as he got out his trusty military issue .45.

Jim downed what was left in his tumbler. "I guess we better hit the road. Just as we got here I got a call that needs some attention. Thanks for the booze," then he joked, "Give us cover with that cannon on our way to the car."

Just about the time Al and Jim reached their car, the two men who had been seen by Bob and Kathy drove down the street. One of them recognized Jim, because he had been given his picture by Arron Jones. Jones had told him, "If you happen to run into this guy, take him out if you can do it and get away clean. He's looking for Bennet, too. Big bonus if you get him."

The man who recognized Jim didn't even ask his partner as he pulled in behind Jim's car. He screeched to a stop just two feet behind it, then pulled his gun as he freed himself from his seat belt. As he started to get out, Jim already had his own weapon out and fired through the small space between the opened door and the frame of the car.

The shot caught the man in the side of the head. Even as he slid to the ground, the other man was out with his gun drawn. He jumped toward the hood of the car to get a better shot at Jim, who by then had shot out the headlight nearest him, and while diving to his right, took out the other headlight. Seemingly all in the same motion, he shot the second man just as Al fired at him, also. They weren't the only two shooting...the husband's "cannon" also fired.

All three shots hit home, with the force of the .45 round being just enough to cause him to slip off the car's hood.

Jim stood up. "Well, I'd say with that bit of excitement over, someone better call the Wentzville police."

Al smiled and replied, "I got it. I'll check the one on this side, you wanna check the other one, Jim? After that, I'll call my cop house."

"Yup. Then I'm calling Bob. I have a hunch these two guys are the ones he and Kathy spotted."

While those two did their checking, and then started making their calls, the husband kept a keen watch to make certain the two men were going to stay down. After Al and Jim had pronounced the two men dead, and were on their calls, the husband checked out both dead men. He noticed where Jim had shot the first man, then discovered all three men had hit the second one.

When Jim had Bob on the phone he asked, "The two guys you saw at Miss Jennings' home, what kind of car, and any plate number you might have gotten, please?"

Bob told him the make, model, and color of the car before he added, "Kathy didn't get a plate number, and I only got the last two digits...89."

"Okay, don't worry about them. They just made a try on Al and me. Didn't go too well for them. After we finish up here, we're on our way back. What have you decided to do about Miss Jennings?"

"Grab a fast bite to eat, then go take the first watch on her place. After we talked it out some, I nearly turned around...with maybe a stop at a fast food joint. You folks at my place can figure out who comes to relieve us...maybe around midnight would be nice."

***

Bob had no way of knowing that he and Kathy would be watching an empty house...so would the team who relieved them, because Bennet and Ellen were long gone by the time Bob parked down the street from Ellen's house.

Bennet had found the money he was looking for, and was stunned at the amount. He didn't actually count it, but knew it had to be well in excess of two million dollars. Had the FBI done a thorough search of Donnelly's house they could have easily found it. The money had been hidden in a false wall inside the master bedroom closet.

When he returned to Ellen's house, she quickly explained about the visit from Bob and Kathy. She also told him about the other car with two men inside that had rushed off, when her two visitors walked out the front door. After telling him about that situation, she added, "I'm ready to go. I don't think I did a very good job of fooling those two who came inside. I packed what I need to take, and have an empty suitcase for you. We can do some shopping to get you some clothes, then go to a laundromat I know to wash them so they don't look new. We can use my credit cards to shop, but when we have everything we want to take with us, I've got a nice little credit card holder that I'll drop someplace where we think it'll likely be picked up by someone who will use them. If the cops ever get around to checking my cards, that'll put them on a wild goose chase. I think we should head south by private plane. I bet I can trade my car for at least part of the cost...I have the title in my purse. We can have the pilot fly us to somewhere. Oh, hold it, I forgot to tell you, but I have a timer on my front room lights, and one in my bedroom. I got them when I went on a trip to Canada. I have the one in the front room set to turn on at five, and off at ten. The one in my bedroom is set to turn on at a little before ten, and shut off twenty minutes later. Anyhow, maybe fly to Mexico City. From there we can get another, local, pilot to fly us wherever you want to go. I think Belize would be good because English is the national language. I don't speak anything else, how about you?"

Bennet burst into laughter, so Ellen asked, "What? What's so funny?"

"You...all that in almost one breath. You have this all worked out...perfectly, I might add. Let me pee, then let's go...you're wonderful, Ellen."

The plan Ellen had come up with is exactly what they did. Two days later they were in Belize, with a permit allowing them to stay for three months. Ellen had a passport she had obtained for a bus trip to Canada. Bennet had a passport and documentation in the name of Melvin T. Carter. When Ellen asked how he got that, he answered, "When I was a teenager, 15, I knew M.T. Carter...actually Melvin. But I used to tease him about going by M.T. I called him Model T. We used to fish together at a pond owned by a mean old man. One day, M.T. went alone, but I came later. By the time I got there, the mean old man was just finished burying him. He turned, saw me, and growled, 'I told you damned kids about fishing my pond. I just buried your buddy, now it's your turn.'

"With that he swung his shovel at me. I managed to duck inside the swing and kicked him in the nuts. He dropped the shovel and grabbed himself down there. So I picked up the shovel and whacked him. In time, and with a few more hits, I had him pretty well out of it. I finished him off, and like a fool kid came up with the idea of burying him, too. I was afraid if I went to the cops, they would arrest me for killing the guy. It was tough on M.T.'s folks, not knowing whatever happened to him. I kept thinking of ways to tell them, but in the end just let it go.

"So anyhow, when I got out of the joint and started planning my revenge on the people who put me in prison, I applied for his birth certificate. With that I got all the identification, and passport, I needed to become Melvin Carter. You think you'll be okay calling me Melvin, or Mel, or something?"

"If I get to call you 'husband,' I don't care what name you use," was Ellen's answer.

Thus, when in Belize, they married and became Mr. and Mrs. Melvin T. Carter. Within three weeks, long before their visiting permit was up, they applied for citizenship. By then they had opened three bank accounts, with over a million dollars in each. Part of the citizenship request included their offer to buy a nice piece of property northwest of Belize City.

***

Meanwhile, back in Missouri the hunt for Jimmy Bennet went on. After the second day of watching Ellen's house, Bob suggested, "I'm thinking maybe we should go into her place to see if anyone is still there. I'm having a sick feeling I should have doubled back when I first had the idea."

At midnight, Bob and Jim did the breaking and entering job. They found what Bob expected they might...it was empty...with no car in the garage. In the morning, Jim announced, "Back to square one, folks. Miss Jennings is gone. She had timers on her living room lights, and one in the bedroom. Someone is sharp as hell, either Miss Jennings or Bennet. So I'm gonna check her financials to see what I can find."

While Jim did that, Sarah was up early in Montana. There was something that had been running around in her mind since returning to the ranch. She and Maggie had traced the outlying family members from the Englishmen, and the Frenchman. But she had only done so with one of the Germen men. Holly had done one for them when she and Jim finished with the Americans, but Sarah was now working on the one she chided herself for not doing in the first place...Maximillian Bachmeier. It was time consuming work, and she had started on Bachmeier's faulty family tree the night before. Three hours into her work, she suddenly stopped and muttered an oath. She thought to call Jim, but knew he would tell her to do what she was already doing.

Maggie answered the incoming call, "Hi, Sarah. What's up?"

"Where are you?"

"In my office having a late spot of tea."

"When's the last time you drank a 'spot of tea.'"

"That's what I'm now calling sour mash."

"Well, never mind. Where do you stand on informing the German Chancellor of this mess?"

"Funny you should ask. The P.M. is at this moment in the air on the way to Germany. Plans to have an early meeting with the Chancellor, spending the night at our embassy. Why?"

"Get that plane turned around. Tell the Germans something has come up, that the meeting will have to take place at a later date."

"Why?"

"While we've been talking I have forwarded what I just found to your computer. Read it...after you get that plane headed back to England."

With full trust in Sarah, Maggie placed a call to the Prime Minister's plane. She had just been connected to the Prime Minster when Sarah's new information came in. She nearly dropped her phone. She quickly recovered, and asked the Prime Minister to have her plane turned around, and to tell the Germans that something urgent had come up that needed her immediate attention back in England. When asked why, Maggie answered, "Just please trust me on this. I have received additional information from Sarah Turner that changes the dynamic of this situation...drastically alters it in fact."

"Does this have anything to do with the Chancellor?"

"Please just come home. I'll explain when you arrive. I'll meet you at Downing Street."

Two hours later, in spite of the lateness of the night, Maggie was shown into the Prime Minister's office. She knew that the office had been updated to be the equivalent of a "quiet room" so she got right to the point. "Please tell me you did not tell the Chancellor the purpose of your visit."

"No I did not. Now just what is so urgent that you had me return home?"

Maggie handed the Prime Minister a printout of what Sarah had sent her. As it was being read, Maggie could see the ashen appearance of the Prime Minster. The first thing asked was, "Are you absolutely certain this is correct?"

"Yes. While waiting on your return, I double checked it. I have already had one of my agents get a DNA sample taken from another family member. Taken in such a matter that it was not known to be done. That agent is at present flying home to have the sample run. I have also checked the money trail...there is no doubt that this group now controls Germany...or at least controls the Chancellor."

"My God! How do we handle this? Surely not like you plan to handle some of the others."

"I don't know. I haven't consulted with Jim Scott yet. I have a few ideas, but don't like any of them."

"Would you like to enlighten me on those ideas?"

Maggie did, and the Prime Minister replied, "I don't like them either. By all means, consult with Mr. Scott. His devious mind will probably come up with something. I would like to have a reasonable plan by morning, if possible."

Maggie thought, "*Yeah, me too,*" but replied, "As you wish."

As soon as she had finished her call to Maggie, Sarah had called Jim. After she filled him in on the new information and what she had done to that point, Jim simply replied, "When Maggie calls, we'll try to concoct some sort of plan...thanks for nothing, Sarah."

Sarah knew Jim was joking, so just wished him a good day before ending the call to see what else she could find to ruin everyone's day.

When Maggie called, Jim answered, "I've been expecting your call. Please tell me the Chancellor never heard of what we know."

"That I can tell you. However, the P.M. wants a new plan by morning."

"You better get busy coming up with same, dear child."

"My plans stink, the P.M. agrees."

"Very well...how does this sound," Jim asked before giving her a plan off the top of his head.

"Doable, but dangerous."

"When have you ever been afraid of dangerous?"

"I'll have to get the P.M. to sign off on it...may as well do all four Germans while at it."

"Understood. Same with me and the President. In the meantime, I'll get my man on the way to me."

As Jim started putting his phone down, he started explaining the latest development to everyone in the room...which was everyone on the property except Clyde, Jo, Bill, and Amanda. When he finished he looked at Holly. "Road trip, dear. You get to brief the President, and get his approval. Pick who you want to be co-pilot."

"Michelle, I guess. May as well dazzle him with beauty."

Michelle blurted out, "As if you can't do that better than me. God, Holly you're a trip."

Jim was smiling when he called the President, who looked at his special phone and sighed. "Yes, Jim."

"Sir, Holly is getting ready to fly out to see you. Michelle Becker is going to fly with her. I would like you to entertain them in the Situation Room...something alarming has come up that will need your approval, as well as the Prime Minister's approval, to take care of. Maggie Littlefield will take care of obtaining that from the P.M."

"I take it I'm not going to like this visit."

"You won't, sir, but it is necessary."

"Very well. I assume there is a reason you aren't making this trip yourself."

"There is, we have a new development with the Bennet situation that needs my continued attention. It appears he's on the run...trying to find out where."

"Have them fly into Andrews. I'll arrange landing rights, and have them brought here. When Holly has her ETA figured out, have her call me."

20.

With Holly headed to her plane, Jim made another call. Richard Newton, a retired international assassin, answered after seeing just the name "Jim" on his caller ID, "Hello, Jim. I won't even ask how you managed to get this new number. What can I do for you?"

"Have a job for you from a fella who lives in a big white house."

"Jim, to be perfectly honest, I had hoped never to hear your voice again. I am retired...period. No jobs for anyone, government or otherwise. I have funds enough to last my lifetime, my children's lifetimes, and my grandchildren's lifetimes. Speaking of yet to arrive grandchildren, I would like to live long enough to meet them."

"You'll take this one, I assure you. That is assuming you can still shoot straight. If you fly in to see what I have, you'll do the job without question."

"Jim, in the first place, I vowed to a very rich and powerful man, one who has friends in big white houses, that I would never set foot in the United States again. There is, in addition, the matter of murder charges hanging over my head in the U.S."

"I can get you a full pardon for any crimes previously committed in the U.S. You can forget the vow."

"No."

"Okay, how about Canada? I'll pay you a million just to look at what we have."

"I don't need your money, Jim. But, I'll admit you have my interest. Question...why don't you do the job. You're more than qualified, I'm certain."

"I will be a guest of my previously mentioned friend, while the job is being done. He and I will be assumed to have been involved."

"Alright, Vancouver, but only to look at whatever it is you have...no guarantees I'll even consider it."

"Edmonton would be better, dress warm...unlike where you are, it is very cold."

"Do tell. Edmonton because it is nearer your Montana ranch. I suppose you want me to arrange my flight, then let you know when I'll be in to meet you."

"Yes, but not me. I'll have a lady by the name of Sarah Turner meet you. She runs things at my place, actually she is in charge of overseeing my financials. She's cheap, keeps cutting my allowance."

"I have a life sized picture of that. I guess it would be a good idea to have your number to call you back. As you no doubt are fully aware, only your first name, with no number, shows in my caller ID."

Jim chuckled before giving Newton his number.

That call finished, Jim called Sarah. "As soon as I know his ETA, you are going to meet Richard Newton in Edmonton."

"Your assassin buddy, right?"

"Yup. Do you still have that ghastly pink overcoat Bear got you one Christmas when he couldn't think of anything better to get you?"

"I have everything Al has ever given me...except my children, who as you know have flown the coop."

Only Sarah called Bear by the shortened version of his given name, so being familiar with that, Jim ignored the "Al" usage as he replied, "Good. Wear it to make you easy for him to spot."

"Do you think it would be a good idea for me to pull up his picture on our computer?"

"Yeah, that, too. I'll get back to you when I know his ETA, Edmonton."

"Do that, though I heard you the first time on the ETA business."

"You sure are awfully feisty today, young lady."

"I miss my husband and the great sex he provides. When can I expect to see him again?"

"Not for a while, hon...sorry."

Jim got to work on Ellen Jennings' financials after talking to Sarah. When he finished, he gathered everyone around. "Okay, someone is sharp. They used her credit cards to buy a number of items, mostly clothing from what I can tell. I'll print out the outlets where they bought what they did. This is a follow-up job for Ken with maybe Bob along to keep him out of trouble."

Ken objected, "I'm a big boy, I can handle it on my own, Jim."

"Probably, Ken, but Bob goes with you. This type of action is a bit above your pay grade. There is no reason to think I'm the only one these boys will target. If Flake was impressed by you, I'd bet you'll be on the take out list. Everyone who leaves this property will have at least one of us who has been to war with these types along for the ride. Am I being overly cautions...yes. But do I think it is necessary...also yes."

With no further argument from Ken, he left with Bob driving, after Jim printed out the list. With them gone, Jim started working on finding Ellen's car. He had no luck, but set up a program in his computer that if any information came in on the VIN number for the car, he would be notified.

During that process, Jim noticed when Hector left the room while reaching for his phone. When Hector returned, Jim paused in his work. "What's the latest on Harris?"

"Still heavily sedated and out of things. As I told you before, he's under twenty-four hours a day observation by the security force."

Jim knew what Hector meant about the "security force." As a matter of course, when the military men who had received bionic limbs were far enough along in their rehab, and had military experience suitable for the task, they were asked to become part of the clinic's security force. This was because Jim knew enough had been said about the operation at the clinic to make it a prime target for a terrorist. In fact, unknown to Jim, that had been on Bassam's list of targets.

Noticing a few questioning looks at Hector's use of the term "security force," Jim explained the arrangement, and the purpose of the cadre of men who participated. When that explanation was completed, Jim realized he had forgotten to tell Bob and Ken something about the list he had given them so he called Ken, who answered, "Yes, Jim."

"I forgot to tell you that you will notice a line under one of the items on the list you two are checking. All the items below that line appear to be strange, that is I'm betting these two got clever, and dumped the credit cards where someone was likely to find them and use for their own purposes. I'd say everything after the first charge under that line, was not made by Miss Jennings and Bennet, so you can stop."

"Got it."

***

While things were moving forward in Missouri, Jones and Flake were meeting in Washington. Jones reported, "The two men who were killed by Scott were the two I sent. Where do you stand with Harris?"

"Haven't heard from him for a while. Tried to call him, but no answer. I'm only slightly worried about that at this point, because he said he was going to put Becker's estate under near constant surveillance, so probably had his phone turned off. With your two guys now dead, I'm thinking we better put somebody else on the Bennet hunt. Which leads to another question: What are we going to do with Bennet when we find him?"

"Get him out of the country with some of our people to oversee him in a nice villa someplace. Then give him a harem of gals to play with until he gets one or more pregnant. When he sires a male child, we take control of the child, and at some point do away with him...Bennet. We'll put someone we can rely on in place to be the guardian of the kid."

"About what I figured. Now the task is to find him. I'm keeping my ear to the ground the best I can on the hunt being led by Scott...without showing an overabundance of interest. Speaking of that, this Agent Langston who is working with Scott's group seems pretty smart. At some point it might not be a bad idea to take him out. In fact, if we have the right people, it might be a good idea to take out everyone on Becker's estate since that seems to be Scott's operational center."

"Not a bad idea, but dangerous. For now, let's concentrate on getting an army of men working on finding Bennet. I can come up with about ten, how about you?"

"If I use some of my FBI people, about twenty, but how to get them on the job with cover is a problem. Let me do some thinking on the subject."

"Alright, I'll get those I can come up with on the way to Missouri in the next day or so. Before we lose sight of it, I'm still concerned about the interest in my financials. I've got some of my geeks working around the clock trying to find out who that was. I'm still thinking it had to be Scott. He absolutely has to be dealt with. If we don't hear something from Harris in another few days, we better get more people on that...maybe your idea of taking down everyone on Becker's estate."

Little did those two know that their concerns were about to grow, and grow rapidly. Maggie had some of her best agents keeping track of the four Germans who each controlled one of the accounts. In the meantime, she and Tony were in France. They had been tailing the Frenchman controlling one of the accounts. He always traveled with a three-man team of bodyguards, one of whom acted as his driver. Maggie and Tony had already decided, that while possible, it would be very hard to get the man at his estate outside Paris. To intercept him on trips to and from the estate seemed to be an easier project. This was particularly true on the last road he took home. It was only about ten kilometers long. The road was a two-lane, tree-lined stretch in an area with very few villas along the route. About two kilometers from his estate, there was a bend in the road. The two had already placed a large charge on one of the trees there. The hope was, that when set off by remote control it would blow the tree with the result of blocking the road, with no villa buildings between it and their target's home.

They had been using a small, highly capable drone produced by one of the companies Jim had a large stake in, to monitor the Frenchman's comings and goings so as to avoid detection. Finally after two days, they caught the break they were hoping for. A major snow storm was brewing, and with their target headed home, the heavy snow started falling. Staying well back of their target, with their drone in operation, they decided to make their move. It was after six, well dark, when Maggie shut her lights off and started to close rapidly. Their only problem was the drone was being unfavorably affected by the snow.

Tony asked, "How say you, Maggie?"

"I say let's do it. Blow the damned tree when we're near enough for the remote to work."

Tony muttered, "Drats...our bloody drone just went down. But I have it pinpointed so we can recover it after..."

"'Drats' he says. Blow the damned tree."

"Blowing tree, dear heart."

When the charge attached to the tree went off, the tree fell across the road. It wasn't square to the road, but near enough that there was no sensible way around it. When the Frenchman's car reached it, the driver came to a sudden stop less than three meters from it. Less than ten seconds later, Maggie stopped a few meters behind the other car.

By then the bodyguard in the back with his charge was out of the car as was the bodyguard in the front seat with the driver.

Tony opened his door and shouted, in his perfect French, "What's the problem?"

As he spoke Maggie got out of their car, too. Both had weapons loaded with, they trusted, non-lethal doses of tranquilizer. Both fired, with both hitting their intended targets. The driver, now alerted exited the car with his own weapon drawn. Maggie shot him with one of the darts and he soon slumped to the ground like the other two.

She and Tony then raced to the car, with Tony sticking his head in as he pointed his weapon at the Frenchman, who just sat there stunned at this turn of events. When Maggie opened the door next to him she softly said, also in excellent French, "Please be so kind as to exit your vehicle with your hands up. When safely outside, please place those hands behind your back."

He started to object, so Maggie smacked him in the forehead with the side of her tranquilizer gun. "Out, now!"

With a subdued and trussed up Frenchman in the rear of their car, with a hood over his head, Tony went in search of the drone. It took him nearly an hour to find it, but by then—thanks in large part to no traffic due to the snow storm—no one was overly concerned about the Frenchman.

When Tony finally returned with the drone, Maggie gave him what for, due to the time it had taken him. "'Pinpointed' my arse. Let's go."

Within the hour they were airborne in Maggie's plane with their passenger safely contained in the cabin with a very snug seat belt, the hood still in place. Maggie flew the plane to the SAS base where she normally parked her plane. Once there, they marched the Frenchman to a very secret holding cell. It was padded, with no windows and only one, solid, door. The interrogation that followed wasn't pleasant. It lasted for several hours, with the Frenchman delirious to the point that he hardly knew his name when it finished. But Maggie and Tony had what they wanted and needed.

Leaving the man, now totally naked with nothing to sleep on other than the padded floor of the room, Maggie left instructions to the General in charge of the base. "The very evil and dangerous man inside the padded room is to be given nothing but a chamber pot, and fed twice a day. He is not to be spoken to, and if he tries to speak have the person delivering the food and emptying the chamber pot growl at him. I am certain he is now so broken he will get the message."

The Frenchman was not the first person to be detained in the room, so the General understood. He had no need to know what the matter was about. Since the P.M. had paid a recent visit to the base in the company of Maggie and Tony, he knew better than to ask any questions.

Alone on the way to their Land Rover for the drive to London, Tony asked, "Are you as disgusted with this plot as I am?"

"Oh, yes. Was before I even had that talk with our Frenchman. I better call Jim to bring him up-to-date. Are you still up for the next phase of our plan?"

"Yes, indeed. These monsters shall all pay a heavy price for their misdeeds, and planned further misdeeds. Timing is going to be delicate, however. We really could use a bit of help, do you agree?"

"I do. I think Jim has that in the back of his mind, even though we didn't specifically discuss it."

At their Land Rover, Maggie asked, "Would you mind rounding up my security team?"

Tony just nodded as he walked off while Maggie called Jim. "Hi, Jim. One Frenchman now in custody. We got more from him than I would like, to tell you the truth. If left alone, they may well have succeeded in Germany, France and England. Basically, they plan to poke and prod the Muslim bear into major actions, allowing the *'knights in white hats'* to take firm control of all three countries. Once in control, a rebirth of National Socialism will be afoot.

"Before I forget it, the new German Chancellor is fully onboard with the plan...is a key part in it. Though, for now, his lineage will continue to be kept secret. On top of all that, I may need some help to make absolutely certain we can wipe out the situation in Germany in one fell swoop."

"With the exception of Holly and me, I'll get you what you need. Just let me know when and how many you'll need."

"Will do. I want to touch base with the P.M. before we make our final arrangements."

21.

While that conversation was going on, Sarah was preparing to meet Richard Newton. She was at the Edmonton airport, wearing her pink overcoat. Having seen his picture, she recognized him walking in her direction. As they met, he smiled. "I love your coat, Mrs. Turner."

"Thank you, it was a gift from my husband. By your smile as you spoke, I guess my boss made some sort of unkind statement about it. Please come with me to my plane. We can go over what I brought there."

"Lead the way."

Wendy Akridge, a retired Air Force Brigadier General, who lived on Jim's ranch with her husband Ray, (the chief mechanic for all the planes Jim had purchased, and were either still on the ranch or given to various people), met them at the top of the plane's steps. Sarah introduced the other two, then added, "Wendy is a pilot. When we fly together we take turns with who is pilot and who is co-pilot. She is fully briefed on the material you are about to look at, as well as the reason for this meeting."

Richard wasn't pleased that still another person knew about what he suspected he would wind up doing, but only shrugged as he was asked to take a seat. When seated, Sarah handed him the now much expanded file on the situation, which included copies of the original document discovered by Maggie. One look at the picture of Hitler (or his twin) caused him to mutter, "Oh, boy," before he started reading.

Two hours later, he looked at Sarah. "I'll do as Jim wants, no questions, no fee. This one I'll do for free. What insanity. Do you actually think they could pull this off?"

Sarah answered, "Yes. The Frenchman has been taken and debriefed. British MI6 Chief, Maggie Littlefield, and the most recent former Chief of that organization, questioned him and are convinced the threat is not only real, but likely to succeed, at least as far as Germany, France, and England are concerned. Rather than using Jews as the whipping boy, they are going to use Muslims...Muslims they did their best to see taken in by those three countries. The U.S. is also involved, but they aren't as far along as the other three."

"What is the timing?"

"Being worked out. You are invited to spend that time at Jim's ranch, but I understand you have no interest in returning to the U.S."

"No, I would just as soon return home, then fly on to Germany. I will call Jim when I am there. I will need a bit of time to plan my part. I'm sure you understand."

"I do, so does Jim. More on timing: the four Germans in charge of the accounts will be picked up just prior to your action. The two in England who are living, and the two in the U.S. will be picked up later...but not much later. There is a third man from the U.S. who has to be found before they are dealt with."

As Richard nodded at the information just given him, Wendy spoke up, "By the way, we are very pleased you missed your shot, or shots, at Michelle Becker. She is a dear friend."

"I am eternally grateful for that as well."

Sarah patted him on the shoulder. "Good thing for several reasons. That you are still alive to take on this new challenge is the main one for now. Please don't miss this shot. I failed to mention that the new German Chancellor is fully aware of the plot, and will play a large part in it. One more thing, he, the new Chancellor is a descendant of either Hitler or the twin, whoever was killed in Brazil."

"In that case, I am doubly in. I'll take my leave now, I have a return flight to catch."

Sarah waited until she and Wendy were airborne before she called Jim. "Newton is in."

"Thanks, Sarah. Talk to you later. I've got some planning to do."

Jim told the others with him about the assassin being willing to take out the Chancellor, without ever mentioning Newton's name. Since it was two days after Bennet departed with Ellen, Jim wasn't the least surprised when his computer sounded with an alert notice on Ellen's car.

He read what was there, then looked at Hector. "If this is Miss Jennings' doing, she is one sharp gal. I've got the name of the proud new owner of her car. How about you, and either Ken or Al, go check it out?"

Al spoke up, "How about Al. Ken's been having all the fun."

Two hours later, having backtracked ownership of the car back to the pilot who flew Bennet and Ellen to Mexico City, Hector and Al were talking to the man. From him they learned how he got the car, and where he had flown the two. At that point Hector asked, "How did Miss Jennings act? I mean did she seem the least bit afraid, or unhappy?"

"Good grief, no. She seemed happy as a clam. If fact she did the negotiating on price, with the car part of it. He was a little bit more restrained, while she was all happiness at the planned trip."

When, back at Bob's place, Hector explained that part of the equation, Jim replied, "Doesn't surprise me. I had a feeling some of this stuff didn't come from Bennet. He's wily and ruthless, with things pretty well planned out, but some of this detail I suspected was beyond him. At any rate, this is a job for you Hec. You better have some backup...Bear, maybe."

"Yeah, since we both look the part, and speak the language. But, as you know, neither of us flies...or at least pilots a plane."

Jim looked at Michelle, who grinned. "Yeah, okay. I better round up Jo. If nothing else, while Hector and Bear do their thing, she can look for junk for her shop...but don't tell I said her artifacts are 'junk.'"

Jim thanked Michelle, then looked at Bear. "You call Sarah. I don't want her asking about you constantly."

Bear chuckled as he took out his phone on his way out of the room.

***

By then, Arron Jones had sent four teams of investigators to Missouri to hunt for Bennet...all with the warning that he was of no use dead. Two teams had two men, while the other two had three men each. All had a lead investigator who, was a well thought of private detective. The best of those four was making progress. With information supplied by Flake, who had also supplied the four detectives with falsified FBI identification, he decided to zero in on the females involved with the original case that sent Benet to prison. He concentrated on the females because of the fluid found on Bassam's body. He easily discounted the court reporter because he had the information about the shootout at her home. After two days of finding no evidence of anyone home at Ellen's house, he decided to break into the house his second night in town. He and his two men found enough evidence of some male having been there, to concentrate on her for the time being. In addition to the clothing left behind by Bennet, they determined that Ellen's clothing had been disturbed in an untidy manner as she searched for the limited amount of her clothing that she would take. The only other thing of note they found was joked about. It was an empty birth control prescription.

While he didn't have a computer anywhere close to the capabilities of the master computer Jim used, he was still able to get her financials, to find out much of what Jim had days earlier. He then checked to see what had been purchased with her credit cards. At one store, the manager made a comment about having already given the information to the FBI. The detective simply replied, "We're going back to the beginning of this case, rechecking everything that's been done to this point, to see if anything was missed or misinterpreted."

After a while of checking on the sales made by whoever found the discarded cards, the detective figured out what must have happened. By then he had come to the conclusion that the woman had left with Bennet willingly. So next, he got on her car. In time he was talking to the pilot, who also commented about having already given his information to the authorities. Again, the same reply by the detective.

With that information he called Jones, both using throwaway phones. "Okay, I've got him and some dame being flown to Mexico City in a private plane. The pilot left them there and came home. I've got a passport, but only one of my men has one. Neither of us have ours with us so we'll have to fly home to get them, then book flights to Mexico City."

"Stop by and I'll give you more expense money. Fly first-class, it'll be easier to get reservations on short notice that way."

Six hours later the detective and one of his men were on the flight to Mexico City, where by that time Hector and Bear had already arrived, but had found no trace of Bennet, or Ellen beyond a few people who remembered them at the international airport where they had landed and passed through customs. The one piece of information Hector had that the detective didn't have was the expected amount of money Bennet had.

Those two had been in the air with Michelle and Jo for less than an hour when Jim thought of the money angle. He soon had a reasonable read on how much the three robbers had stolen, and how much had been recovered, as well as a guess as to how much they had spent supplying Bassam. He also knew a good deal of the money had been "laundered" through the car dealership, but there was still close to three million dollars unaccounted for. That figured out, he sent Ken and Bob to check out Donnelly's house, while he went to Cardin's house with Al and Emil. As to taking Emil, he had joked, "Someone who spent half a lifetime in the Navy certainly should know where to hide things."

Emil asked, "What are you talking about?"

"All the booze and contraband you shouldn't have had hidden aboard ship."

"Oh."

It took Ken and Bob less than half an hour to find where the now empty hiding place was located. Bob called Jim. "Found their stash. Plenty big enough for several million. Bet Bennet took the dough, but didn't hide the fact. He left it wide open for anyone to see where it was. Not too smart, but I'd like to think we'd have found it anyhow."

Jim called Hector. "Hec, he's probably traveling with two or three million bucks. It's why they probably used a small plane for their trip."

Hector gave the matter some thought after the call. "Hey, Bear, if you had a couple million, and a gal you seemed to be hung up on, would you decide to live in Mexico?"

"Nope. Also, the way these two have been operating, I bet they figured someone would probably be on to them at some point, so decided to throw anyone looking for them a curve."

"Just what I was thinking. Okay, then if they are traveling with all that much money, how did they get through customs? Coming in on a private plane sure would help. So, going to their next destination they would do the same thing."

"Which, dear Hector, leaves a lot of small planes to check out in a place as big as Mexico City."

"Yeah. This could take months."

"It better not."

Hector and Bear started off checking with the charter pilots at small airports in and around Mexico City. At the end of the day, Bear had a thought, one he didn't like. "Uh, Hector, I hate to say this, but as sharp as those two were to this point, what if they drove, or were driven, to somewhere else to find a charter plane?"

"I hate for you to say that, too. That awful thought crossed my mind earlier, but I didn't want to ruin your day. We'll just plod on for now. While we could certainly use some help, Jim and the others are gonna be busy with the men they know where to find. I'd bet he's scrambling to find enough help to take care of the situation in Germany as it is."

Jim was indeed having trouble coming up with a way to provide the help he had promised Maggie. He was at the point that he was rethinking his desire to be in the White House when the German Chancellor was killed by Newton. To pull off the German plan, each man in charge of one of the four accounts needed to be taken at nearly the same time the Chancellor was taken out. He was also considering calling Hector and Bear back to lend a hand. But, unless they took down Jones and Flake first, finding Bennet was equally important. That thought in mind, he also considered taking care of Jones and Flake first, but decided that whoever they had on the Bennet hunt might help them in finding the man somehow.

Finally, he decided to take a walk with Holly. As they walked around a portion of the property, they discussed the situation. Holly came up with an idea that she ran past Jim. "Honey, why don't we just forget the White House? Let Jones and Flake leak the idea of you being responsible for the German operation to the press, if they want. Proving it is another matter, and they'll be taken care of soon after anyway...if Hector has Bennet by then. Plus which, I don't think they'll even do that. I bet they'll be too busy trying to stay alive. You and I could hide out forever if push comes to shove. I doubt those two have a clue on how to do that."

"Yeah, you could be right. I've been thinking that. As Maggie might say, I'm just being too cute by half with our planned visit to the White House. You know, honey, I might be getting too old for this business."

"No kiddin."

"Thanks, I needed that...smartass."

Back in Bob's home, Jim called the President. "Holly and I won't be visiting you. We're off to Germany...Maggie needs help."

"I never thought your plan to spend the night here was necessary. I can handle the damned media if it comes to it. Good hunting."

Next Jim called Maggie. "Holly and I'll be heading your direction shortly. We'll bring Bob and Clyde with us."

"Figured you probably would. That night in the White House was too cute by half."

"Please tell me why everyone knew that but me?"

"Because you're getting too old for this stuff."

"Ouch. The four of us gonna be enough help?"

"Oh sure. We'll meet you at the SAS base."

On the trip to the SAS base, Holly, Jim, and Bob did the flying so everyone was well rested when they arrived. While Bob preferred to fly piston aircraft, he *could* fly jets. His time at the controls on this flight was limited sitting in the co-pilot seat.

Being met when they landed, Jim grinned when she saw who was with Maggie and Tony. Two retired SAS Sergeant Majors, Cyrus Squires and Oscar Aldridge were standing on either side of Maggie. After handshakes with the two men, Jim introduced them to Bob and Clyde who had not previously known them. Then after Holly kissed both men, full on the lips, Jim asked, "How did this black-haired vixen talk you two into this enterprise?"

Cyrus answered, "Was rather easy, old chap. She showed us the documents you lot have developed, and after we read them she asks, 'You in'?"

Jim nodded, as he asked Maggie, "What's the plan?"

"On the plane, Jim. We're a bit pressed for time. Tony can fill you four in while I fly. I thought I'd take my plane. Give you some rest on the flight to Berlin. I've been in contact with Newton. He wants to take his shot between eight and nine tonight...if we can get ourselves ready by then. He said the nearer eight, the better. Sarah did a nice job of arranging things with him, by the way."

During the flight to Berlin, Tony filled everyone in on the timing of the kidnappings of the four Germans in charge of accounts. Since, during their flight to the SAS base, Jim had spoken to Maggie, she knew neither Bob nor Clyde spoke German. That being the case, Bob would team with Holly who spoke it well, like she did most languages, while Clyde would be with Jim. Language was also part of the decision to have fluent German speakers Maggie and Tony each with one of the two SAS men...Cyrus with Tony, Oscar with Maggie.

Maggie's field agents had done a very good job in pinpointing where each of the four targets was likely to be at 8:00 PM on Tuesday nights, which would be the case for this mission. Two would be easy...they were most likely to be home. The other two would be more difficult. One would be taken by Maggie/Oscar and the other by Holly/Bob because a woman on the team would make doing the deed a bit easier, as Tony had put it during his briefing.

When all four teams were in position, and convinced they could bring off their part of the operation, they would check in with each other, then Jim would call Newton to let him know he could take his shot as planned.

The four teams were prepared for the light snow they were encountering as they made their way to their respective locations. Jim and Clyde were both wearing light colored clothing as Jim parked the car he had in a pre-selected spot of concealment, less than five hundred feet from the mansion of their target. Cyrus drove with Tony sitting next to him to a similar location near their target, but with less than three hundred feet to traverse to reach the rear of their target's mansion.

At nearly the same time, Maggie and Oscar, in proper attire, walked into the beer garden their target made a habit of visiting on Tuesday nights. They had gone over well detailed plans of the building with care. Oscar did speak enough German to order a stein of beer for each of them after they were seated.

By then Holly and Bob, in fine evening dress, had entered the very expensive restaurant where they immediately saw their target sitting just four tables away from where they were seated. Holly had done the speaking, stating that Bob was a visiting friend from the U.K. They, too, had carefully gone over the plans of the location.

Three brief calls were made to Jim, who in turn called Richard Newton. "Anytime you chose. Good hunting."

22.

As he took the call, Richard had the Chancellor in his crosshairs. The Chancellor was an exercise fanatic, who insisted on a nightly run to start at precisely 8:00 PM every evening when he was in the country. He loved running through the park where he was starting his run tonight. He chose to run no matter the weather, so the light snow was no real burden for him, though his two trailing bodyguards were less happy with running in the weather. Richard's car was parked not ten feet from the tree he sat in. He had his hands-free phone ready for the call, so without bothering to answer Jim's comment immediately, he squeezed off his shot.

With the bodyguards pulling their weapons and looking around when their charge dropped dead like a sack of potatoes right in front of them, Richard hopped down from his perch. As he did, he replied to Jim, "Shot taken, on my way to my car. Good luck."

Jim nudged Clyde as the started walking toward a side sliding door, while putting his phone away after whispering into the conference call with the other three teams, "Go."

Tony nodded to Cyrus as he, too, put away his phone while moving toward the rear door they sought.

Holly, simply removed her earbud and placed it in her purse, the signal to Bob to move into action.

Maggie did the same with her earbud, sending the same message to Oscar.

Maggie had four men setting up the situation. One waited for Maggie and Oscar outside the beer garden, while another waited a few blocks away to hear from the first man. Holly and Bob had the same two-man backup arrangement, while the other four men had no backups.

On Maggie's earbud signal, Oscar reached into his pocket and depressed a button on a remote unit. Instantly there was an explosion, resulting in the lights of the building going out. Outside in the getaway car, the man there called his partner. "Now."

Seconds later all the lights in the block also went out. With pandemonium going on in the building, Maggie and Oscar calmly stood up as they put on their overcoats...and night vision gear. Then they walked to their target, who was standing next to his table. Maggie put the silenced gun in her right hand in his ear as she whispered into his other ear, "I would very much like to collect the ransom I plan on asking for you. But if you misbehave, I will simply kill you and suffer the losses I will incur for setting this up."

The man said nothing as he felt Oscar pull his hands behind his back to secure with a plastic restraint. That done, Oscar draped the man's overcoat, that had been loosely hung on the back of his chair, over his shoulders. Thus adorned, he was led toward the front door where several people were fumbling their way outside. The captive's two bodyguards were lost in the confusion as Maggie and Oscar led him to their getaway car. Once inside, their backup drove to a predetermined place to find his partner patiently waiting on his ride.

Away clean, the driver headed to Maggie's plane.

Holly and Bob had much the same experience, except no overcoats were involved. Once in their getaway car, they hurriedly put on coats waiting for them since their overcoats were still inside in the cloak room, as was the coat of their captive.

On reaching the sliding glass door, Jim tried it to see if it was unlocked. With no luck on that score, he sighed as he took the risk of shooting out the locking mechanism with his silenced gun. He quickly pulled the door open and was followed inside by Clyde. The door was an entryway into their target's den. From there, on hearing no alarm sounded for their forced entry, they went in search of the man they sought. Jim was pleased that their luck was holding, as they found him in a parlor sipping sherry, smoking a cigar, and listening to Bach. His wife was helping their two children with their studies in another room specially set up for that purpose. When the man saw them, Jim held a finger to his lips, as Clyde raced forward with a pre-cut piece of duct tape, which was soon placed on his mouth. Jim took the cigar and put it in a nearby ashtray, before Clyde stood the man up to secure his hands behind his back with a plastic restraint. A hood was soon placed on the man's head, then he was led through the house the way Jim and Clyde had used to enter and find him. Retracing their steps to their car, they were soon headed toward the plane.

Tony and Cyrus weren't as lucky in their portion of the mission. At the rear door they went to, they discovered an alarm system. The detector Tony had brought along on warning from Maggie's team, gave him the information he needed. With perfect timing, Cyrus picked the lock and opened the door, with Tony rushing in to silence the alarm box before it went off. That obstacle out of the way, they soon found their target in a massive living room...with ten other people present. Tony was peeking around the corner of an opening into the large room. He pulled his head back, and using hand signals, let Cyrus know of the problem.

They eased back from where they were to discuss the situation. Whispering, they decided to go with the kidnapping for ransom cover story for their actions. Both men already had on black surgical gloves that stood out from their light clothing. They also both were wearing light colored watch caps, that when pulled down were actually ski masks. They pulled them down, drew their silenced weapons, and marched into the living room.

Since he spoke by far the most superior German of the two, Tony did the talking. "If anyone would like to play hero, please do so now, so we can kill you before getting to the matter at hand."

As he spoke, Cyrus noted two men standing to the right of the others. He thought they were probably bodyguards. He waggled his gun in their direction as he shook his head. The two men saw

Tony's gun pointed directly at the host of the gathering, who was also the man they were paid to protect. Seeing that, and fearing any movement might mean his death, they stood frozen in place.

Tony noticed Cyrus' action so glanced at the two bodyguards. "Starting with you two, everyone on the floor with hands well out in front."

After the two bodyguards were on the floor, Tony instructed each of the other people in the room to do the same...except for their target. Both men had carried several plastic restraints, which Cyrus started using to secure hands behind backs. He, of course, started with the two bodyguards. He only had four restraints, so at one point gave a shrug. Tony understood and gave him the four he had. With two still to be restrained, Cyrus went to a curtain and cut a long section of the cord from it. When the last two people, including their target, had their hands secured, Cyrus started using still more of the cord to secure the feet of everyone except for their target. The target's head was bagged, then Tony announced, "A ransom request will be made in a day or two....goodbye."

That said, Tony and Cyrus led their target to their car. From there they drove to the plane. By the time they reached it, all manner of alarms were going off in Germany. Not only had the Chancellor been assassinated, three very rich men had apparently been kidnapped. The authorities were investigating the assassination, and three kidnappings, when word came in of the fourth.

By then, Richard Newton was happily in the air on his way home. As he fell asleep, most of the cars used in the abductions had been driven to various locations and left behind. On the flight to Germany, once in French airspace, Maggie and Holly had flown her plane at treetop levels to their landing site. It was a very small, private landing strip not too far outside of Berlin. Maggie's field team had systematically disposed of the cars until they had only two left, including the one Tony had driven up to the plane. Her four man team left in those two cars after being told by Maggie, "When you leave the last car, please be so kind as to come home at your earliest convenience. Do so no more than two on a flight."

The four captured men were secured in the rear of the plane, all with bags on their heads as Maggie took off. She and her team left behind pandemonium...which was to get worse in the coming days. The authorities eventually found all of the cars used in the mission, but were never able to trace them to any real person as fake identities had been used to purchase or rent them. Unreasonably high ransom demands were made within 48 hours for all four men. None, of course, were ever paid, and no word of the four ever surfaced. By the terms of the original contracts, without bodies to prove death, the accounts of all four men went dormant...to the joy of the banks servicing those accounts.

By the time Maggie landed her plane at the SAS base, her four men were on the way home, all on different flights.

On landing, the four captives were hustled to separate SIS safe houses, where they were in turn interrogated by Tony and Maggie...not a very pleasant experience. Before those questioning periods commenced, Holly was flying her plane back to Missouri, with Jim and Bob lending a hand with the piloting. Clyde slept.

On returning to Bob's living room, Clyde announced he was heading to his home to catch up on his sleep, which drew hoots and hollers from his co-travelers. During the flight, Jim had contacted Hector to let him know the trip had been totally successful. Hector replied, "Yeah, good for you. We're getting nowhere, but doing so at a slow pace."

"You need help?"

"No thanks, Jim. You just spend your time trying to figure out how to take down Jones and Flake, now that they are fully alerted they have a major problem. I bet Maggie takes care of her two before you figure out how to deal with our two."

"No bet. We'll need to keep an eye on Jones and Flake to make sure they don't go to cover...but how I haven't exactly figured out just yet."

***

Well before they were being discussed by Jim and Hector, Flake was meeting with Jones. While not in a panic just yet, Flake invited himself up for drinks. When he arrived, Jones offered the suggested drinks, then got right down to the matter at hand. "The situation in Germany and France is beyond a major concern. Those five were in a position to start their plan when the collective Fourth Reich board agreed. We are now down to just us, and the two members in England...and, of course, the one and only Jimmy Bennet. My two men in Mexico City are continuing to dig, but need help to expedite the process. I have recalled the others I had in Missouri, and those who have passports, five of them do, will be off to Mexico City by later tonight."

"That's good, but what can be done about the five accounts now in limbo? It'll take forever to get those five declared dead if their bodies never turn up. Now that a ransom demand has come in on our Frenchman, we can bet there will be the same for the four Germans. That will only muddy the water further. You don't have any illusions that the French ransom demand actually came from that terrorist organization, do you?"

"Of course not. My money is still on Scott being up to his neck in this. How he or anyone managed to discover who we all are, or about the accounts, if they know about them, is beyond me."

"It had to have something to do with that unannounced meeting at the White House. If so, the Brits are deeply involved, also. I have spoken to our two living members in England intent on warning them. I needn't have bothered, they're almost in panic mode...which might not be a bad idea for us."

"Barton, my friend, if you are even considering flight, I suggest you forget about it. I have an idea no matter where we might flee to, that damned Jim Scott would find us. To stay alive, we simply must take down Mr. Scott."

"Have you given any thought to leaking, or planting, the suspicion that the President, in conjunction with Scott, is behind the mess in Germany...and France?"

"Yes, a great deal of thought. But since we have lost our ears and eyes in the White House..."

"What are you talking about, Arron? What lost?"

"Oh, didn't I tell you. He had the feeling the roof was about to collapse on him, so I got him sent to my hunting cabin in upstate New York, where he is to stay until further notice. It might just be prudent to eliminate him where his body can never be found...but I haven't made a final decision on that."

"You better do it. He gets caught it might do more damage than we can deal with right now."

"As you wish. I agree actually, but he has been such a loyal servant I hate to lose him if we can find a use for him later on."

"There is not going to be a 'later on' if we don't come up with a plan of some sort to deal with Scott...if it is Scott behind our problems."

"It's Scott, I'd bank your life on it...mine too if you come right down to it."

"Very decent of you to include yourself in that thought. Assuming it is Scott, back to my idea to somehow get the media on the premise that the President and Scott are behind the assassination of the German Chancellor, and the kidnaping of our five board members."

"We have absolutely no proof that Scott has anything to do with this. We can't even use the White House meeting because the records show no such meeting took place...unless we keep the just discussed witness that the meeting did happen alive...and use him somehow."

"I see your point about keeping him alive for now. Okay, so as of right now, we're down to only four of the original 12 accounts that can be used. I think we might consider just pulling our horns in, except for finding Bennet, until we have more information. Where that might come from I have no idea."

"I don't think that is wise. We need to figure out a way to eliminate Scott."

"Scott again. I'm thinking you're too fixated on him to think properly."

"And I'm thinking you better become so, and help me find a way to deal with him. How many men do we have who would be willing for an all-out attack on that Becker fellow's place in Missouri...when we are absolutely certain Scott is there? I can probably come up with around a hundred or so who are totally committed, and capable of this type action."

"I don't have near that many who are capable, but do have more than that number who are totally committed."

"Maybe we should consider the use of some of these so-called militias we've been secretly funding for years."

"I'd be scared to death to use them for something like this. The FBI has an entire, very secret, program of infiltrating such groups, both left and right leaning. It is my understanding that they have close to 1,000 agents involved. Personally, I think the best bet, if we're going to use force on Scott, would be lone assassins, even if Cam Harris failed. Which, by the way, we must assume he ran into trouble. I'd bet he's buried somewhere where no one is ever going to find him."

"Alright, assassins it is. I have about ten at my fingertips, but none as capable as Harris. I have heard of one, by the name of Richard Newton, who is considered to be the best ever at this type of matter. I know a man who might be able to reach him. I'll take care of it first thing."

"Okay, and I have any number of those types that would be more than willing to handle the job. But we need to send no more than one at a time, or they would wind up falling all over each other. You find out about this Newton fella, then we'll go from there."

It was only to take one day for Jones to find out Newton was absolutely out of the assassination business. But the man who handed out that piece of information was still a friend of Richard. He gave him a call. "Hi, Sir Newton."

"Hello, old friend. How are you these days? Prospering, I assume."

"I'm fine, thanks in large part to that wonderful trust account you set up for me when you decided to get out while you still have your skin. Speaking of which, that is why I'm calling. You'll never guess who wanted to hire you?"

"Arron Jones, or Barton Flake would be my first two guesses. Then I can think of a couple of Englishmen who might be interested."

"Are you a witch, or do you know something I obviously don't?"

"That would be 'warlock' my friend. As to the other, I know quite a few things you don't. If you're looking for a direct and truthful answer to your question, you're not going to get it. But, I have one for you, which one...Jones, or Flake?"

"Jones. And, before you ask, the man he had contact me wanted you badly enough to reveal who he was asking for, even though we both know that is a no, no."

"Target?"

"Jim Scott. I had a hunch you'd want to know."

"Thank you, my friend. I have to go now, have a nice day.

23.

Five minutes later Jim was talking to Richard. "Hello, Jim. I have some information for you. But first, I was very clear when I spoke to your messenger, Sarah, that there would be no charge for the last little job."

"So send the money back."

"You know I have no way of doing that, since the account it came from doesn't seem to exist."

"Fine, then set up an annuity for your children."

"Very funny. Arron Jones wants you dead...wanted me to do the job."

"I sincerely trust you declined, and this isn't a warning that my days might be numbered."

"Yes, I declined, or rather my former go-between declined for me, because of my assurance to him that under no circumstances would I take any job from anyone. Knowing what I know after I read the material Sarah showed me, I will be more than happy to take care of Mr. Jones for you...if you can herd him out of the U.S. Maybe even if I have to break my vow to you."

"No thanks. Him dead doesn't eliminate the problem of the account he controls."

"I assume the four missing Germans shall stay missing for eternity, which is brilliant on your part, since you brought it off. Therefore, I understand there is no need of my services. Thank you, I shall now go back into retirement. If you should ever call again, please do so to ask if I would like to spend time on your yacht."

"Ah, you know about the Holly? Keeping track of me in case you ever change your mind?"

"No, simply out of interest. A retired man has to find something to do with his time. It was nice of you to name the boat after your wife. Good luck with Jones, *et al.*"

Jim quickly passed on the information Richard had given him, and after a few comments from the others, he joked, "Okay, I guess they want my hide...so let's be on alert, but I'm not going to worry about it too much. Next item of business..."

His comment was cut off by his phone. He looked at his caller ID, and knew the call was from the clinic, so he simply answered, "Yes."

It was one of the members of the security force. "Hello, Jim. Doc says it's time to take this guy off the sedatives. He wants him up and walking around when he comes up for air. Should we just do as told, but keep a close eye on him?"

"Yeah, thanks. When he's able, I guess we'll bring him over here. Let me know."

"Will do."

Jim then looked around the room. "Harris needs to be taken off sedatives, and pretty soon we'll have to bring him here."

Holly shook her head. "The security guys over at the clinic can watch him there as well as we can here. We suddenly need to run off somewhere, he would be a problem here. Though, I guess we could take him to the ranch."

"You make a good point. In the meantime, they've got the keys to the handcuffs on his good hand, so when the cuffs are taken off for him to walk around, they can lock him up to something over there and keep up with the 24 hour surveillance. At some point I want to talk to him, but I guess I can just go over to the clinic."

Bob suggested, "Yeah, but with care. Don't forget Flake and Jones want you dead."

"I haven't forgotten, but thanks for the concern."

***

While that conversation was going on, progress was being made in Mexico City...by the detective Jones hired. He and the man with him had found the pilot who flew Bennet and Ellen to Belize. They had been told by someone else at the small airport about another man having flown a guy and girl somewhere in the last few days. As he walked up to this pilot, the detective held out his false FBI ID and introduced himself as an agent on an international manhunt for a man who had killed several people, including a woman and her two children. The woman he was traveling with had assisted in the murders of the woman and children.

The detective had learned to speak Spanish on the mean streets of New York, but while not fluent, could make himself understood. The pilot wasn't impressed, with either the man or his Spanish. He was even less impressed when the man had added the part about the woman (Ellen), because the pilot found her to be charming, even if her poor attempts at Spanish left a good deal to be desired. But, he hadn't let that bother him because he realized his English wasn't the best. With his dislike of the detective, and the fact that he had offered nothing for what information the pilot might have, the pilot did as Bennet had asked him to do if ever questioned...with $2,000.00 handed over as he made the request. In Spanish he replied, "I know who you are probably talking about. I flew them to Costa Rica. It was my understanding that the man had a friend, or friends, living there."

The detective nodded and soon left with his companion. They went to a cantina they had seen outside the gates of the airfield. Over their meal, the detective asked, "Do you feel like a trip to Costa Rica?"

"I do. How the hell do we find him there is the question?"

"It may take a while. I better call Jones for directions."

"Yeah, good idea," the companion replied in a manner suggesting he didn't hold out much hope for finding Bennet there, especially if he had friends.

The detective waited until they finished eating and were in their car before he called Jones to report their progress. Now more worried about his own hide than anything else, Jones was still gladdened by the call and information. He replied, "It just so happens, *I* have a few friends there. I'll give you their names and contact information. I'll also forward another $50,000.00 in expenses. Charter yourselves a plane to fly you down. In addition, your promised bonus is now twice what it was. Good job. Let me know when you're ready to write down the info I have for you."

"I'm ready."

With that information taken, the detective informed his friend about the conversation. The other man, still not convinced of their chances of success, was at least somewhat pleased with the new arrangements...especially since Jones had friends in Costa Rica.

It was two more days after that took place before Hector and Bear finally tracked down the pilot. After exchanging names with him, Hector, in his perfect Spanish, explained as he showed a picture of Bennet and Ellen to the man, "We are looking for this couple. It is my understanding that you flew them somewhere. Is it possible you might be willing to tell us if this is true?"

"You, sir, are the second man to ask me that in the last two days. This gringo claimed to be with the American Federales." Then after he spat, he told what the detective had told him, and then added, "I did not believe him. Maybe the man might have done such a thing, he had a hard veneer to him, but not that charming woman."

Hector thought a moment before he asked, "If you are not too busy, may I pay you for some of your valuable time?"

As he spoke, Hector reached into his pocket and pulled out a wad of U.S. currency. The pilot's eyes twinkled as he answered, "I am not too busy right now."

Hector handed him a thousand dollars. "Is this enough for the next two hours of your time...perhaps over lunch and tequila at a place of your choosing?"

"Come with me, I know a nice place not too far from here."

The walk to the cantina the pilot had in mind was more than a half mile, and while Hector would have preferred to drive, he walked along. During the walk, Hector asked, "Tell me about this gringo who spoke to you, if you don't mind?"

The pilot described the detective then added, "The gringo with him was shorter."

Hector then took out his phone, explained he had a call to make, and called Jim. Still using Spanish, he said, "Hey, amigo. Need you to check something for me. Find out if the FBI has anyone, or anyone authorized to do so, in Mexico looking for Bennet. Call me back. I'm going to lunch with the pilot who flew them somewhere."

Jim knew by the way Hector worded his request, that the pilot must still be with him. He told Hector he'd get the info as soon as possible.

Inside the cantina, the pilot ordered what he wanted to eat, along with tequila. Hector and Bear both ordered the same thing. While waiting on their meals to arrive, the pilot noticed Bear was slow to drink the liquid fire so he asked, "Is something wrong with my choice of tequila?"

Hector answered for Bear, "My friend here has become addicted to something else by a friend...in fact the friend I just called. I must admit I have grown used to drinking the same thing, but still enjoy a good tequila, which this is."

The pilot smiled. "What is this drink you speak of that your friend, Bear, enjoys?"

Bear answered, in *his* excellent Spanish, for himself this time. He gave the name brand of the most widely known sour mash, though not the one Jim...or his friends, normally drank.

The pilot called out to their waitress to ask if they carried the brand Bear had just given him. When she replied in the affirmative, the pilot ordered some to be brought to his friend, as he pointed at Bear. With the sour mash on its way, the pilot reached for the glass of tequila. "Since you won't be needing this any longer, I will take it."

"Be my guest," Bear replied with a smile.

As they ate, Hector asked the pilot, "Since you sent the men who spoke with you two days ago on a wild goose chase, may I ask a few questions while I wait on the call back from the friend I called?"

"Yes, ask away."

"Did the couple speak Spanish?"

"No. The young woman tried her best using one of those little books. She was so cute, making funny faces as she did. Finally, I decided my awful English was better than her even worse Spanish, so we muddled along to arrive at what they wanted, where they wanted to go, and that I was to tell anyone who asked that they had been taken to Costa Rica."

Hector sat straight up in his chair as a thought ran through his mind. "Did you tell the gringo that you spoke English, and that the couple did not speak acceptable Spanish?"

"No, he did not ask. He used a version of Spanish, that while not well spoken, at least I could understand. Now I have a question. I told you the gringo told me this man had killed many people and that the young woman helped. Is that true?"

"Part of it is. He has killed a few people, but none were children. The woman has killed no one, nor helped him in any way except to escape. The reason we are looking for him at this time is of a different nature. Without his knowledge, a relative of his passed away, leaving behind an account of vast holdings. The man in question now has control of that account, but as I said, is not aware of the fact. This account is beyond your wildest dreams. Also, he need not return to the United States to claim control of the account. It is held in a Swiss bank. All the proof he needs to take control of the money is a blood sample showing he is the relative of the deceased man. I am certain that if the men you spoke with earlier find him before we do, his life will take a far different turn than if we find him first."

Bear nearly smiled at the way Hector worded what he had just said. He had not lied to the pilot, yet had told him only part of the story...not the part where Bennet was likely to spend the rest of his life in prison, or face execution. Then it suddenly dawned on Bear that with the account in his control, Bennet might very well avoid that fate somehow.

The pilot, for his part, was stunned at what he had just heard. Yet he believed what he had been told by this man who he had some sense that he could trust.

While he was mulling that over, Hector continued, "Now we have another little problem, my friend. Are you married?"

"Yes."

"Children?"

"Yes...two."

"How would you like to visit the United States until this is over? What I am thinking is at some point the men you spoke with will realize they didn't ask you about languages and will come back to ask. Also, if they don't like what you have to say, harm may come to your family. Another thing is the call I made to my friend may reach the ears of the man—a very evil man—who sent those two to find you in the first place. If they realize you have spoken to us, as they very well might, it could be bad for you and your family."

"I would love to visit the United States, but how is that possible? Aren't you Mexican?"

"I am Mexican, but a citizen of the U.S. Was born there as were my parents, and grandparents. We are all legal citizens of the U.S. As to how it is possible, the man I called earlier can and will arrange it. We can probably fly you out of here yet today, or you can fly your own plane. Where you will stay is lovely, though a bit cold this time of year. They also have an excellent airplane mechanic who can take care of any problems you may have with your plane...I'd bet on a complete retrofit if you want it."

"I would be forever in your debt. What would you want in return?"

"I obviously want to know where you took the young couple, but that is not tied to this offer. I think I may have unwittingly endangered you and your family. Even if you do not tell me what I want to know, the offer stands. For now, I need to call my friend to get this underway. You better stop drinking if you're gonna fly all the way north...hold it...is there room in you plane for your family and another pilot?"

"Yes, but crowded," the pilot answered, though stunned at what he had just heard.

Hector called Jim. "Hey, Jimbo, I may have goofed. But, first let me tell you what we've found out."

When he finished speaking, Jim laughed and then cut him off. "I called the President, before I called our friends in Washington to find out if the FBI is looking for Bennet out of the country. Take your pilot to our embassy there in Mexico City. Show your White House pass at the gate to bypass any lines. Visas will be forthcoming. Have him fly to the ranch, directly. After you give me his plane's call sign, I'll have it cleared to bypass customs. I still haven't heard back about FBI interest, but Ken tells me no one from St. Louis is on any such search."

"Jim, you're the best. Sorry I screwed up, amigo. I'll get right on it."

Hector tossed well more than enough for their meals and drinks on the table, then looked at Bear. "Call the gals, tell them to meet us at the plane, but that we'll be a while."

It was a good thing Jim and Hector were acting so fast, because even before anyone got back to Jim on his request, an FBI agent who was part of Flake's network called him. "Jim Scott is trying to find out if we, the FBI, have any agents in Mexico looking for a guy by the name of Bennet. Mean anything to you?"

"Hell yes it does, good job."

Ten minutes later after the information was passed on to him, Jones called his detective, who was already in Costa Rica. "The pilot you spoke to must have told some associate of Scott's what he told you. I'll get some guys on the way to take care of him to shut him up, but I have a question. Did you discuss the matter of languages with the pilot? It would be a good idea to know if Bennet or that dame speak Spanish."

"Shit, sorry, but no I didn't ask. I was so glad to find out where he took them, I didn't even think of it. I spoke Spanish to him so don't even know if he speaks English."

"Don't make any more mistakes, please. I'll have the men I send find out."

The detective looked at the dead phone in his hand, and a bead of sweat broke out on his forehead. His companion noticed and asked, "What's up?"

The detective explained, then added, "So I'd say it would be a very good idea to find Bennet before anyone else does."

"That's nice, but the friends of Mr. Jones haven't been much help. How do we proceed?"

"With a good deal of intelligent haste."

"Okay, let's think about what we have. Nothing."

"Had you made the phone call I just made, you would be a bit more inventive than that. For starters, let's go over what we know. We know that damned pilot flew them down here to Costa Rica. We also know we have found no record of them ever having passed through customs, unless the money I spread around for that information was wasted and we were lied to. So..."

"Hold it right there, boss. Do we know the pilot actually flew them here? No. You didn't give him any money for his information. What if Bennet paid him a nice bonus for keeping his mouth shut, or lying about where he took them."

"You have a point. I'm thinking we keep looking for leads here, but waiting until the guys Jones sends down to have a further conversation with the pilot turn up something before thinking about our next move. But, let's keep in the back of our minds that if he did lie to us, where was he likely to have taken them."

"If they don't speak anything but English, I'm betting on Jamaica since it is English speaking."

"Is there any other English speaking nations down this way?"

"I don't know, you're the brains of this operation...but I'd still go to Jamaica first."

24.

When Hector arrived at the U.S. Embassy in Mexico City with his group, which consisted of Bear, Michelle, Jo, the pilot, and his family, he produced his White House pass. The Marine he showed the pass to snapped to attention and smartly saluted. Hector said, "Stand easy, Marine. I'm just an old retired Master Sergeant...Marine Master Sergeant. Semper fi."

"Master Sergeant, sir, you are expected. Please go through the side door over there, rather than through the front door."

Hector looked where the Marine guard had pointed, and told his group to follow along. Inside, one would have thought the group was royalty the way they were ushered into a large conference room, with many kind words being spoken.

What followed was almost comical. Two embassy officials came in to handle whatever was needed. Hector explained that the pilot had a passport, so would only need a visa...one valid for one year. His wife and children, however, did not have passports so Hector requested that they be given U.S. passports. The Ambassador himself walked in at that point to hear the last of Hector's comments.

Mindful of the President's orders that every courtesy be shown to those in the group and that any request Hector made be granted, he stammered, "The President spoke personally to me on this matter. He mentioned visas, but not that any non-citizen be granted a U.S. passport."

Hector was no stranger to dealing with officialdom, so he replied, "I am aware this is far beyond the norm, sir. So if it will help solve the matter, I will be happy to call the President myself and make the request to him."

As he spoke, Hector took out his phone. The Ambassador thought fast, realizing that to gain admittance as he had, Hector had to have shown his White House pass. Therefore, he replied. "That will not be necessary. The President told me personally to grant any request you made. They will have the passports, but, please, Mr. Garcia, do not let these passports be abused. And please see that they are destroyed when the matter at hand is completed."

"Thank you, Mr. Ambassador. Your wishes, orders, will be seen to, I give you my pledge. Actually, if these fine folks wish it so, I'm certain the President will expedite a request for citizenship for all four of our protected guests. Please be aware that the reason for this extraordinary handling of the matter is truly a matter of life and death."

When the requested documents were given to the family, Hector requested, "May we now please have some privacy in this room to discuss our plan to extricate these folks from harm's way?"

Left alone with his group, Hector organized things. Jo, since she had her own propeller-driven plane, would fly with the Mexican family as co-pilot. That plane would follow Michelle's plane to Jim's ranch. It would fly slightly behind, well off to her left where Michelle could keep an eye on it. This was an extra precaution because Jo knew where they were going and how to get there.

The pilot, who Hector was rapidly befriending, would tell some of his friends at the airport that he had been hired for the next several months by a rich lady who was on the hunt for Mexican artifacts. This fine lady had been kind enough to pay for all expenses of his family on the extended trip around Mexico.

The pilot had already told that story to a friend and neighbor who had been given the key to the family's home with instructions to take all foodstuffs out of the home because of the extended trip. The neighbor had also been given $1,000.00 in cash to keep an eye on the property during that time. The neighbor had also been told to be forthcoming with anyone coming around looking for the pilot or his family.

All that settled, Hector called Jim with the call signs of the two planes, and Jim assured him that they would be ignored when crossing the border, without having to stop at any normal entry points to the U.S.

While Michelle's plane could make the trip without a fuel stop, the smaller plane would have to make a re-fueling stop. That being the case, once they were in the air and had crossed into Texas air space, Hector would call a friend in Kerrville, Texas to arrange having a fuel truck standing by for the re-fueling of the smaller plane. Michelle's plane also would land, though it would not need fuel.

The last detail was for the Mexican pilot to file a flight plan for a point northwest of Mexico City, while the actual flight would be almost due north to Texas. After the fuel stop, the on-going flight would be north and slightly west.

Hector, satisfied he had left enough bread crumbs to throw off anyone Flake or Jones sent to deal with the family, the two planes took off from Mexico City...from different locations. It took a while for them to join up in formation, but from that point on the flight went without a hitch.

As they approached the area of Jim's ranch, the Mexican pilot noticed all the snow below and glanced over at Jo. "If this landing strip you told me about has all that snow on it, this plane will have difficulty landing...as will the plane of your friend."

Since Jo spoke Spanish fluently from all her time searching for artifacts in countries south of the U.S. border, they had been speaking that language on the flight. She replied, "As a redheaded pilot I know likes to say, 'piece of cake.' Actually, do not worry. The airstrip is heated."

Nearing the ranch, Jo called Sarah using her special phone. Sarah who had been briefed by Jim on the situation and had been expecting the flight, answered, "Hi, Jo. Are you finally here?"

"Yup. Mercy flight for landing. Michelle dropped back behind us once past Billings. We're gonna land the small plane first."

"Good. The door to one of the underground hangars is open, just pull on in. One of your planes better damned well have my husband aboard."

Jo laughed, "Michelle has him flying co-pilot."

"That should be good. Please tell me she isn't planning on having him do the landing."

"Nope, she doesn't have a death wish."

As they neared the landing strip, Jo suggested, "I better take her in because I know where to park her."

"Please do. Thank you."

When Jo pulled into the hangar and cut the engines, Michelle was already landing her plane, which would stay outside. As those in the small plane got out, Sarah was there to greet them. She introduced herself in Spanish, then continuing on in that language, she added, "Please follow me."

They all walked to and through the building attached to the hangars. It housed ten bungalows in the direction they were headed, with a swimming pool, firing range, and workout area in the other direction. Once past the bungalows, they came to the large computer room on one side with a conference room, dining room, and kitchen on the other.

There Sarah halted the procession to wait on the others to catch up. Seeing Bear, Sarah ran up to him to give him a large hug and long, passionate, kiss.

About that time others staying on the ranch appeared. Michelle and Jo were surprised when Jim's father-in-law Drew Hollins and his wife Pepper (both retired from the CIA), and Boris Telman (retired from the KGB) and his wife Suzan (a former Marine Captain), were introduced to the Mexican family. Noticing the looks from Michelle and Jo, Sarah muttered softly in English, "Added security for the next little bit. We've got more company coming."

That out of the way, Sarah introduced Ray and Wendy Akridge, explaining Ray would be doing any work needed to be done on the plane at no cost to the family. Then, after taking a breath, Sarah told the Mexican family what was in store for them. "You will be living with my husband and me for a while. Once I have shown you how everything works, there is another house almost identical to mine that you will be living in. Is that okay?"

Yes it was more than okay was the reply with many added thanks for how everyone was treating them. At that point, Hector asked Sarah to get the wife and children settled into her home while he had a brief conversation with the pilot. Hector added, "When we are finished, I'll have Bear bring him up to your place. Michelle, Jo, and I are gonna bunk down here until morning...they need some sleep after the long flight. And I need some because I'm old."

As the others started leaving, Drew and Boris stayed behind to talk to Hector when he finished his conversation with the Mexican pilot. Offered a drink, the pilot accepted, so Hector poured him a healthy amount of tequila, while the other two men poured themselves a drink also...sour mash for Drew and vodka for Boris. Hector opted for tequila, also. Bear begged off.

With all four seated, Hector got to the point. "If you feel obligated not to tell me where you flew the two people we're looking for, can you at least tell me if I should look someplace other than Belize. That seems to me to be the logical place for them to settle since they don't speak Spanish."

"I trust you, so I will tell you what you want to know. I did fly them to Belize, but only after going on to Honduras...Tegucigalpa, to re-fuel. The lady thought that would be a good idea to throw off anyone searching for them."

Hector laughed. "That girl is a pip. Drew, Boris, either of you would have been proud to have her working with you in the old days. Thank you, my friend. Now let Bear take you to his home."

The pilot gulped down his tequila, then left with Bear. The three remaining men then chatted for a while, with Hector filling in any blanks they might have in the entire story to date. The two old spies explained their presence in detail, then told him who else would be coming in soon, which included ten young Cherokee Indians from north of Jim's ranch. The Cherokee tribe was very close to Jim, and amongst other things manned the small arms plant he owned in partnership with the Cherokees near the town they called home. Whenever Jim was expecting trouble, he always knew he could count on the Cherokees to help out.

After saying good night to the two men, Hector headed down the hall with the bungalows. Jo had taken the first room on the right, while Michelle had taken the second. Hector figured they would have taken the first two on one side of the hall or the other, so he went to the third one on the left for no particular reason other than figuring neither lady would be in the third on either side of the hall.

In the morning, Michelle and Jo were first up in the bungalow section of the estate.

They started checking other bungalows until Jo tapped on the door of the one Hector was in and peeked inside, then nearly shouting, she called out to Michelle, "Found him. Sound asleep."

Hector growled, "No longer, young lady. Get. I'll be along in a while."

Those three were eating breakfast in the dining room of that complex when others started wandering in. Bear was first to arrive, noted they were eating, and announced he was off to clean horseshit...caring for the horses there was his main job on the ranch.

While the two ladies started cleaning up, Hector called Jim. "Okay, amigo, what's the plan?"

"You are aware that day after tomorrow is Christmas, are you not?"

"Yeah. I wondered when you'd get around to that. For my money, I'm ready to head home for the holidays. That darn Ellen planned so well it'll take anyone Jones and Flake has looking for them several months to get even a faint smell. But if you want to take down those two just mentioned fellas, I'm game."

"Nah. After the first of the year will do. Let them sweat for a while wondering if we know they're involved. Same deal with Maggie's two. I was about to call her. Get someone to fly you home. We'll be flying to the ranch later in the day. Get your pilots on the way home when they're ready."

Jim and his people weren't the only ones deciding to take a rest over the holidays. The detective Jones had working on the hunt, called. "Mr. Jones, we're gonna come home for the holidays. We both need some time to clear our heads. We're getting nowhere here in Costa Rica, but I'm not ready to give it up."

"Just as well. Perhaps after the first of the year, you and I can sit down and have a discussion on this matter. By the way, the men I sent to speak with your pilot friend discovered he has disappeared. They found out he had taken on a job to fly some rich dame around Mexico looking for artifacts. The flight plan he filed either was bogus, or he landed at some private strip. They can find no trace of him, but they, like you, want to be home for the holidays. If Scott's people get enough from the pilot to find Bennet, they have such a big head start on you that they almost certainly will find him first. If so, we will have to deal with the matter when they bring him back to the U.S. to face justice."

Even as he spoke, Arron Jones realized the man might not be brought in to be turned over to the authorities if found by Scott. It all depended on how much Scott knew. Since no effort had been made to capture or kill him or Flake, or for that matter the two living men in England who were part of the arrangement, it was actually possible the events in France and Germany were unconnected to the Fourth Reich. That was especially true if the ransom demands on the five kidnapped men were to be believed.

But the five men designated to replace the kidnapped five had gotten together and come up with a plan. They marched themselves to Switzerland to speak to the Swiss bankers where the money was held. They pointed out that the men almost surely had been killed, since it was likely connected with the assassination of the German Chancellor. That logic fell on deaf ears since the bankers were just as happy to have the accounts go dormant.

The bankers were even less inclined to listen to such "nonsense" when the carefully orchestrated ransom demands started reaching the families of the kidnapped. Ransom demands for amounts ranging from $90,000,000.00 to $110,000,000.00 (the different amounts were simply requested to confuse the matter still further) started arriving while the five designated men were still in Switzerland. Thus, the five made requests for those amounts from the Swiss bankers. Those requests were all replied to with the same short answer: "no."

Before leaving for home, the five were each told when proof of death could be supplied they would be put in charge of the account they were designated to take control of.

***

Before Jim returned to the ranch, he called Maggie. "Hi, hon. We're hanging it up for the holidays. I think you should do the same."

"Been planning on it...but have been summoned to #10. Will see the P.M. then head home, unless, of course, I get direct orders otherwise of some sort."

"Good luck. By the way, I've been meaning to ask if you have been looking for the original documents responsible for what you found?"

"No, Jim. Why would I do that? Just because they might shed more light on how the accounts are set up?"

"Sorry."

"Good. Anyhow, to answer your stupid question, Tony and I have been pulling our hair out trying to find them. Tony remembered long ago, when Sir Alistair was turning SIS over to Tony, Sir Alistair told him of some secret vault. He didn't say so, but Tony got the impression the same former chief who died while in this office may have mentioned it to the man who succeeded him, but not where or what it was exactly. Before Sir Alistair retired he came up with the idea that the Royal Family might know, so he asked the Queen. She claimed to have no knowledge of any secret vault, so the matter died there. While it is possible she lied to Sir Alistair, I doubt it...so does Tony. Since SIS has been in this building for the longest, it is assumed the vault should be here. Tony and I have almost literally torn this building apart looking for the blasted thing."

"Not wanting to be taken to task again for asking 'stupid' questions, I'm very reluctant to ask this, but have you checked with all the banks holding MI6 accounts about any secret vault?"

"Yes, we have...including the unofficial accounts. But most of those have been set up with your help since you started pouring found money our direction when Sir Alistair was still around...which I continue to thank you for. It drives the bean counters nuts when we're always on budget, without ever asking for the extra pound. Driving bean counters nuts is one of my favorite things about this job."

"I guess you've thought to look around our favorite SAS base?"

"Yes, Jim. Looked under my bed, too."

"Testy, testy. I'll stop now. Have a Merry Christmas and Happy New Year. I'll call

Tony in a while to wish him the same."

"Everyone involved with this deal on our end will have a good New Year if we solve this problem. By the way back at you...where do we stand on timing for the last four? That question might come up with my conversation with the P.M."

"Fairly soon after the New Year. I've decided there is no real reason now not to take them down because of the Bennet concern. Hector came up with a pretty good lead on finding him...a lead the opposition cannot get."

25.

After ending her call with Jim, Maggie looked at the large clock on the wall of her office and realized she had to hurry to be on time to visit #10 Downing Street. As it was she arrived just three minutes early.

Shown into the Prime Minister's inner office, she accepted the offer to sit. Tea was offered and accepted. As the two sat sipping their tea, the Prime Minister got right to the point. "On the matter of our two naughty boys, where do we stand? I'm interested in timing, and the matter of you being absolutely certain MI6 will not be operating in this country."

"The second inquiry first: as you may remember from the meeting with the U.S. President, it has always been our intent that no one employed by our government, MI6 or others, will take part in the abduction of those two...nor will they be housed in the U.K. after being abducted. As to timing, we plan to take the last four of these men out of circulation sometime after the first of the year. After that, we will start rounding up the designated replacements. As I told you the last time we spoke on this matter, the five men next in line for the five accounts from France and Germany have visited Switzerland inquiring about a way around the rules governing the accounts. They were rebuffed, but after a certain period of time, the five, while still alive, will be declared dead...our ransom nonsense notwithstanding."

"Very well. Have a nice Christmas and make everyone's New Year a happy one."

Realizing she had just been dismissed, Maggie left her unfinished tea where it sat as she stood and returned the holiday wishes.

She didn't even return to her office before heading to her home.

***

On January 3rd, Arron Jones summoned the detective who had been in the forefront of the Bennet search to his Washington penthouse. Once seated with drinks, Jones asked, "What are your plans to find Bennet?"

"Since, due to my oversight, we don't know what language Bennet, or the gal he's with, speak besides English, I did some research. You told me he has plenty of dough, so if it was me, I'd go where they speak the language I speak. In that part of the world, it would be Jamaica, Belize, or further south, Guyana. Again, it was me, I'd pick Jamaica, or Belize...so I think we'll start on Jamaica because if he's in Costa Rica it might take forever to find him. Having no idea what name he's using, we have to hope the gal at least is using her own name. No one by the name of Jennings cleared customs in Costa Rica in the right time frame. So that's where we'll start...in Jamaica, but if no luck there, head on to Belize. Of course, no guarantee she's using her own name either. I think we showed their pictures to everyone who works customs in Costa Rica just in case she is using a different name. The pilot we talked to didn't seem to know their names, but he may not have been straight with us. On the way to Jamaica, I'd like to stop in Mexico City to ask that guy some questions if he's returned from wherever he got off to."

"Do that, but if he isn't there go on with your plan. It seems to be well thought out on the surface. I asked Flake to see if he can find out if either of them is known to speak a foreign language. He couldn't find out anything on that score, so our best bet is the pilot. If he is back, don't ask him nicely. In fact, if he's back from the deal with the dame he's supposedly flying all over Mexico, press him on Costa Rica. If he's not there, I'll send someone else to find him. Like the plane I've made available for you, I'll give them one, also. How are you on expense money?"

"Should be okay. We passed out quite a bit to the customs people in Costa Rica, but still have plenty left."

"I understand from my friends in Costa Rica that they checked out property sales that might be suitable for a guy with plenty of money, but came up dry. Did you do any checking on that score yourself?"

"Yes, nothing. There is no telling how much he'd want to spend since whatever money he took with him has to last a lifetime, unless he finds a way to make money wherever he ends up."

"On that score, I'd think Belize or Guyana would offer more bang for the buck, so to speak, when buying property. Actually, I would guess Guyana would be the cheapest."

"I hadn't thought of that, well I did think Jamaica might be a bit pricey. That's why I don't plan to spend much time there if we strike out with customs. Checking all the custom agents takes time in its own right, so we can do some other snooping around waiting to make sure we interview all custom agents."

"Very well, at least you have what seems to be a workable plan. Two questions: would you like more help; and when do you plan to start?"

"I don't think I need additional help...too many cooks in the kitchen, et cetera. I thought we'd head south in the next few days."

After the detective left, Jones invited Flake to visit. On arrival, Flake immediately asked, "What did your great detective have to say?"

"Actually, I was rather impressed with his next plan," Jones answered before recounting the conversation he had with the detective.

Finished with that, Jones asked, "Have you heard anything on Scott and his team's efforts to track Bennet down?"

"No. The lead agent on the case, that fellow Langston, reported in that not much was going on. He told his Agent-in-Charge, who passed it on to the Director, that he felt it was a longshot that anyone would ever find Bennet. He reports that Scott and his people feel

Bennet had a well-conceived escape plan in place and has used it to good advantage."

Of course, what Flake had no way of knowing was that almost those exact words had been requested by Jim for Ken to utter when he reported in. Jones then asked if Flake had developed any new information on the language situation, which Flake had not.

At that point, Jones brought up the matter the two men had discussed often, "About Scott, do you think he is on to us?"

"I don't know. I've been looking over my shoulder for days. I'd like to think that if he's coming for us, he would have done so by now. Speaking of Scott, the assassin I sent after him reported in that trying to take Scott out would be the hardest job he had ever undertaken, and he had great reservations about continuing. I had told him what Harris had planned, so he went to the site Harris had planned to use. What he found didn't encourage him to continue with the effort. He found where someone, almost assuredly Harris, had set up shop to spy on that Becker guy's property. Once there he discovered what had to be equipment left behind by Harris...and a lot of dried blood. Evidently the large snow storm they had early last month has pretty well melted, or frozen, but there was still blood evident. His guess was Harris was badly wounded, or killed."

"Is he going to continue?"

"In a halfhearted way would be my guess. He did say that executive jets come and go from the property. He stayed around long enough to witness that from 'a damned safe distance.'"

"Have you been paying attention to the ransom situation on our five men?"

"Oh yeah. It's reached the almost comical stage."

The original ransom demands told family members of the five now-detained in England men to place an ad in various newspapers when they were ready to proceed. When no ads were placed, the next round of ransom notes sent more evidence of the men being alive, and urged a report on social media...as outlined by the ransom request. Those social media statements said the amount of money demanded was out of the question, simply not available. The next ransom demand included still more evidence of the men still being alive, but this time rather than hair samples as had been used earlier so DNA could be checked, chunks of skin had been included.

The bottom line was the ransom requests never allowed for any possible decrease in the amount demanded. But each time, social media pleas were posted about the impossibility of raising the kind of money being demanded.

Actually all five families were scrambling to come up with the money. In fact the five men who went to Switzerland had contacted Jones to ask for help. Jones and Flake both had funds available to cover the demands, but both men felt the likelihood of ever seeing the men alive was beyond slim. Thus Jones had told the five designated men that he simply did not have the funds needed, that his account and the account controlled by Flake were being pressed to the limit being used to set up things in the United States for eventual success. What was left unsaid was that they might be able (and willing) to help out one of the men, but which one was the question.

Therefore Jones and Flake were waiting for the five to come up with that idea on their own and get back to them. They had agreed to pay the ransom for one of the men, and then consider doing the same for another man if the first one was released. That very idea was being discussed by the five designated men at the same time Jones and Flake were having their present conversation.

The five agreed to pull the name out of a hat for the one man to use as a test sample. Had Flake known about that, he would have stated his "almost comical" could be changed to "comical."

The five agreed that the designated man for the chosen abductee would fly to England, and then on to the United States to offer that proposal. The feeling was being that with all five of the account holders onboard, the amount of the ransom demand would be easier to obtain. The timing of that planned trip was then discussed, and the five decided to wait for the next round of ransom demands which were expected in less than a week...just to see if the last pleas to lower the amount would be agreed to.

***

The next day, Hector called Jim. "Okay, amigo, Rosa (Hector's wife) says she's tired of me being underfoot, so I guess I'm ready to renew the search."

As he spoke, Rosa slapped him in the back of the head for that lie, even as Jim replied, "Yeah, I'm about ready to get back in the saddle myself. I'm still at the ranch, so Holly and I'll head out in the next little bit to pick you up. We'll bring your sidekick, Bear, with us. I want to talk to Harris before I leave. I've been letting him sit in the 'bad guys' cell at the end of the hangars without being spoken to since we came home."

Before leaving Missouri, Jim had asked the security team at the clinic to bring Harris to him. When they arrived with the man, his mouth was duct taped shut and a hood was on his head. He also had shackles and chains joining his legs together at the ankles. Thus outfitted, he was put in a seat in the cabin of Holly's plane where he was secured with a tightly drawn seatbelt, with his one hand handcuffed to the armrest. On arrival at the ranch, Harris was driven in one of the dune buggy-type carts on the property to a special cell not too far from the end of the underground hangars.

The cell had been dug out of the side of the same hill that had been used for the hangars. It had a rock base, with an underground stream running by. There were iron bars inset all the way across, and deep into the base, including well into the bed of the stream. There was a trap door above the cell. Harris was led there and undressed.

The hood came off last, then the duct tape was pulled off his lips. As he did that, Jim held his fingers to his lips. When Harris started to say something, Jim doubled up his fist and shook his head "no." Next the escape hole above the trap door was opened. There was a chair inside, which Harris was put into before it was lowered through the trap door. Harris figured, correctly, that he was to get out of the chair. As soon as he did, up went the chair. The trap door was then locked from the outside before the escape hole was closed.

Bear, who had been helping Jim, muttered, "I sure hope you never get pissed at me."

"I've been pissed at you several times, but don't worry...this is only for really bad people. Come on, let's climb down and pass his goodies through the bars."

Down at the front of the cave, Jim opened one of the sliding doors hiding the cell from observers. When it was wide enough for what he wanted, Jim handed in a sleeping bag, an extra thick blanket, a bag of sandwiches, and a plastic cup. Then, still not having spoken, he shut the sliding door, leaving Harris alone in the cell. There was a light in the earthen ceiling, and a vent that controlled the heat, or air conditioning depending on the season. The cell temperature was maintained at around 70 degrees.

Harris looked at the bag of sandwiches and decided to eat. When he had finished them the next day, he looked at the pile of wrappers and nearly threw them in the stream, but thought better of it. The last thing he wanted to do was irritate Scott.

After that day, and until the day Jim was ready to head back to Wentzville, either Jim or Bear brought him replacement food. Each time they would indicate they wanted the empty bag before handing in the next bag of food. Never a word was spoken by either, though for the first couple of days Harris spoke to them, which was ignored.

Finally, on that last day, Jim came down with a chair. He opened one of the sliding doors, sat down, and said, "Okay, Harris, here's the deal. I'm not certain just what to do with you. Killing you has some appeal, but I might have other uses for you. That I am aware of, you are the first man who has tried to kill me who has lived. Please keep that in mind as we speak. Both my friend and I who interviewed you, noticed that you were very forthcoming with the information you gave us. I seriously doubt that you did so in hopes of gaining favor. So I will ask this only one time...why?"

Harris thought the question over for a few moments before he answered, "You may not like some of what I say, and probably won't believe some of it either."

"Try me."

"Okay, Jones and Flake are convinced you took out a bunch of rich guys they were involved with. You probably killed my half-brother or had it done, but..."

"Hold on right there. Let's make sure your facts are correct. To the best of my knowledge, the conclusion the authorities in Nevada reached is probably correct...he killed himself. Two men I have total trust in, took him into the desert to some old abandoned bar, but left him there alive, with twenty grand getaway money. But he was a broken man. With the exception of the twenty grand, we had his money, and there was no going back to Las Vegas. So there he was, alone, without real friends and nowhere to go on twenty grand. If someone else came along and killed him, they did him a favor. Back to what you were saying."

"Okay, about him. We weren't close. He had all the money in the world, and only threw me crumbs once in a blue moon. So screw him, which I was about to say before you cut me off. Anyhow, back to the two who sent me after you. When Flake sent me to kill you I figured why not...just another rich bastard, and it would help me do what I wanted to do. By the way, before I forget it, a few of the things the cops think I did but they couldn't prove, was because I didn't do them. The worst stuff. Somebody did a fine job of drawing interest in me, but didn't leave enough proof around for the cops to nail me...because there wasn't any proof.

"Okay, that aside. I figure Jones and Flake got my half-brother killed. While I didn't much care for him, there was the matter of blood...which also figured in my willingness to kill you. But the main reason was whatever those two are up to, I'd hate to see them get by with it. Them, my half-brother, and that bunch you took down are, or in some cases were, one helluva lot more ruthless than I ever dreamed of being. I figured by taking you down, I could get in tighter with them, and in time find out exactly what they're about, then blow the whistle on them. Well, not actually blowing the whistle, but getting enough on them to pass on anonymously to the cops.

"For what it's worth, other than being one-handed, I'm glad I *didn't* get you. You may be rich as hell, but you're a different kind of rich. The people at that clinic where you took me, or had me taken, think you're the second coming. What you've done in that place helping out our service guys who have lost limbs sets you apart."

"Well, thanks for that. You about ready to get out of your cage?"

"That's a dumb question."

Jim laughed, "You're the second person in the last little bit to accuse me of asking dumb or stupid questions. Let me go up above and send down your ejection chair...I've got your clothes with me."

After Harris was extracted from the cell and dressed, Jim jerked his head. "Come on, follow me."

"Yeah, okay, but what happens now?"

"That's, in part, up to you. But if you go along with my little plan, I'll forget about the little incident in Missouri, and if you live through this, you get a new hand."

"I thought that clinic of yours was only for service guys."

"It is...but I have some influence with the doctor who runs it, so I guess I can talk him into putting a new hand on you."

"I bet you can. Who do I have to kill? Please tell me it's Jones or Flake, or both."

"Kill...neither. But help me nab both of them, from where they'll wind up in a nice place like you just left. Well, not as bad, but they'll never see the light of day again."

"Done deal."

26.

An hour later, Holly was flying to Los Angeles to pick up Hector. Aboard the plane with her were Jim, Bear, and Cam Harris. On the flight, Jim called Maggie from the cockpit so Harris couldn't overhear the conversation...not being a hundred percent certain Harris could be trusted. "Hi, Maggie, dear. You ready to rock and roll?"

"Yup. I'll round up Tony, Cyrus, and Oscar. When?"

"Tomorrow night."

"Okay, we'll have them under surveillance until then. Bye."

After picking up Hector, Jim and Holly flew the plane to Bob's estate. In the cabin of the plane after he came aboard, Harris looked at Hector. "You're the guy who blew my hand off, aren't you?"

"Yes, I am. Had Jim not wanted to take you alive, I would have killed you. I certainly hope you behave, and haven't sold Jim a bill of goods. If so, I will not have any restrictions this time. I'm not too fond of people who try to bring harm to my friends."

"I can understand that. I'll behave...whatever it is he has in mind for me, I'll do without question."

"Good."

Arriving at Bob's home, Jim gathered everyone around, except for Emil and Harris who were invited to enjoy the game room. Alone with the rest, Jim laid out the plan. When he finished, Amanda shook her head. "I don't know how you guys dream this stuff up, or how you bring it off like you always seem to do. Egads, I'm glad I'm not a bad guy in your crosshairs. If you'll excuse me, I'm gonna go home and have nightmares. But, before I go, thanks for what you folks do to rid the world of evil...even if it's scary as hell."

Bill left with Amanda after wishing everyone good luck. Before the door closed behind them, Ken groaned, "Here I am sworn to uphold the law, and I'm busy applauding the fact that in less than a month you will have kidnapped nine of the richest men on the planet...bravo. What do you want me to do, Jim?"

"Stay here until we return. There is the little matter of the possibility of someone after my hide being stupid enough to make a try for me here...even though I won't be here. Bill and Amanda can use some help warding off anyone who tries. For the next forty-eight hours they'll be here alone with no else but Al, Kathy, and Emil. Speaking of Emil, Bob, have you shown him the gun ports and how to use 'em?"

"Yeah, Al, Kathy, and Ken, too. With Al and Kathy staying in their place, with Bill and Amanda in theirs, and we'll have my home protected by Emil and Ken...it should be enough."

Al joked, "With the rest of the Wentzville Police Department a phone call away. But, hell, old Emil could probably handle anything that comes along by himself."

Jo stood up. "Come along husband, I want to use you before you split. See you in the morning, Hector, you too, Bear."

Clyde was laughing as he followed Jo out the backdoor.

Holly looked at her watch. "To make this work timing wise, Jim, we really should be out of here by two in the morning to give us time for any weather problems we might run into. Maybe get up by midnight, eat, and then hit the road. That builds in two hours 'oops' time."

"Yeah, okay. Bob, call Clyde and let him know to be up here by midnight if he's planning on eating with those of us who are leaving."

Michelle joked, "I hope nobody is expecting me to get up at midnight, get you folks gone, then leave out of here whenever Hector wants to go."

Bob shook his head. "Nope, darling. I'll try to be quiet when I get up. Jim, what about sleeping arrangements?"

Hector answered for Jim, "If welcome, I'll bunk with Al and Kathy."

Bob smiled, "Actually my first concern is Harris. What about him, Jim?"

"He can sleep in the maid's room since Hector is gonna bunk out. Uh, can you lock the gun ports, Bob?"

"Yeah, good point."

Everyone going to England was up and ready for breakfast just after one. Jim did most of the bacon and eggs cooking, while Holly organized toast, with Bob handling coffee and juice. Clyde put out plates and coffee mugs. Harris sat there watching and thinking, "*I've got a life-sized picture of my stupid half-brother, Jones, or Flake ever doing anything like this.*"

It was 2:20 AM when the group headed to Holly's plane. On the flight east, Holly, always careful when it came to fuel, decided to stop in Virginia to re-fuel, even though she knew she had plenty to make the trip. They landed at a small airstrip at Marine Base Quantico, where they had more-or-less permanent permission to land. The re-fueling proved to be a slight problem, but their tanks were eventually topped off. But the stop cost them a bit over an hour. Holly wasn't concerned, because she knew she had built in plenty of time for things like getting away a bit late, then spending so much time on the ground in Virginia.

When they finally reached the SAS base outside London, Holly was to be congratulated for arriving with perfect timing. Maggie was there to greet them, and was laughing as they deplaned. Jim first down the steps of the plane asked, "What's so funny, Maggie?"

"I'll tell you in a while."

By then everyone else was off the plane, and Jim introduced Maggie and Harris. In a flash after being told his name, Maggie walked up to Harris and punched him square on the lips. "That is for trying to kill the best man, other than my husband, that I have ever known. Had you succeeded, I would have tracked you down and peeled the skin off your torso. Then I would have poured salt in the open wounds before I continued on until you died a horrible death."

While the blow had not broken the skin, Harris certainly felt it, but he said nothing until Maggie completed her rant. Convinced she meant what she said, and probably could have tracked him down, he replied, "I was glad I missed before now, but I am now doubly glad."

"Very well, if Jim has seen fit to forgive you, or at least put it aside, I shall bow to his judgement. Now, then, Jim, let's retire to the entertainment center you so graciously funded for the troops here."

Jim glanced at his watch. "Shouldn't we get a move on, Maggie?"

"No rush. Follow along, you lot."

Inside the large room with several easy chairs, a bar, and open kitchen, Maggie asked, "What will everyone have?"

Everyone asked for coffee as they sat down around a large table. Maggie enlisted the help of Holly as she started bringing coffee mugs, all with the SAS emblem on them. Everyone, except Jim, who had asked for coffee soon had it. For Jim, she poured a healthy portion of sour mash for him and herself. As she sat the drink down in front of him, Jim shook his head. "You know I don't drink just before starting a mission."

"Ah ha," Maggie replied, "no trust amongst friends. Drink up."

Jim shrugged and did as ordered, then the group sat around talking about next to nothing having to do with the coming events. About the only thing Jim said in that regard was, "Maggie, Cam will be staying behind with you. Try not to damage him while we're gone...I have a use for him when we return to the U.S. Now, we really should get this show on the road."

"In due time, in due time. We'll wait here for Tony, Cyrus, and Oscar."

"Where are those three, by the way? I thought they were supposed to make sure our targets were in place, then come to round us up."

"Change of plans. They'll be along in a jiffy."

"A jiffy" turned out to be little more than an hour after the plane landed. When notified the two cars she expected had cleared the main gate, Maggie led those with her outside. In a few minutes the two cars pulled to a stop several feet from the group. Tony, Cyrus, and Oscar got out first, then helped three men in hoods out. Each of those three had their hands secured behind their backs.

Maggie asked, "Which one is mine?"

Cyrus pushed one of the three hooded men forward. "This one, lass. Should I take him to the interrogation room?"

"Yes, Cyrus. Thank you."

By then Jim was smiling, as was Holly. Both knew who two of the men had to be, but even then it hadn't occurred to them who the third man was. Maggie soon explained, "That chap Cyrus is hauling off, paid a visit from Germany. He's one of the five designated replacements. We'll find out shortly what he was doing here, but it must have been important because your two targets got together to talk to him. My darling friend, Sir Anthony, had the presence of mind to swoop in and nab all three. He called me with the good news when he was on his way back...the call came in about ten minutes before Holly landed. So wonderful man, Jim, you can now turn around and go home."

Jim asked, "Don't you think it would be a good idea for us to take down the other four before they get wind of this, or at least wonder what happened to this one?"

"We can handle it. You better get back before your two birds hear about this somehow and land up on the run."

"Only four of you to do nearly simultaneous raids is cutting it a bit thin, even for such more than capable folks, Maggie."

"Not only the four of us, Jim. My four guys you met, and another four have been keeping an eye on the five designated replacements. That's how we found out who was with our two original targets. My guys are quite capable. That's nine of us to round up four...go home. Take this trash with you. I love you all...well except for Mr. Harris, him I only tolerate because Jim does."

Jim asked, "Are you sure, Maggie?"

"As a certain redheaded pilot likes to say, 'piece of cake.' Go."

Jim replied, "Load up the trash folks, let's hit it."

Harris, who had heard no news since his hand was shot nearly off, was mystified at what was going on, and who the two hooded men about to be loaded on the plane were, but kept silent...thankful that none of these people were after his hide. When the two captured Englishmen were snugged into rear seats of the plane, he did ask Jim, "Just who is that lady...other than Maggie?"

"That, my friend, is Margaret Littlefield, Chief of SIS...otherwise known as MI6."

"I guess you'll tell me sometime what this is all about."

"Perhaps, perhaps not...we'll see."

Before the plane was even out of sight, Maggie and Tony were "interviewing" the German.

By the time the plane landed at the same CIA controlled airstrip outside D.C. as it had on the outgoing flight, he had been bled dry and Jim had been given the information from that interrogation. It was a little before 9:00 PM local time when Jim, Bob, Clyde, and Harris deplaned. Holly was left aboard with the two prisoners.

Jim had arranged two SUVs and the four men left in them, with Jim driving one. Harris was with him, and the other two men were in the second vehicle. Harris had told Jim where he and Flake normally met, so that was the destination. When they arrived, the vehicles were well hidden before Harris did as had been drummed into him by Jim during both directions of the just concluded flights.

He took an unlisted cell phone from Jim and called Flake. Flake, not recognizing the number nearly didn't answer, but on impulse did. "This is Barton Flake, whose calling?"

"Mr. Flake, this is Harris...Cam Harris. I've had a terrible time, but have some great news for you. Scott is dead, but I had one helluva time getting away...and not in one piece. I've managed to make my way from Missouri without a weapon, phone, or any money which is why I haven't been in touch. Rode most of the way with a trucker who I fed a line of crap to. I have a file folder of documents that I do not have any way of understanding...they're in some other language...maybe German. Before I killed Scott, I heard him mention something about some damned twin, but don't know who the twin was or anything. I'm using a phone I took from the guy who I carjacked locally, after making my way back here. I also got the guy's gun, but he had only about six bucks on him. He had credit cards, but no way in hell am I gonna use them. His car ran out of gas about a mile from here at our normal place to meet. I need some help. Can you come out...now?"

At the mention of documents...in German, and a twin, Flake was very excited. He assured Harris he would be on his way to him within five minutes, then added, "Just hang tough...good job. Uh, when did you kill Scott?"

"About a day ago. I'd say maybe 22 hours."

Still excited, Flake again assured Harris he was on his way, but before he left he called Arron Jones. "Great news, fantastic news! Harris somehow managed to kill Scott yesterday, about 22 hours ago he said. But, even more exciting, he has a folder with documents he believes are in German that he took from Scott! He also heard Scott mention something about a twin! I'm going to see him now to get the documents."

"My God man, this is wonderful news. Do you want me to come with you?"

"No need. I'll get the documents, then bring them to you. What should I do with Harris?"

"After what he's done, I hate to say it, but he may know too much."

"Understood, I agree."

While Flake hurried to the meeting place, Harris was being congratulated on his "fine job of acting" by Jim, who added, "One more great performance, and I'll grant you a full pardon for trying to kill me, and your life will take a great turn for the better...so long as you agree to be a good boy going forward."

"Mr. Scott you're the first man in my life who scares the living hell outta me. You tell me to shit, I'll..."

"I get the picture. Okay, guys let's take our positions."

When Flake arrived, he pulled to a stop not ten feet from Harris. As he walked toward Harris, Flake reached into his shoulder holster. Harris thought, "*That dirty son-of-a-bitch*" just as Bob, who had hidden nearest where Flake parked rushed forward to hit the man's gun wielding hand with his own pistol. As Flake screamed in pain, Clyde was around his car coming up from behind. In seconds, they had his hands (one broken) secured behind his back with a hood over his head. Jim walked forward, pulled up a pants leg and injected him with a very strong sedative.

Harris asked, "What did you shoot him with?"

Jim answered, "Something that'll keep him out of commission for about two hours...of course it means we'll have to carry him to one of our SUVs. You ready for act two?"

"Damned right I am. This bastard was gonna shoot me."

"I figured he might have that in mind. That's why we were deployed as we were, so at least one of us would be near enough to disarm him before he did so."

As prepped by Jim, Harris called Jones. In a fake weak voice he started "act two," "Mr. Jones, this is Cam Harris. We just had a big shootout with some guys. They must have followed Mr. Flake here. We're all shot up, need help. Mr. Flake took several hits. I've managed to stop the serious bleeding but he needs a doctor fast. We sure as hell can't call the cops or an ambulance. The three guys who we got into it with are all dead, so how would we explain this away without all hell breaking loose? Can you bring a doctor or someone with some sort of medical experience for the two of us? Please. Oh before the shootout started, Mr. Flake asked if there was anything else I remembered Scott saying. A couple of things I heard and reported to him seemed to get him all excited...hold it, did you hear that?"

"Hear what?"

"Mr. Flake's phone is going dead. I better hang up fast. Do you know where we normally meet?"

"Yes."

"That's where we're at. Better go now."

Arron Jones nearly threw the dead phone in his hand at the wall, but knew time might be running out on both men, so sprang into action. While he didn't have a doctor nearby, he did always have a former paramedic on his staff. She was summoned from her living quarters in the penthouse, and those two left in one of his cars. He thought to take his bodyguards with him, but the fewer people who knew about this situation, the better. As it was he would probably have to kill the paramedic, as well as Harris after he told what he knew that had Flake so excited.

As Jim would say later, "That was almost too easy."

Jones walked right into the trap. When he stopped he noticed three bodies lying around the area as the paramedic jumped out of the car to hurry toward Harris who was slumped over Flake to hide the fact that his hands were secured behind his back. When she ran past one of the bodies (Jim) he tackled her and she went down face first. In seconds her head was bagged and her hands secured. Another body (Clyde) jumped up to nab Jones, and give him the same treatment...with a fast arriving Bob to lend a hand.

After finding her cell phone and tossing it a long way, Jim took the keys to both cars and tossed them as far as he could. Next, Bob and Clyde went for their SUVs.

27.

As Holly's plane flew westward, with Jones and Flake in seats facing the two Englishmen, Jim sat next to Holly in the right seat of the cockpit. He called Maggie first to let her know all was well, then called the President. "Sir, the nine men each in charge of one of those accounts are now out of circulation. Maggie Littlefield and her people already have one of the designated replacements in custody, and are at present after the other four for those over there. We'll get around to our designated replacements, and Maggie's, in the next few days. But from what we now know, this is gonna take a while to wrap up."

"Good job. Keep me up-to-date, please."

"Will do, sir. In a few days, I'll stop by the White House to give you a full briefing."

"You haven't mentioned it, so I assume that the original documents have not been found."

"Alas, sir, you assume correctly."

On arrival at the ranch, the four captives were unceremoniously placed in the cave cell...naked, with sleeping bags and one extra blanket each. None had been spoken to since their capture, but that was about to change. Before that, Jim wanted to sit down with Cam Harris and have a long discussion with the man.

With drinks in hand in the swimming pool area of the complex, Jim asked, "You ready for a new life?"

"Yeah."

"Okay, here's what I propose. We take you back to the clinic, and you get a new hand. I've gotta tell you the rehab is long and hard, while trying to learn how to use your new appendage. But when you have done so, I will set you up with a tidy sum do with as you like. Do you think you can live out your life happily on a couple of million?"

"If that's dollars and not pesos, hell yes...maybe even if it *was* pesos."

"Okay that's settled. Now, next question, do you think any of Flake's people, or anyone connected to Jones will come after you when you surface a year or so from now?"

"Could be."

"Okay, we'll cross that bridge when we come to it...get the new hand working before we worry about it. Ridding the woods of all the snakes may take more than a year if I can't figure out a way to let the proper authorities deal with them."

Through with that conversation, Jim approached his father-in-law, Drew, and Drew's next door neighbor, Boris. "Okay, gents, I think the threat of attack on this place is pretty well over. I sent the Cherokee fellas home with thanks as soon as we got back. But, I would appreciate it if you would have a chat with each of our prisoners. Bear and I'll bring 'em down to the barn one at a time for you."

Drew looked at Boris, who nodded, so Drew responded, "Bring 'em on. We haven't had any real fun in a couple of years."

Boris growled, "Speak for yourself, old man. I can still get it up."

Both men were nearly the same age, but in their eighties. Drew just looked at his friend and shook his head without reply.

Jim joked, "You two *young* gentlemen both probably engage in that wonderful exercise more than most men half your age. I hope you can get something worthwhile out of these guys. But the one thing none of them have is any way of solving the aggravating situation poor Maggie has. She's been searching SIS Headquarters high and low, with Tony's help, looking for a hidden secret vault. It might hold additional information to the particulars of how these accounts are set up as far as succession of control."

Drew rubbed his chin. "You know, son, any such vault just might be in the section of the SIS building that OSS once occupied. During

WWII, OSS had a couple of offices at SIS Headquarters. It seems to me that sometime back in the 50's, when I was just a pup, CIA finally moved out into new digs. I heard some comments about leaving all the wartime documents jointly gathered in some vault in the OSS/ CIA section. Mind you I was never in the building, so this is just wild speculation from my fading memory."

Jim shrugged. "I'll pass it on to Maggie after we get your first subject in the barn. Are you gonna have your ladies lend a hand with the interrogations?"

Boris answered, "Good God, no. Suzan is occupied catching up with everyone here, and Pepper would pluck their eyes out, or worse, the first time the one we're working on paused before giving an answer. That woman is hell on wheels...scares the dickens outta me. I still have nightmares over what she did in Bolivia."

Coming from a former KGB agent, who had killed many over the years, and had even tortured a few along the way, that statement about Pepper might seem a bit strange. However, both Jim and Drew knew exactly what he meant. On a mission to Bolivia to take down an al-

Qaida drug operation, Pepper had grown tired of terrorists, and began cutting heads off several, then placing the heads between the legs of one body or the other and placing a lower reproductive appendage in the mouth of a head not belonging to the body it was being attached to. Her intent had been to enrage and terrorize the terrorists. She succeeded in both, to the point that the terrorists lost focus on what they were trying to accomplish...which was her intended goal.

When the first of the four captured men was secured in the barn, Jim did call Maggie with what Drew had told him about a possible location of the vault. Her reply was curt, "You might have asked him about this earlier. That old section has been used for storage for years. I've never even been in it until Tony and I went through all the files we found there. If there's a vault in there I'll puke...right after Tony and I jump up and down in glee."

Two hours later, Maggie called back. "Okay, we found it. Had to tear out a wall, but found a vault in one of the rooms. Now the problem is getting inside it without the combination."

"Margaret Doyle Littlefield, do I have to do everything for you? In the margin of one of those pages you found is a series of numbers. They had nothing to do with what was written, but I have a hunch that they might have been scribbled there as a reminder of where the original documents were, or something of the sort."

"Now that you mention it, I do remember seeing those numbers and wondering what the heck they were for. I'll get back to you."

It was two days later, with only three of the four prisoners finished with their "questioning," when Maggie called back. "You getting any more out of those gentlemen in your control?"

"Not much, just verification of what Drew and Boris have already come up with. The last one, Flake, is being interrogated by Pepper...Drew and Boris claim to be too tired to continue. I think Drew just wants to let Pepper in on the fun."

"But for who he is, I'd say pity poor Flake. Oh, by the way, Tony and I just found the original documents. We thought we'd have a drink before starting to read them."

"Goodbye, rat."

Maggie was laughing as Tony poured the drinks they fully intended to sip on as they read. After all the work they had gone through to find them, they figured they deserved something for their efforts. As he handed Maggie her tumbler, Tony asked, "Was Jim glad to hear we found the Crown Jewels?"

"No, he was a bit put out that I waited so long to tell him we had found them."

***

In Belize, the detective employed by Jones, who had no idea the man who sent him had "disappeared," was closing in on Bennet with his partner in this venture. They had gone to Jamaica and struck out there, so decided to try Belize before considering Guyana. They had spent several days without much success, when they stumbled onto their first break. While having breakfast in a small café they had found and enjoyed utilizing, they overheard a delivery man telling the owner of the café that the American couple who bought a certain piece of property had sent thanks for the recipe he had sent them. The delivery man had taken a load of supplies out to their home, and was just in the café to eat. From there it had taken three days of careful questioning to find out more about this couple. They weren't convinced it was Bennet and Ellen, but decided to drive out to the property Bennet had purchased.

Hector and Bear had taken a different approach. One of the things they had been checking was—on the assumption Bennet and Ellen might settle there—real estate sales people. The very day the detective and his partner had set out for Bennet's property, Hector struck pay dirt when he found the agent who had sold the property to Bennet. Even though Bennet had a light beard when he passed through Mexico, it was now full. The pictures Hector had showed three different facial appearances...one was with full beard. Assured Bennet was the man the agent had sold to, Hector and Bear drove to the property...roughly fifteen minutes after the detective got behind the wheel of his rented car.

Hector and Bear had one advantage...they were in a rented SUV and the roads were not what one would call first-class once out of the city. They still arrived after the other two to find a full scale gun battle in progress.

Bennet had been told by the delivery man that two Americans had shown interest in him, so he was prepared for the possibility of an unwanted visit. Thus he had taken to going around his homestead fully armed. When the detective and his partner got out of their car in the circular driveway of Bennet's property, Bennet was standing next to a rock wall he was building. He called out, "Who are you, and what do you want?"

The detective took another step without answering and Bennet took out his weapon to fire a shot at the feet of the man. The detective stopped dead in his tracks, as he replied, "Just want to talk to you if you're Jimmy Bennet, as you appear to be. Some very rich men wish to speak to you. It seems a man of great wealth has died, and you are his only living relative."

"Bullshit. You take another step and you fall dead."

The detective's partner had been easing to the right and was considering the options. Jones wanted this man alive, but he didn't say it had to be in one piece. A properly placed shot might convince the man to drop his weapon and listen to reason. One thing he knew for a certainty was he wasn't gonna get gunned down like some dolt, because Bennet decided to fire first and ask questions later.

As he started to ease his hand toward his shoulder holster, Bennet noticed and shot him in the leg. Then as that man yelped, Bennet swung his gun toward the detective, who was backing toward his car with his hands out in front of him. "Don't shoot, we're leaving."

In Bennet's mind these two men had to be cops of some kind to come up with that kind of silly story. He knew the only chance to protect what he had was to kill them, and get rid of the bodies. This reasoned out, he shot the detective, but his aim was less than spectacular. He had intended to shoot the man in the heart, but instead only hit his left arm.

Soon both visitors to the property decided the hell with what Jones wanted, they weren't gonna die here, so the battle was on...though in fairness, both men were trying to wound Bennet, not kill him. Bennet had no such idea once he fired at the detective who was partially shielded by the car door he was trying to hide behind. The shot went through the door and was deflected upward into the man's neck. It hit in a vital spot and the detective flopped to the ground.

At that point Hector and Bear arrived, stopping less than fifty feet from the car. They both got out and Hector growled, "Drop your damned weapons, you two!"

As Hector spoke, the detective, sure he was dying decided to get even and fired one more shot, this one catching Bennet in the stomach. As he did that, his partner turned to fire at Bear.

Bear beat him to the shot, firing a killing shot into his forehead. Meanwhile, the dying detective tried to raise his weapon to fire at Hector, and was hurried to death by another head shot, this from Hector's gun. Bear and Hector finished the gun battle with one shot each because they had both been trained by the Marine Corps, and had spent countless hours refining their skills under the tutelage of Jim Scott. The other advantage they had was being nearer the two men, than had been the case of the other three shooters who were roughly eighty feet from each other.

Hector, certain the two men were dead called out, "Hey, Bennet put your gun down, we don't want to kill you. Actually neither did these two. I don't know what they told you, or how this all started, but you're in line for control of one very big Swiss account. It's a long story, but I'm thinking you better let us take a look at you to see if we can patch you up."

Ellen was already at Bennet's side, and she shouted, "His gun fell out of his hand, I think he's hurt real bad. Please see what you can do to save him."

Bear reached into the rear of the SUV where his war bag was and took out his first aid kit. But when he and Hector reached Bennet, they both looked at each other after seeing the amount of blood he had already lost. Bear shrugged while Hector knelt down next to the killer. Hector didn't bother saying anything because he knew Bennet was dying.

Instead, he put his arm around Ellen and whispered, "I'm sorry, but there is nothing we can do."

Realizing Hector was right, because she knew Jimmy Bennet had just died, Ellen didn't fight him when Hector started helping her to her feet. She wasn't sobbing, but tears were running down her face. Hector took out his handkerchief and dabbed those tears while steering her away from the area.

With those two inside the house, Bear quickly took blood samples, then took a photo of Bennet lying there dead. After putting the samples and first aid kit in the SUV he went inside the house, also.

Hector was quietly talking to Ellen, "So you really can't stay here, Ellen."

"How do you know my name? Sorry. Stupid question. If you know how to find us, you must know quite a bit about us."

"We do. Now then, what I propose is for you to come back to the U.S. with us. You don't have to worry about being charged with anything. We have a feeling you haven't done anything wrong, except maybe helping him escape the law. Whatever money he had, will be yours to keep, since I guess none of it is the original money he came down here with, right?"

"Yes. He's been buying a lot of gold which is here in a safe we bought. The rest is in three bank accounts, in different banks."

"Okay, here's the story we'll tell the local authorities. We found you running down the road, and pulled over to see what the problem was. You told us two men were trying to kill your husband, and ran off seeking help. By the time we got you home, all three men were already dead. While they are trying to sort things out, we'll explain that we're gonna check you into our hotel until further notice. In fact, we'll load you, and your gold, up on our plane and head back to the U.S. I can guarantee you'll never be extradited if it ever comes to that."

As he spoke, Hector took out his White House pass and showed it to Ellen. "The President knows we have been trying to find you and Mr. Bennet. He'll go along with whatever I decided to do, okay?"

"The President? What, why...I don't understand."

"It's a long story, one you may never be told...or at least not all of it. Come on now, let's load up your gold before we call the authorities."

Both Hector and Bear policed their brass, then started the process of loading up the gold, computer, and whatever Ellen wanted to take. During the process, she asked, "Do I really have to go back to the U.S. with you? I think I'd like to live out my life here."

Hector answered, "Not a good idea, Ellen. In the first place, you could easily face charges down here. For starters, the matter of how you aided Bennet enter the country illegally...using false identification. Then there is the matter of the money...ill-gotten money. Come with us and I can help you get it...illegally, but without a trace of where it went. I'm certain the local authorities can come up with other things to charge you with. At home, I can solve those problems for you, but not here...sorry."

"Okay, I get it."

With everything loaded up that needed to go, Hector placed a call to the local police. When they arrived Hector explained that he and his companion had been driving along with they saw "the lady" running for help, or just to get away from the gunfight. He told the officer he spoke to that by the time they arrived back at the house all three men involved were already dead. The police bought the story, and after Hector suggested he take the lady to their hotel to give the police time to do their work, they agreed.

While all that was going on, Bear called Michelle and told her to check everyone out of the hotel and make tracks to the plane.

She replied, "Your timing is pretty good. Jo just came back with her purchases of the day. We'll see you at the plane. I take it you had success?"

"Of a fashion. Bennet is dead, two of the guys Jones probably sent down here, got into a gun fight with him...all three are dead. Hector is bullshitting the cops so we can get away clean."

When all was said and done, Michelle and Jo were flying Ellen, Hector, and Bear back to the U.S. Just as they took off a big storm started pelting the plane with a downpour of rain. Ellen said, "Jimmy used to call storms like this Mother Nature having an orgasm," then she started to cry, so Bear held her close to comfort her.

During the flight, Hector called Jim to fill him in, then asked him to transfer the money in the three accounts Bennet had set up to somewhere where it couldn't be found. Jim was very adept at such maneuvers.

By the time the plane landed at the ranch, the money was in an offshore account of Jim's, to eventually be transferred into an account set up for Ellen.

Also, by the time the plane landed, Maggie and Tony were on their way to the ranch in Maggie's plane with the original documents. Boris, Drew, and their wives had returned to their homes in Sedona, Arizona. They left behind recordings of their "interviews" with the four captives.

In Wentzville, Al and Kathy started house hunting, and when they found one they liked, they bought it and moved in...with thanks to Bob for his hospitality. Emil returned to his home, with the same thanks for his stay on the estate.

28.

At Jim's suggestion, and offer to do so, Ellen agreed to live on the ranch until "things settled down" as Jim put it. She was taken under the wing of the three ladies on the ranch who lived there full time. Before Maggie arrived with Tony, the Mexican family who had been staying on the ranch returned home (leaving behind the U.S. passports)...much richer than when they arrived. Also, their plane had undergone major repairs, just short of a total retrofitting.

Knowing there was still much work to be done to round up as many of the adherents to the Fourth Reich idea as possible, Jim took a deep breath and exhaled it when Maggie did arrive. Coupled with the information gathered from the interrogations of the nine captives, the original documents shed still more light on the overall operation of the accounts. In some cases those documents had information that was unknown to the nine men who still had control of their respective accounts.

The one key piece of new information was what happened to the accounts that had gone dormant. Unknown to anyone but the Swiss bankers, money from dormant accounts could be moved into one of the other accounts. When he saw that information in the original documents, Jim laughed, "Those wily bastards in Switzerland are greedy and unethical, but just as well, I guess. With what we have here, I see a way to get at least some of this money away from them under the threat of this document being made public."

Maggie asked, "What shall we tell the President and Prime Minister about this new information?"

Jim grinned as he answered, "Not a thing for now. Let's not start a food fight over this money. Nobody but us knows you've found this document, right, Maggie?"

"Correct...and I agree with you about keeping it to ourselves, until we come up with some clever plan on how to squeeze the Swiss bankers."

That discussion completed, the next several weeks were spent rounding up many of the people who had been so carefully selected to be part of the Fourth Reich. By the time they had found ways to deal with that group, Ellen Jennings, who had decided to use her maiden name, found out she was pregnant.

This happy event caused Jim to come up with a devilish idea, but one that had to wait until she successfully delivered a bouncing baby boy. Only then did he contact Maggie with his idea. She happily agreed, so next he talked the matter over with Ellen, who said she would have to think about it, but probably would go along.

Jim then called Benjamin (Ben) Schiller, who was a retired number two man of the Israelis' Mossad. "Ben, old friend, this is Santa Claus. Would you have time to visit my ranch for your gift?"

"Jim, I hate to point this out, but I am Jewish, so don't observe your Christmas. That being said, if you want to play games, I take it you have something for me of interest, so trusting you as I do, I will be in the air within the hour."

Jim also called Maggie and asked her to visit...with both documents, the original one and the handwritten one she had found in her desk. She of course agreed, especially knowing what Jim had in mind.

Maggie arrived first, was introduced to Ellen, and the three of them sat around a large table in the conference room of the computer complex. Ellen was given the handwritten document to read. She did a double take on seeing the picture of who she assumed was Hitler. Then she started to read. As others before had, she made several comments of awe as she read. When she finished, she asked, "So this is what is behind everything involving Jimmy...I mean about the guys who killed him?"

Jim answered, "Yes. But, there is more for you to read."

Maggie, at Jim's request, had prepared a duplicate of the original document, but in English. Jim explained the other document was written in German, so this was a translated copy as he handed it to her.

Ellen was only a few pages into that document when Ben Schiller arrived. After fast introductions, he was given the handwritten document. He raised an eyebrow at the photo of the dead man with a neat bullet hole in his forehead, then commenced reading.

Ellen finished her reading project before Ben did and muttered, "This, while in more detail, says about the same thing as the other one."

Jim patted her on the shoulder. "There is one very significant thing in there, Ellen. But we'll wait to go over that until Ben has finished reading everything."

Finished with the first document, Ben was handed the second one after he made a few comments on what he had read. As she handed it to Ben, Maggie asked, "Do you speak and read German?"

"Yes, to a degree."

"Would you like a translated to English copy?"

"I think so."

While he was reading, Jim switched from the coffee everyone had been drinking to a tumbler of sour mash for each. Ellen sipped it and made a comment about it being a bit strong for her, but continued sipping it while Ben continued to read. When he finally finished, he looked at Jim and asked, "What of the men with control of these accounts?"

Jim answered in Hebrew, "Two are totally dormant, because the males of the family tree have all died out. One we will get to in a while. The other nine are presently in our custody...I have four, Maggie has five. Maggie has been sending ransom demands, with a freshly plucked piece of hair or hunk of skin, since they were taken by us."

Ben understood the use of Hebrew, assuming Ellen didn't speak the language, because he knew Maggie did. In English, he asked, "What about the twelfth one, Jim?"

"That is where Ellen comes in, or at least her son does. He is the only living male of that family tree. We have DNA evidence of the family tree taken from both his father, and him. Now a question for you to make certain I have this right. Ellen's grandmother was Jewish, her mother half Jewish. With Ellen 25% Jewish, is she automatically a citizen of Israel?"

"Yes, if she asks for it."

Ellen asked, "How did you know my grandmother was Jewish, Jim?"

"Through a lot of research, Ellen. I didn't go looking to see if that was the case, just stumbled onto it in researching your family tree. I did that to make sure no money from any of these twelve men ever wound up with anyone in your family. I was convinced you were not involved in any way with this mess."

"Oh...I guess."

Ben asked, "I'm starting to get an idea, one that I think may explain your 'Santa Claus" comment, Jim. But how do we go about it if what I'm thinking is correct?"

"I have spoken to Ellen. If she surfaces here in the U.S., she may face a few difficulties, not the least of which is using any of the money she will control at some point. It was all stolen by her now deceased husband. If she was to move to Israel, I know you can gloss over the problem of the money, and where it came from. It is more than enough for her to live out her life and raise her son in comfort. Young James, that is her son's name, as a citizen of Israel, would live out his life never knowing his father was a murderer and thief, or that he had been born in the U.S....if Ellen chose to make it so."

"I do," Ellen chimed in.

Ben nodded. "Okay, so far, but where does 'Santa Claus' come in? There is the matter of the living account holders."

Maggie, using Hebrew, spoke up, "They aren't going to live forever. Every living male member of their family trees who has any idea these accounts even exist are now deceased...or soon will be. Before they became so, they were carefully questioned as to who knew of the accounts. Those who knew are also deceased. You may have noted that any inaction of an account for the period of one year puts it in the dormant stage...subject to being moved into a live account."

At that point, Ellen asked, "Why are you using some language I don't understand?"

Jim replied, "To protect you. You don't need to know what we've been saying, are in fact better off not knowing. In spite of what you've been through, some of what we've done would probably shock and sicken you. We're doing our best to eradicate a cancer, but the best way to make certain to kill this cancer is to keep them from the vast amount of money in the accounts you read about."

In English, Ben asked, "Just how much money are we talking about, Jim?"

"At the present time the twelve accounts total somewhere north of 221 billion dollars. You have to give these guys credit, they invested wisely over the years."

Ben agreed, "I'll say. That's a tidy sum, Santa."

The four at the table talked for over an hour after that, and in the end it was agreed: Ellen and her son would travel back to Israel with Ben. At the appropriate time, Ben would travel to meet with the Swiss bankers and deliver an ultimatum. By then Ellen and her son would be citizens of Israel, with Ellen appointing Ben to act on behalf of her son. The Swiss bankers would decide amongst themselves which bank would have the single account to be controlled by Ben on behalf of young James Jennings (a birth certificate issued by the Israeli government in that name was for the correct date, but fudged a bit in that the birthplace was shown as Israel).

As Jim said when asked "why" he wanted to settle the matter in this way, his answer was, "No doubt a good deal of the money for these accounts was stolen from Jews by the Third Reich, so it is only fitting that it benefit Jews in their homeland.'

After the fact, Jim, Holly, and Maggie met with the President and Prime Minister. Jim told them what had been done with the accounts, which drew a few grumbled comments from the Prime Minister, but hearty congratulations from the President. At that point, the Prime Minister reluctantly agreed that Jim's solution was "perhaps for the best."

Eventually Ellen re-married, to an Israeli soldier, and her son grew into a fine young man...never knowing about the vast fortune that was now controlled by the Israeli government. Ben had had a long drawn out negotiation with the Swiss bankers to reach an agreement. Each bank would set up an account with the money they already had. As soon as the new accounts were opened, the Israeli government would have full control of the accounts, but with the agreement offered by Ben that they would only be drawn on when needed.

Shortly after that agreement was reached, dead bodies of the nine men who had been in charge of the previous accounts started showing up...inside their original countries.

the end

Don't miss out!

Visit the website below and you can sign up to receive emails whenever Mike Jackson publishes a new book. There's no charge and no obligation.

https://books2read.com/r/B-A-ZBKV-AEHFF

BOOKS 2 READ

Connecting independent readers to independent writers.

Milton Keynes UK
Ingram Content Group UK Ltd.
UKHW030912121124
451094UK00001B/130

9 798227 490926